P9-CDT-494

Dangerous Alterations

"Elizabeth Lynn Casey keeps her readers entertained with *Dangerous Alterations* through her wonderful storytelling skills that feature light humor, gentle romance, and always an intriguing, suspenseful mystery to be solved. What more could you ask for in a cozy mystery?" —*Fresh Fiction*

Deadly Notions

"I always enjoy visiting Tori and her friends in Sweet Briar. They are their own band of sisters who squabble and pick at each other yet will drop most anything to lend a hand." —*Once Upon a Romance*

"A perfect addition to the Southern Sewing Circle series. With strong personalities vibrating off each page, the twists and turns of the story line, and the exceptionally exciting ending, this one will please them all!" —*The Romance Readers Connection*

Pinned for Murder

"[Mixes] a suspenseful story with a dash of down-home flavor . . . Visiting with the charmingly eccentric folks of Sweet Briar is like taking a trip back home." —*Fresh Fiction*

"A relaxing and pleasurable read. Ms. Casey has sewn together a finely crafted cozy mystery series." —*Once Upon a Romance*

continued . . .

"An excellent read for crafters and mystery lovers alike. Elizabeth Casey has a knack for threading together great story lines, likable characters, and surprises in every page. The women in the Southern Sewing Circle are friends we all wish we had. This book was terrific from beginning to end."
                                    —*The Romance Readers Connection*

Death Threads

"A light, fun mystery with southern charm and an energetic heroine."
                                    —*The Mystery Reader*

Sew Deadly

"Filled with fun, folksy characters and southern charm."
                                    —Maggie Sefton, national bestselling
                                    author of *Cast On, Kill Off*

"Sweet and charming . . . The bewitching women of the Southern Sewing Circle will win your heart in this debut mystery."

                                    —Monica Ferris, *USA Today* bestselling
                                    author of *Threadbare*

Berkley Prime Crime titles by Elizabeth Lynn Casey

SEW DEADLY
DEATH THREADS
PINNED FOR MURDER
DEADLY NOTIONS
DANGEROUS ALTERATIONS
REAP WHAT YOU SEW
LET IT SEW

Let It Sew

Elizabeth Lynn Casey

BERKLEY PRIME CRIME, NEW YORK

THE BERKLEY PUBLISHING GROUP
Published by the Penguin Group
Penguin Group (USA) Inc.
375 Hudson Street, New York, New York 10014, USA
Penguin Group (Canada), 90 Eglinton Avenue East, Suite 700, Toronto, Ontario M4P 2Y3, Canada
(a division of Pearson Penguin Canada Inc.) • Penguin Books Ltd., 80 Strand, London WC2R 0RL,
England • Penguin Group Ireland, 25 St. Stephen's Green, Dublin 2, Ireland (a division of Penguin
Books Ltd.) • Penguin Group (Australia), 250 Camberwell Road, Camberwell, Victoria 3124, Australia
(a division of Pearson Australia Group Pty. Ltd.) • Penguin Books India Pvt. Ltd., 11 Community
Centre, Panchsheel Park, New Delhi—110 017, India • Penguin Group (NZ), 67 Apollo Drive,
Rosedale, Auckland 0632, New Zealand (a division of Pearson New Zealand Ltd.) • Penguin Books
(South Africa) (Pty.) Ltd., 24 Sturdee Avenue, Rosebank, Johannesburg 2196, South Africa

Penguin Books Ltd., Registered Offices: 80 Strand, London WC2R 0RL, England

This is a work of fiction. Names, characters, places, and incidents either are the product of the author's
imagination or are used fictitiously, and any resemblance to actual persons, living or dead, business
establishments, events, or locales is entirely coincidental. The publisher does not have any control over
and does not assume any responsibility for author or third-party websites or their content.

LET IT SEW

A Berkley Prime Crime Book / published by arrangement with the author

PUBLISHING HISTORY
Berkley Prime Crime mass-market edition / November 2012

Copyright © 2012 by Penguin Group (USA) Inc.
Cover illustration by Mary Ann Lasher.
Cover design by Judith Lagerman.
Interior text design by Laura K. Corless.

ISBN: 978-0-425-25171-3

BERKLEY® PRIME CRIME
Berkley Prime Crime Books are published by The Berkley Publishing Group,
a division of Penguin Group (USA) Inc.,
375 Hudson Street, New York, New York 10014.
BERKLEY® PRIME CRIME and the PRIME CRIME logo are trademarks of
Penguin Group (USA) Inc.

PRINTED IN THE UNITED STATES OF AMERICA

10 9 8 7 6 5 4 3 2 1

ALWAYS LEARNING   PEARSON

For Emily,
who was more than willing to wonder along with me
when it came to the notion of Christmas in Sweet Briar.
Now we know, Emily, now we know . . .

And for Erin and Jennifer—you make every day magical.

Chapter 1

There were certain things that simply went together.

Milk and cookies . . .

Music and dancing . . .

Hugs and kisses.

You know, tried-and-true matches capable of withstanding the test of time and serving as beacons of normalcy when life got crazy. To mess with one of them was akin to turning one's personal snow globe upside down and giving it a violent shake.

At least that's what Tori Sinclair told herself as she lowered her uneaten candy bar into her lunch sack and sealed it up tight, her appetite suddenly depleted.

"Ain't no need to quit your horrible eatin' habits on account of me, Victoria." Margaret Louise Davis dropped her polyester-clad body onto the concrete step just below

Tori and released a weighted sigh. "I just need a little fresh air is all."

"Margaret Louise? Are you—"

"And maybe a few nips of Gabe Jameson's moonshine while I'm at it."

She gestured over her shoulder to the stately brick structure at the top of the stairs. "Last time I checked, the Sweet Briar Public Library only offers books, exceptional customer service, and an occasional cup of coffee depending on whether Dixie is working or not." Tori brought her hand back to her lap and leaned forward. "What's wrong, Margaret Louise?"

The sixty-something woman shifted her plump form ever so slightly until her back was propped against the staircase wall. "Wrong? Who said anything was wrong?"

Extending her finger outward, Tori did her best to nudge her friend's mouth into a smile but to no avail. "*This* did." Margaret Louise's brows furrowed as Tori abandoned her efforts. "Your smile. It's *gone*."

"You're darn tootin' it is."

"Is it the kids?"

Margaret Louise shook her head. "My grandbabies are doin' just fine."

"Melissa?" Tori asked quickly as a flash of fear reared its head where the woman's pregnant daughter-in-law was concerned.

"Melissa is fine. Carryin' number eight like it's her first."

Tori's shoulders slumped. "Phew. That's a relief."

"Ain't nothin' wrong with Jake, neither," Margaret Louise said, referring to her one and only son.

Tori studied her friend closely, trying to make sense of the nonsensical. "Then if it's not the kids, and it's not

Melissa or Jake, what on earth has got you looking like . . . *that*?" Again, she pointed at the frown on her friend's face.

"It's not a *what*. It's a *who*."

And then she knew.

In fact, now that Jake and his family had been systematically eliminated as potential culprits, there was only one person who could possibly be responsible for Margaret Louise's frown.

"What did Leona do now?" she asked even as her thoughts began filling in potential possibilities where Margaret Louise's night-and-day-different twin sister was concerned.

"It ain't Leona."

Okay, now she was stumped. "Then who?"

"Name's Maime Wellington. Though I've got me a few names that fit better."

"Maime Wellington?" she echoed.

Margaret Louise merely nodded. Sadly.

"My sister always was far kinder than she should have been." Leona Elkin climbed the first five steps of the library and sank onto the step beside Tori, her breath coming in soft little gasps. "Good . . . heavens, Twin. I realize one of us . . . wears jogging suits . . . on a regular basis . . . but I don't clothe myself in Donna Karan . . . so I can . . . sweat my brains out . . . chasing you across the town square!"

Tori stifled the laugh that lay in wait halfway down her throat, opting instead to tip her head in the direction of the latest newcomer to her lunch-that-wasn't. "Leona."

"Victoria." Smoothing her freshly manicured hands down the sides of her hunter green suit jacket, Leona pursed her lips around one final dramatic inhale before addressing her sister with a knowing look. "Avery Jordan isn't thinking with his brain. And when a man isn't thinking with his brain, he's ripe for the picking." Crossing her ankles and tucking them primly to the side, Leona batted her eyelashes ever so coyly. "If they weren't, my passport wouldn't be so well stamped."

That did it. Tori laughed.

Leona turned a disapproving eye in Tori's direction. "You disagree, dear?"

"No. I—"

"Lulu is gonna be heartbroken when I tell her," Margaret Louise moaned.

The mention of number five in Margaret Louise's lineup of grandchildren brought her up short. "Lulu? What's Lulu got to do with all of this? I thought you said the kids were fine."

"They are. But I promised Lulu she could help this year. And since I told her that, that child's been jottin' down all sorts of decoratin' ideas in that little notebook of hers. Course, there's an inordinate amount of candy canes makin' their way into the mix, but still, it's a start."

"Candy canes," she whispered. "I don't understand . . ."

Leona bent her fingers so as to afford a closer inspection of her nails. "Avery Jordan has replaced Margaret Louise on the Sweet Briar Christmas Decorating Committee."

Tori drew back, images of her first two Christmases in Sweet Briar lining up in her thoughts one picturesque memory behind the other. "Replaced *Margaret Louise*? Is he nuts?"

"That's one word for it, dear. Others would include clueless, desperate, pathetic, and predicable. All of which I tried to share with my sister during our sprint across the

Green, but none of which seemed to have helped," Leona said.

"But w-why?" Tori sputtered.

Margaret Louise's mouth dipped still further. "Officially? Councilman Jordan thinks it's time for a change."

"And unofficially?" she prompted, knowing full well who would answer.

Leona didn't disappoint. "Unofficially, Councilman Jordan met some little hussy on one of those Internet dating sites and she's finagled not only an invite to live with him and his son, but also Margaret Louise's prized role as Chairman of the Sweet Briar Christmas Decorating Committee."

"O-kay." She worked to take in everything she was hearing. "So he moved his girlfriend into his house. What does that have to do with Margaret Louise's committee spot? Giving it to his girlfriend doesn't make any sense."

"It does if you're Maime Wellington and you want so desperately to"—Leona hooked the index and middle fingers of both her moisturized hands in the air—"fit *in* in your new hometown."

"So she ousts the one woman who makes Sweet Briar look like something out of a Dickens classic?" Tori heard the disbelief in her own voice, knew it would be mirrored in that of every resident of Sweet Briar, except, perhaps, Councilman Jordan and his new live-in girlfriend.

"That 'bout sums it up." Margaret Louise tipped her head back against the wall and looked up at the charcoal-streaked clouds. "Why, I even offered to stay on and help in whatever capacity this woman needs, but he said no. He said it might make it too hard for the other committee members to see her as the decision maker if I'm nearby."

"Maybe that should tell him something." It was all Tori could think to say.

Leona threw back her shoulders. "Which is why *I* volunteered to help this year."

Tori choked on a swallow. "*Y-You*, Leona?"

"That's exactly what I said." Margaret Louise rolled her eyes. "After all, Leona's first and only order of business when it comes to all things decoratin' is to call a decorator. Who, in case you're curious, Victoria, is number five on my twin's speed dial."

Leona made a face at her twin sister and then held it as she swept an offended glance in Tori's direction. "I barely have room in my schedule for a pedicure this month and this is the thanks I get for keeping Maime Wellington on her toes? Doesn't bode well for you, either, Victoria."

"Me?" she echoed.

"Do you really think she volunteered alone, Victoria?" Margaret Louise asked.

She looked from Leona to Margaret Louise and back again, her mouth gaping at the reality. "You volunteered me for the Christmas committee? Are you crazy? The Holiday Book Extravaganza is coming up! I can't take on any other responsibilities right now."

Leona waved Tori's worries away. "Don't worry, dear. Rose and Dixie will be there to help us both."

Tori worked to moisten her throat. "You volunteered them, too?"

Leona beamed. "Think of the fun we can have with the councilman's little hussy . . ."

Propping her elbows on her knees, Tori dropped her head into her hands. "Ugh. Ugh. Ugh, Leona. How could you do this?"

"Easy. I simply gave the councilman's secretary our names and numbers. When she was done writing that all down, she welcomed us aboard."

Tori pulled her head from her palms and rose to her feet, her thoughts ricocheting between the upcoming holiday book event and her own plans for a special Christmas with her fiancé, Milo Wentworth. "Leona, I can't. I can't do this. It's too much."

Leona, too, jumped to her feet, the click of her Prada shoes reverberating against the concrete. "Taking a few minutes out of your precious schedule to be my sister's voice on the Christmas committee is too much for you?"

She felt her face warm as Margaret Louise lowered her gaze from the sky for the first time in ten minutes. "Leona, stop. Victoria doesn't owe me anything. She's got enough on her plate—"

"I'll do it." The words slipped between her lips, unfiltered. "I'll do it. I'll find a way to make it work."

Leona's smile returned. Only this time, it was dripping with self-satisfaction. "I knew Margaret Louise could count on you, dear." Before Tori could respond, Leona clapped her hands in rapid succession. "Ooooh, just think of all the new gossip we're going to get for our sewing circle meetings. Things have gotten so drab in there lately with Rose always wincing, Dixie and you blathering on about the book fair, and Melissa talking about her pregnancy."

"I just want to talk about decorations . . ." Margaret Louise's words trailed off as the peal of her cell phone took over. Sighing, she retrieved the royal blue gadget from her purse and checked the caller ID screen. "It's Rose."

Approaching her mid-eighties, Rose Winters was one

of Tori's dearest friends. Equal parts prickly and sweet, the retired schoolteacher turned matriarch of the Sweet Briar Ladies Society Sewing Circle was a force to be reckoned with whether she was working in her garden, sewing away the hours, or hooked up to an IV drip pole for one of her rheumatoid arthritis treatments.

"Shhhh," Leona said, quieting her voice as she continued. "Don't tell her I volunteered her for the Christmas committee. I want to do that in person when I can watch the old goat's reaction with my own two eyes."

"Leona!" Tori reprimanded despite the smile that let the woman off the hook. Leona Elkin and Rose Winters were like oil and vinegar. If Leona wasn't taking potshots at Rose, then Rose was taking some at Leona. It wasn't always pretty, but it was almost always amusing.

Leona cocked her head and batted her eyelashes innocently. "What did I say?"

"Oh, put a sock in it, Twin." Margaret Louise snapped her phone open and held it to her ear. "Is everything okay, Rose?"

Ever the grandmother, Margaret Louise slipped into nurture mode with quiet ease, casting away her personal troubles in favor of making everyone else's life better. It was one of probably a zillion reasons why Tori treasured her so.

She studied the twins closely as Margaret Louise paid full attention to the voice on the phone and Leona stood idly by, trying not to get caught eavesdropping. Born on the same day, to the same mother, the women, who were three decades Tori's senior, had little in common beyond their shared birthday. Where Margaret Louise was stocky, Leona was trim and toned. Where Leona tended to be

prim and proper, Margaret Louise was loud and boisterous, always ready to have a good time regardless of their
surroundings. Where Leona wore the latest styles and
trends with an artist's eye, Margaret Louise was lovingly
disheveled at best. Where Margaret Louise could spend
hours playing on the floor with one of her grandkids,
Leona looked aghast at the mere mention of anyone under
the age of thirty. And while Margaret Louise was content
to live her long widowed existence surrounded by family
and friends, Leona lived her never-married status to the
fullest, winking and blinking her way toward free dinners
and movies with just about any uniform-wearing male
regardless of whether he was twenty or seventy.

"I didn't realize she was that bad," Margaret Louise
said.

Something about the tone of the one-sided conversation she was hearing snapped her into the present. A quick
glance in Leona's direction told her she wasn't alone.

"When is the wake and the service?" Tori felt the help-
less churn of her stomach as Margaret Louise paused long
enough for her tone to switch from dismay to disgust. "I
wouldn't imagine that worthless young man *would* make
the arrangements . . ."

Another pause quickly disappeared. "Well, thank
heavens for Jerry Lee. I'm not sure what Charlotte would
have done these last few years without his guidance . . .
Yes, yes, of course, Rose. We'll let everyone know at
tonight's circle meetin' . . . Yes, it's at Georgina's place . . .
Do you need a ride? . . . No, Rose, I don't think you're an
invalid." Margaret Louise closed her eyes. "Yes, yes, I
know you can get there yourself . . . Okay, I'll pick you up
at seven, then."

Parting her short, stubby eyelashes, Margaret Louise snapped her phone shut and shoved it into her oversized tote bag–turned-purse. "Charlotte Devereaux died last night."

The name, while oddly familiar, didn't stir up anything specific. "Who's Charlotte Devereaux?" Tori asked.

"Charlotte, along with Rose, Dixie, Georgina, and myself, founded the sewin' circle to which you now belong, Victoria." Margaret Louise huffed and puffed her way to her feet. "She retired from the circle 'bout five years ago when Parker up and took off."

"Parker?" she repeated.

"Her husband of almost fifty years. Provin', of course, that good men are as scarce as deviled eggs after a church picnic."

"That's why you never give a man more than five dates. Six tops." Leona turned on the soles of her expensive heels and made her way down the steps. "They can't hurt what they don't have."

Tori watched Leona swing her hips down the sidewalk and disappear behind a series of hundred-year-old moss trees, her destination either the antiques shop she owned on the town square or whatever lunch date she'd been invited to by some unsuspecting man. "Margaret Louise? That sister of yours is a piece of work."

When there was no response, Tori turned back to her troubled friend and focused her attention where it was due. "Was Charlotte sick?"

Margaret Louise nodded. "She had Alzheimer's and it was gettin' pretty bad. I just didn't realize she was so close to dyin'. If I had, I'd have gotten my hide over there sooner."

She reached for her friend's hand and gave it a gentle squeeze. "Hey. Go easy on yourself. Between your grandbabies and your mother, you barely have time to breathe. Besides, if she was as bad off as you say, she might not have even known you were there."

A beat of silence was soon followed by a soft tsking sound. "Victoria, I can only hope you're right. Because maybe, if she couldn't remember nothin', her heart wouldn't have been hurtin' so much at the end. That alone would have made her Alzheimer's a blessin'."

Despite the fact that she'd never met Charlotte Devereaux, Tori couldn't help feeling bad for a woman who had spent her last five years on earth aching over a loved one's betrayal. It just seemed unnecessarily cruel. "She was surprised when he left?"

Margaret Louise snorted. "More like shocked. We all were. She adored the ground that man walked on, and we all thought the same thing 'bout him."

Tori swallowed back the lump that threatened to make speaking difficult, her own experience in the blind-sided-by-love department bringing Charlotte Devereaux's plight much too close for comfort. "Tell me she at least had someone by her side at the end. Some children? A sibling? Someone?"

Hoisting her tote bag onto her arm, Margaret Louise turned in the same direction Leona had gone and made her way to the sidewalk below, stopping to readdress Tori at the bottom. "Considerin' what she had *by her side*, as you say, Charlotte would have been better off on her own. Far, far better."

Chapter 2

Tori reached her hand into the center of the wreath and pumped the brass knocker up and down, careful not to dislodge the smattering of berries that popped out proudly against their autumn-leaf background. She knew the decoration was designed to give guests a seasonal welcome, but for her, it ushered in a momentary rush of inadequacy.

Despite the ever-growing collection of holiday decorations she housed in color-coded bins in her own attic, Tori tended to put off their unearthing until it made more sense to wait until the following year. Only the following year always brought its own lineup of busyness capable of making time disappear from between her fingers. And so the cycle continued . . .

"I'm glad to see I'm not the only one running behind." Tori shifted the plate of homemade brownies from her

left hand to her right and gave Debbie Calhoun her cheek
for the inevitable kiss that was sure to follow. "A box of
Colby's latest book arrived just as I was trying to get dinner on the table for him and the kids and, well, I couldn't
resist looking at one . . . and then reading the dedication . . .
and the acknowledgments . . . and looking at my handsome husband's photo on the back jacket. Before I knew it,
dinner was pushed off by thirty minutes."

She had to laugh. "I wish I could say my reason for
being late was equally noteworthy, but it wasn't."

"Oh?" Debbie narrowed her pale blue eyes at Tori.

"I was looking at my calendar and getting stressed."

"About what?"

She opened her mouth to answer but left the explanation unspoken as the massive oak door that welcomed
guests to Georgina Hayes's home swung open, revealing
the sixty-two-year-old mayor of Sweet Briar herself.

"Victoria! Debbie! Come in, come in." Stepping back,
Georgina swept her hand down the long hallway in front
of them, the sound of chatter from the study making its
way in their direction. "Everyone was just saying how
much they hoped you'd make it tonight."

"We're here." Debbie trailed Tori through the door and
handed two powder blue boxes to Georgina. "The top
box has some pastries, and the bottom box has a French
silk pie."

Tori's stomach rumbled. "Did you say French silk
pie?" she asked as Georgina took the plate of brownies
from her hand.

Wrapping her hand around Tori's arm, Debbie fairly
tugged her down the chandelier-lit hallway, the bakery
owner's laugh echoing against the mahogany-paneled walls.

"I will never understand how you can eat the way you do, Victoria, and stay so slim."

"Same way you do, I guess."

When they reached the study, all chatter ceased as the members of the Sweet Briar Ladies Society Sewing Circle looked up and smiled. Rose Winters, the matriarch of the group, was the first to speak, patting the empty sofa cushion beside her frail body. "Victoria, I saved you a spot right here next to me."

"Thank you, Rose." Extricating her arm from Debbie's gentle hold, Tori set her tote bag on the floor beside the sofa and claimed her reserved spot. "I'm sorry I'm late. I got"—she glanced over at Debbie—"sidetracked."

Nestling into the empty armchair between Margaret Louise and Melissa, Debbie grinned back. "I believe you said you were sidetracked by stress."

Just like that, every pair of eyes in the room was on Tori. Waiting.

"Did you hit a snag in your wedding plans?" Dixie Dunn mused over the pillow cover she was hand stitching.

Tori met the woman's questioning eyes and couldn't help smiling at the memory of her very first sewing circle meeting—a meeting Dixie had avoided out of anger. At Tori.

Now, two years later, Dixie had not only reconciled with the notion of Tori serving as head librarian at Sweet Briar Public Library—a position the seventy-something woman had held for more years than Tori had been alive—but also seemed to genuinely like her.

Part of that, Tori knew, came from the many efforts she'd made to draw Dixie back into the day-to-day operations at the library. The move had smoothed the woman's ruffled feathers and proven invaluable to Tori when her assistant, Nina Morgan, left on maternity leave. The other part, she knew, had come from their mutual respect and love for books—something that had proven to be an irrefutable common ground between them.

"Because if you did," Dixie continued, "maybe I could help."

"Wedding plans are moving along just fine," Tori said. And they were.

"Is it the holiday book fair?"

Tori shifted her focus to the far corner of the room and the quiet brunette who sat hunched over a portable sewing machine, working on what appeared to be a costume of some sort. Beatrice Tharrington was the youngest of the circle, her meek demeanor and British accent a stark contrast in a room of boisterous southern women. "The book fair is stressful, yes, but Dixie has been a huge help these past few weeks in helping to tie up all the loose ends."

Dixie beamed at the praise, her needle-wielding fingers moving even faster as they zipped above and below the pillowcase taking shape in her wrinkled hands.

"Then what's wrong?" Melissa asked from her chair to the left of Debbie, the woman's eighth-time burgeoning belly peeking out from beneath a partially hand-sewn teddy bear.

"Just trying to figure out how to juggle everything I have to do."

Georgina lifted a glass of water to her lips and took a sip, setting it back down on a nearby end table. "Maybe you should have held off on helpin' with the Christmas committee until next year or maybe the year after that."

Rose drew back. "You're helping on the committee, Victoria? When did you decide to do that?"

"She didn't," Leona interjected from behind her latest travel magazine. "I decided *for* her. And for you, too, Rose."

Dixie stopped sewing and pinned the cover of Leona's magazine with a death glare. "You volunteered Victoria for the Christmas committee when we've got the Holiday Book Extravaganza in two weeks?"

Leona's voice rose above the edge of the magazine. "With you helping her in both capacities, Dixie, it won't be so bad."

"Both capacities?" Dixie echoed.

As Rose's sputtering came to a stop, Tori leaned her head against the back of the couch and waited for the inevitable war of words she knew was coming.

Rose didn't disappoint.

"Are you telling me you volunteered Victoria, Dixie, and *me* to be on Margaret Louise's Christmas committee without asking?" Rose hissed through gritted teeth.

"It ain't my committee no more." Margaret Louise closed her eyes and inhaled sharply before releasing it throughout the room with a sigh to end all sighs. "It was snatched clear out of my hands by Councilman Jordan just so his online girlfriend can feel . . . special."

A hush fell over the circle, followed by a domino of gasps.

"But that's *your* committee, Margaret Louise," Debbie rasped. "You make Sweet Briar so . . . so perfect at the holidays. Like something out of a fairy tale."

Rose and Dixie turned a collective glare on the evening's hostess. "Georgina? You allowed this?"

Georgina's broad shoulders rose and fell. "He took it to the council as a whole and they agreed."

"But you're the mayor," Beatrice protested in very un-Beatrice-like fashion.

"I'm the mayor, not a dictator," Georgina reminded them.

Margaret Louise held up her pudgy hands. "This ain't Georgina's fault. Besides, no one ever said it was my committee for life."

"Well, they should've," groused Rose before turning an evil eye in Leona's direction once again. "Why on earth would you volunteer us for a committee that was just taken away from your sister? Are you really that heartless?"

Leona tossed her magazine onto the coffee table. "The way I see it, you old goat, having the three of you on the Christmas committee will give Margaret Louise the say she's earned and keep this—this Maime Wellington person from getting too full of herself."

"I'll do it." Dixie set her pillowcase to her left. "When's the first meeting?"

"Tomorrow evening."

Margaret Louise looked a question at her sister. "Tomorrow evening? But that's Charlotte's wake."

That's all it took. Suddenly, all talk of Christmas committees and online hussies gave way to news of the latest passing in Sweet Briar—a passing that touched nearly every member of the circle.

"Do you realize, we wouldn't all be sitting here together right now if it weren't for Charlotte Devereaux?" Melissa volunteered.

Dixie made a face. "Rose and I had something to do with creating this sewing circle, too, you know."

Heads nodded.

Tori reached into her tote bag and pulled out the wooden sewing box Leona had gifted her shortly after moving to Sweet Briar. Setting it on her lap, she allowed her finger to trace the horse and buggy carved into the lid of the simple antique box as a question formed on her lips. "Why did Charlotte leave the group? Was it her health?"

"At the time she quit? No." Rose pulled the flaps of her thin cotton sweater more closely against her chest. "The Alzheimer's came later."

"Then why did she leave the group?" she asked again.

"Because she'd been humiliated, that's why." Dixie wiggled her way forward on her chair and then pushed off the edge. "She worshiped the ground her husband, Parker, walked on for five decades and then, one day, he up and walked out. And he did it with some little thing he met while traveling for his computer business."

Rose took the ball from Dixie and ran with it, her own voice suddenly thick with anger. "She came home from a circle meeting one night and he was gone. Yanked her heart and her spirit right out of her body when he left."

Tori sucked in her breath. "That's awful."

"We tried to convince her to keep on sewin', to use us as a soundin' board 'bout that pig," Margaret Louise explained, "but she just shut down. Never really talked to me none after all that."

"She stopped talking to all of us after Parker left." Georgina stretched her trouser-clad legs in front of her and stifled a quick yawn. "Guess she was afraid we'd be looking at her funny or something."

It was a notion Tori understood. Because even though her late ex-fiancé had cheated on her in the coat closet at their engagement party, she, too, had felt as if everyone was staring at her over the days and weeks that followed. In fact, she'd been so certain of the pitying looks, she'd spent virtually every nonworking hour holed up in her then Chicago apartment.

It had been about avoidance.

And feeling sorry for oneself.

Fortunately, Tori had just been starting out in life, and after pulling herself up by the boot straps, she'd set herself on a different course—one that brought her to the head librarian job in Sweet Briar, South Carolina, and into the welcoming arms of her fellow sewing circle sisters and her soon-to-be husband, Milo Wentworth.

Being in the late sixties at the time of the betrayal, though, had to be rough. It made starting over so much harder. Tori said as much to her friends.

"What made it hard was that she didn't see it comin'. None of us did."

"Margaret Louise is right." Dixie made her way slowly around the room, stopping every so often to take a closer look at everyone's sewing project. "Why, we all thought Parker was head over heels in love with Charlotte. Least that's how he acted."

"What was he like?" Beatrice asked.

"He was a real straight arrow," Georgina said by way of explanation. "You know, the kind who didn't ruffle feathers, didn't complain for the sake of complaining. He just ran his computer company and looked after his family."

Debbie nodded. "Every night, after his hip replacement, I'd see him and Charlotte going for a walk past the bakery, hand in hand."

"Someone should have told him how ridiculous he looked wearing those dark brown leather shoes with shorts." Dixie continued her meandering around the room, her anger over her late friend's mistreatment rising with each step. "But that would've fallen on deaf ears, I'm sure. He didn't go *anywhere* without those shoes."

"None of us thought less of Charlotte when he up and took off." Margaret Louise threw herself over her knees and reached into the sewing bag propped on the floor at her feet. "We just felt sorry he left her with the headache of runnin' a company she knew nothing 'bout and skipped out on the family as a whole—leavin' her to deal with that no good-for-nothin' son of theirs all on her own."

Tori offered a distracted nod as the woman pulled two green-checked strips of stocking-shaped fabric from the bag and sat up tall, smoothing them across her legs with a quick swipe of her pudgy hand. Intrigued, Tori opened her mouth to inquire about Margaret Louise's project, but was thwarted by the woman's daughter-in-law.

"Have you ever met him, Victoria?"

Pulling her focus from Margaret Louise's lap, Tori fixed it on Melissa instead. "Who?"

"Ethan Devereaux?"

"Charlotte and Parker's younger son," Dixie clarified.

"I don't think I've ever met him. The name isn't . . . wait. Ethan Devereaux. Why does that sound familiar all of a sudden?"

Dixie spun around from her spot in front of the large plate glass window overlooking Georgina's dimly lit French patio and shook a finger at Tori. "It's familiar because Ethan Devereaux is the reason the library board insisted on our patron conduct policy."

Melissa scrunched up her pretty face. "There's a patron conduct policy at the library? I didn't know that."

"That's because it was put in place for Ethan Devereaux and it's never been needed for anyone else," Dixie said. "Folks around these parts are usually smart enough to throw their gum in the wastebasket and to refrain from accessing the computer to watch shoot-'em-ups with the volume turned on high."

"Sounds like my Break-You-Buy policy at the antique shop. That, too, was put in place because of Ethan Devereaux. He broke an antique mirror from the late 1800s shortly after I opened the shop. Ethan being Ethan, he refused to help me clean it up." Rose tsked under her breath as Leona continued. "Of course, Charlotte hurried over and made amends on all fronts."

"She's been doing that since he was two." Rose shook her head sadly. "And I suspect she was still doing it until the day she died . . . or at least during any periods of lucidness she may have had."

"How old is this kid?" Tori finally asked, anxious to put an age-appropriate image to the name being bandied about the room.

"He's not a kid," Melissa answered. "He's got to be in his late thirties, at least."

Georgina quickly concurred. "Brian is coming up on fifty-five, I believe, so that would make Ethan about forty-one, forty-two."

Tori pushed Margaret Louise's stocking from her mind once and for all. "Who's Brian?"

"Charlotte's older son. He's mentally challenged but quite high functioning." Dixie wandered over to the stone hearth and peered at the various framed photographs displayed across the mantel. "Charlotte never said it, but I always assumed Ethan was pampered the way he was because he was . . ."

"The normal son," Rose finished. "The one who would eventually take the helm of Parker's company, though from what I've heard, Ethan sits at a desk and watches TV most days while Brian and Jerry Lee keep things running."

"Jerry Lee?" It was like Tori's first sewing circle meeting all over again. So many names she simply didn't know.

Dixie shuffled her way along the length of the mantel, studying each photograph with the carefully culled skills of a busybody. "Jerry Lee Sweeney. He was Parker's best friend and right-hand man."

"And a saving grace for Charlotte once Parker took off for the hills." Rose periscoped her head over the back of the couch and narrowed her gaze on Dixie. "What in heaven's name are you doing over there, Dixie?"

"Just looking, I guess. Charlotte's passing has me feeling a little restless and out of sorts."

"When *aren't* you out of sorts?" Leona quipped.

Anxious to avoid the war of words that was sure to follow, Georgina, too, stood, the warning glint in her eyes aimed at Leona even while her words were meant for Tori. "It's a shame you never got to know Charlotte, Victoria. She was a true talent with a needle *and* a pencil."

"Oh? Was she a writer like Colby?" Tori asked.

Debbie shook her head at the reference to her author husband. "No. Charlotte was a gifted artist. That pencil sketch of my bakery that hangs on the wall beside the front door was done by Charlotte as a gift shortly after I opened."

re   that drawing there"—Georgina pointed toward
e   tel—"by Dixie's right hand? That was done by
            te as well."

            studied the framed sketch of the Sweet Briar
        Hall and marveled at the details. The trees, the
        alk, the building, and even the cracked window
        skillfully drawn.

Resting her hand along the back of the sofa, she ges-
red toward the picture with her chin. "What's with the
crack in the front right window?"

Georgina laughed. "Charlotte was a stickler about
details. You remember what it was like when Tropical
Storm Roger came knocking, Victoria?"

"How could I forget?" she asked. The storm had caused
some flooding damage to the library as well as extensive
tree-related damage to Rose's neighborhood.

"Well, we had one like that here about seven years ago.
In that one, a tree had fallen against that very window of
Town Hall just days before she sketched this picture. Fortunately for us, the tree had been removed. But as you can
see, the crack remained."

"She couldn't simply draw the window without the
crack?" Tori asked, her curiosity aroused.

Leona lowered her magazine to her lap. "Charlotte
called a spade a spade when it came to her art. If the crack
was there when she sat down to sketch, the crack was part
of the drawing."

Rose rubbed at her arthritis-ridden fingers and did her
best to disguise a wince. "Too bad she didn't employ that
same attention to detail where Ethan was concerned.
Might have saved her some heartache."

"Not to mention embarrassment." Dixie stepped back

from the mantel and came to stand beside Tori. "I su
hope you take good care of that sewing box Leona ga
you after you moved here. It meant a lot to Charlotte ev
if she wouldn't admit it."

Tori looked from her sewing box to Dixie and back again
her fingers instinctively reaching out to trace the horse
and-buggy carving once again. "I don't understand . . ."

Leona set her magazine on the end table to the left of
her chair and sighed. "Remember how I told you Charlotte made amends after Ethan broke that antique mirror?" At Tori's nod, Margaret Louise's twin continued.
"Well, one of the ways she did that was to give me that
box for my shop. I refused to accept it at first on account
of not wanting to be burned at the stake by certain women
in this room if I had, but Charlotte insisted I add it to my
inventory. I never felt right about it, though, even going so
far as to turn down a number of offers from interested
customers. But then, when you came along and fell in
love with it, I knew I'd found someone who would treasure it for more than just its antique value."

She let her hand glide across the legs of the horse and
the wheels of the buggy, the sensation beneath her fingertips transporting her back in time to some of her earliest
memories of her late great-grandmother—the woman
who had taught Tori how to sew.

Blinking against the prick of tears that threatened to
bring down the mood of the room, Tori found her smile
and directed it up at Dixie. "Charlotte's sewing box is safe
with me. You have my word on that."

Chapter 3

One look around the funeral home and it was apparent Charlotte Devereaux had been a well-loved member of Sweet Briar. Council members, business owners, and residents alike mulled around the viewing room with story after story to share of a woman Tori had met only through the eyes of her sewing circle sisters.

But just as Rose's and Dixie's stories stopped at the time Charlotte left the circle five years earlier, so, too, did everyone else's. And it wasn't hard to understand why.

Charlotte had married her husband, Parker, when they were just nineteen. The next five decades together yielded a family and a lucrative company dreamed up over a shared glass of wine. Based on the snippets of conversation Tori heard throughout the night, they were the epitome of the perfect couple.

So it made perfect sense why Charlotte had retreated

from the world when one half of that perfect couple simply up and walked out on her with nary a hint as to his plans. To venture out her door after that would have been akin to ripping off her heart's Band-Aid again and again and again.

"If you keep frowning like that, dear, no amount of makeup advice I give will have even a hope of making a difference."

Tori released her lower lip from its nibbled hold between her teeth and glanced up at her self-appointed life coach on all things southern and beyond, shrugging as she did. "Don't you find it so sad that Charlotte lived the last five years of her life in so much pain? I mean, think about it. Those six months or so after I caught Jeff cheating on me were virtually unbearable. I can't even imagine five years like that."

Rose elbowed her way between them to claim a pair of white folding chairs to the left of Tori. Pointing a middle-aged black woman to the one in the middle, Rose slowly lowered herself to the other. "That's why the Alzheimer's was actually a blessing in disguise. She was able to forget the pain at times, wasn't she, Frieda?"

Before the woman could answer, Rose grabbed hold of Tori's white silk blouse and tugged. "Victoria, this is Frieda Taylor. Frieda was Charlotte's personal nurse right up until the very end, isn't that right, Frieda?"

Her face grim, Frieda nodded. Slowly. "That's right, Mizz Winters."

Margaret Louise cleared the receiving line and pulled up a chair, her feet looking more than a little out of place in black patent leather dress pumps. "Did ya'll see Ethan just now? Why, he was textin' up a storm while the lot of us were waitin' to offer our condolences to him and Brian." Pulling her hand down the front of her face, Margaret Louise took in a deep, deliberate inhale. "You'd think he was sittin' on a park bench instead of mournin' the mama that catered to his every whim."

"What's going to happen to Brian?" Leona asked.

One by one, they all turned in the direction of the receiving line, their collective gazes moving from the well-dressed, albeit despised, Ethan to his slightly rumpled, yet older, brother, Brian. In contrast to the younger Devereaux, Brian's focus was trained on the face of each person who stopped to shake his hand, his expression serious.

Rose sighed. "I imagine Ethan will shove him in a group home for the mentally challenged."

An uncharacteristic cluck emerged from Leona's mouth but was quickly dwarfed by a garbled sound from Charlotte's nurse.

"Frieda?" Margaret Louise leaned across the circle of chairs and laid a calming hand on the woman's knee. "Is everything okay?"

Laying a hand across her mouth, Frieda shook her head, her long dark lashes mingling atop her cheeks before parting to reveal a pain so raw, so real, it drew a gasp from Tori and her friends. "Mizz Devereaux was convinced Ethan would step up and take care of Brian when she passed. She believed it so surely she insisted on making a list of all Brian's likes and dislikes just so Ethan would have them to consult as needed." Frieda dropped her hand to her lap, her already hushed voice morphing into a near whisper. "She used one whole day's energy writing that list."

"I knew Charlotte was sick and that she wasn't doing well, but I had no idea she was so close to death." Rose's hands shook ever so slightly as she pulled the flaps of her cotton sweater close against her delicately patterned floral housedress. "If I'd known, I would have stopped by to see her."

"I didn't know she was so close, either." Frieda looked up, her large eyes moving from face to face, searching for something Tori didn't understand. "Every day she had a good spell. She'd tell stories—mostly about her husband, Parker."

"She shouldn't have wasted her spells." Leona's voice dripped with the unmistakable bitterness of one who understood the kind of hurt Charlotte had endured at the hands of her wayward husband. "He didn't deserve them."

"Some days, I worked up the courage to say those exact words. I even tried to encourage her to use her energy on other things—like accompanying me on a walk around the property or doing something simple like icing cookies or playing a game with Brian when he wasn't working . . . but then she'd ramble on about mistakes, looking at me with the most heartbreaking emptiness in her face."

Rose and Margaret Louise exchanged looks as Frieda continued. "That's when I started to realize the emptiness came *after* Mizz Devereaux rambled."

Tori looked at the faces assembled around them but saw the same confusion she knew was mirrored on her own.

"I tried to tell Ethan some of the things she said, but he chalked it up to the Alzheimer's just like Mr. Sweeney, and the night nurse, and the doctor, and even"—Frieda worked to contain the emotion that permitted a tear to slip down her round cheeks—"*I* did for far too long."

Leona backed into the upholstered chair behind her and sat down. "What are you saying, Frieda?"

The nurse lifted her head and looked toward the receiving line, the sight of Ethan texting and Brian still greeting mourners relaxing her too-rigid shoulders a hairbreadth. "Miss Devereaux was insistent that Mr. Devereaux loved her."

"It's called denial. It's one of Kübler-Ross's grief phases." Leona rubbed her heavily moisturized hands against one another. "Charlotte was just too old and too sick to reach the acceptance phase, that's all."

Frieda leaned forward across the center of the circle, her hands nervously clenching and unclenching in her lap. "I don't think it was denial. I think it was real."

"If that louse truly loved her, why did he walk out?" Leona hissed.

Frieda swallowed. "I asked her that. Many times, in fact. And every time I did, she answered the same way."

"And what way was that?" Rose asked.

"She would say, 'Parker loved us both.' And then, when I would question her words, she would say, 'I did as he would have wanted.'" Frieda swiped at her face as a second and third tear rolled down her cheeks. "But then she'd get this fearful look on her face and she'd quit drawing completely, mumbling over and over about being a fool."

"You tend to feel that way when you've been dumped." Leona shot a pointed look in Tori's direction. "It's the anger phase—only in the case of a broken heart, the anger tends to go inward as much as it goes outward."

Margaret Louise held her hands up, successfully cutting off her sister mid-tirade. "Wait just a minute. Charlotte was drawin' while she was sick? I didn't know that was possible."

"She wasn't dead, Margaret Louise," Rose groused.

Frieda straightened up once again, this time reaching her hand into a large black purse she'd set on the ground at her feet and pulling out a leather-bound book. "I bought this book for Mizz Devereaux about four or five weeks before her death. I'd had an Alzheimer's patient once who seemed to come alive when he painted. When I saw all those lovely sketches Miss Devereaux had made over the years, I hoped a sketchbook might do the same for her. I guess there was a part of me, too, that hoped it would help her communicate more effectively."

Realizing the nurse was holding the book in her direction, Tori took it from the woman's hands and unsnapped the tab that kept it closed. The first page showed a picture of a fireplace that played host to a series of tiered candles where a fire would normally burn. All but one candle was lit, casting the scene in a magical glow of warmth and peace. The mantel above held framed sketches, various knickknacks, and even a carelessly placed piece of paper dangerously close to the far edge. Tori brought the book closer, squinting at the framed sketches in the background.

"Did Charlotte draw all of these?" She heard the awe in her voice and knew it was well deserved.

Rose peered over her shoulder, her breath warm against Tori's cheek. "You mean the ones on the mantel?"

Tori nodded, her gaze skimming across the main sketch as she drank in still more details—the empty rocker in the corner, the sleeping cat on the hearth, the stethoscope lying on a table beside the rocker . . .

"She did," Rose confirmed as Margaret Louise left her

seat for a better view. "See that one right there?" Extending her bony index finger toward the book, Rose pointed at the framed photograph on the far left of the mantel. "Don't you remember that picture Georgina mentioned at the circle meeting last night? The one Charlotte drew of Town Hall with the crack in the window? That's the original right there. And do you see the one right next to it?"

Tori followed Rose's finger from one sketched photograph to the next, marveling at the perfect scale. "That's the Gazebo in the town square during a festival!"

"*That* one there is my favorite." Margaret Louise reached over Tori's shoulder and indicated the picture in the center of the mantel. "I reckon that's because it captures just how purty Sweet Briar is during the holidays."

Margaret Louise was right. It did. Right down to the perfectly decorated tree in the middle of the Green.

"I like that one." Leona's chin jutted in the direction of the second-to-last frame on the right. "Something about seeing the Sweet Briar Fire Department just makes me feel . . . warm."

"I reckon that's because you've spent the past five years or so datin' your way through the volunteer ranks, Twin." Then, without giving Leona a chance to respond, Margaret Louise continued. "Charlotte sure did love this town. Loved the buildings. Loved the people. Loved the spirit. Cryin' shame Parker had to humiliate her the way he did."

Tori heard the words yet didn't respond, as her attention had shifted to the final frame. "Oh, my gosh, that's my building. That's my library!" Leaning still closer to the original sketch, she took in every detail of the smaller, framed sketch in the background—the hundred-year-old moss trees that graced the grounds, the steps she'd sat on for lunch nearly every day despite the picnic table the Friends of the Library had donated three years earlier, the large stately windows that overlooked the town . . .

It was all there.

Picture perfect.

"Beautiful, ain't it?" Margaret Louise asked.

Nodding, Tori looked up from the first page of the book and sought Frieda's eyes. "Where is this?"

"You mean the fireplace?"

"The fireplace. The mantel. The room. All of it," she answered.

"That's Mizz Devereaux's study. That's where we went when she had her clear moments. She was sitting in her favorite recliner when she drew that. That's why the recliner isn't in the picture—because that's where she was sitting. In that one, I'd gotten out of the rocker to get her some tea yet left my stethoscope on the table." Frieda's shoulders dropped, her words, her tone taking on a broken quality. "By the time I got back with her tea, she'd slipped away again."

Silence blanketed the space between them as each woman took a moment to study the picture one more time, the nurse's words reminding them of the reason they were there and Charlotte was not. Then, with a determined inhale, Tori closed the book and handed it back to Frieda. "Thank you for sharing that with us."

"But what 'bout the rest of the pictures?" Margaret Louise protested. "Can't we see the rest?"

Reaching up to her shoulder, Tori rested a quieting hand on Margaret Louise's. "Frieda needs to get home and get some rest."

And it was true. One only had to look at the woman's

eyes to see the pain and the sadness. It was obvious Frieda Taylor had lost far more than a patient when Charlotte Devereaux passed away. She'd also lost a treasured friend.

The picture book could wait.

Compassion couldn't.

Tori rose to her feet, extending a hand in Frieda's direction. "I'm so sorry for your loss, Frieda. If there's anything we can do, please let us know."

Chapter 4

Tori could sense the tension in the room as surely as if it were a living, breathing person sitting alongside them in the ten-by-ten-foot meeting room of the Sweet Briar Town Hall. It had clenched fists compliments of Rose, drumming fingers thanks to Dixie, and more than a few noticeable sighs from Leona. Yet at that moment, it still lacked a face.

"I suppose when you're canoodling with a councilman, you can afford to be late to your own committee meeting," Leona drawled, glancing at the fourteen-carat gold souvenir from her latest male conquest while her pet bunny, Paris, sniffed her way around the room. "It's nearly seven forty and the holiday-stomping hussy is nowhere to be seen."

Rose released her fists long enough to point an accusing finger across the rectangular conference table. "I'm not quite sure why you're complaining, Leona. You're the one who got us into this mess in the first place."

"As if you have something more pressing to do on a Thursday night." Rolling her eyes skyward, Leona snorted. "Let's be honest, you old goat. If you were home right now, you'd be sitting in front of your television with your head tipped forward. Snoring."

Tori placed a calming hand on her elderly friend's arm while giving Leona her best evil librarian eye. Sure enough, all insults turned in her direction.

"Victoria, have you not figured out that your crow's feet come from making faces like that?" Without waiting for a response, Leona touched the outer corners of her eyes with her fingertips and tilted her chin upward. "I have three decades on you and I don't have lines like that."

"Don't you mean three decades and a gallon of Botox?" Dixie quipped from her spot at the far end of the table.

Leona's mouth gaped, only to shut and gape again as the door of the conference room opened and a five-foot-two overperfumed blur breezed into the conference room, dropping a stack of magazines and a leather-bound appointment book at the head of the table.

"Good evening, ladies. In case you don't know who I am, I'm Maime Wellington, Chairperson of the Sweet Briar Christmas Decorating Committee." Placing her hands on her hips, Margaret Louise's holiday nemesis flashed what Tori imagined was a smile, but it was hard to be sure. It had been so slight and so fleeting it could have been a figment of her imagination. "If you brought ideas with you, put them aside. I've got more than enough of my own."

Maime shifted her appointment book to the side and began picking through the magazines, the momentary lull providing just enough time for Tori to glance around for any sort of confirmation that she wasn't alone in her shocked confusion.

Avery Jordan was a fairly attractive man. Not without flaws, but certainly worthy of a double take from women who were drawn in by pretty eyes and nice hair. His new live-in girlfriend, however, was an entirely different matter.

Built like a pit bull, Maime was nearly as wide as she was tall. Her hair, which could best be described as the color of scorched pumpkin, was short and lifeless, providing an ill-fitting frame to a face that was more than a little nondescript with the lone exception of the dime-sized mole on the side of her nose.

Once more, Tori placed a calming hand on Rose's arm, only this time, instead of staving off a war of words, she prayed her touch would prevent a second and more noticeable shudder.

Maime looked up, her dark-as-mud eyes skirting their faces with an air of hostility that was thinly disguised by a syrupy sweet voice more befitting a preschool teacher than the woman standing in front of them now. "In the interest of those, like myself, who despise all things hokey, this year's Christmas in Sweet Briar is going to be different."

"Different?" Rose rasped before clearing her throat with a cough. "Different how?"

"Different in every way possible." Flipping her appointment book open, Maime reached into the built-in pocket on the inside front cover, extracted a thin stack of pictures, and dropped them onto the table in front of Tori, Rose, Dixie, and Leona. "We're going to decorate differently and host entirely new events."

Maime flicked her fingers across the stack of photographs, scattering them in various directions. "I mean, look at the lampposts surrounding the town square. Green garland and red bows? Don't you think that's rather . . . *stale*?"

"Nooo, I find it to be Christmas-y just like it's supposed to be." Dixie raked two or three of the pictures in for a closer look. "People in this town look forward to the telltale signs of the holidays. It's a *tradition*. Just like caroling in the Gazebo, and the holiday food drive, and Santa's ride atop the fire truck the week before Christmas."

Straightening up to her full minuscule size, Maime clapped her hands together. "And just like the green garland and red bows, those events will be changing as well. Out with the old and in with the new!"

Rose's jaw dropped.

Dixie laid her head on the table.

Leona pushed back her chair and stood, all hint of lingering shock gone in favor of barely restrained anger. "You can't do this. This isn't even your town."

Narrowing her eyes to near slits, Maime gave Leona a dismissive once-over. "I'm quite sure the postal carrier who delivers my mail each morning would beg to differ with that assessment."

"You're living with Avery on a permanent basis then?" The beaten tone of Rose's question caught Tori by surprise, prompting her to shoot a worried look in Dixie's direction.

But it was too late.

Maime held up her left hand and wiggled her ring finger back and forth, the overhead light catching hold of the woman's diamond ring and casting shimmering sparkles across the plain white walls. "I most certainly am."

"B-But he just met you," Dixie stammered.

Rose raised her elbow to the table and rested her forehead in her wrinkled hands. "Is his little boy okay with this?"

Waving off the question, Maime readdressed an eerily silent Leona. "So, as you can see, Sweet Briar is every bit as much *my* town as it is yours. And since my fiancé is a *council member*, my say actually counts."

"I can't believe Avery is okay with this." Dixie pushed back her chair and drew her purse onto her lap. "Okay with your attitude."

Like a passing cloud giving way to the sun, Maime's face broke into a plastic smile. "Avery is thrilled that I am embracing Sweet Briar and that I'm eager to make it the perfect home for our new little family."

"Avery and his son have been a family forever." Slowly, Rose lifted her head from her hand and pinned Maime with bifocal-enlarged eyes. "There's nothing *new* about that."

And just like that, any hint of sun—artificial or otherwise—was pushed from the sky by the kind of cloud that sent people scurrying for the nearest basement.

"You just wait," Maime hissed from between clenched teeth. "By the time I'm done around here, there won't be a single shred of Avery's former life *anywhere*. And that includes inside your precious little Sweet Briar."

Despite the presence of a brownie, a slice of apple pie, a blueberry scone, and a piece of chocolate fudge, the mood around the table was dour at best.

Every few minutes, Dixie would start a sentence, only

to shake her head and go back to poking at her scone. Rose didn't even attempt to speak, her lips pursed tight in a visible mixture of grief and anger. Leona, on the other hand, had no trouble speaking at all, her play-by-play recap of the Christmas committee meeting pouring from her mouth with little to no filter.

"Can you believe the nerve of that woman? Who does she think she is, blowing into town like that and changing everything to suit her evil ways?" Leona pushed her plate of fudge into the center of the high-top table and folded her arms around a sleeping Paris. "She didn't listen to a word we said. Not one."

Tori forked off a corner of her brownie and popped it into her mouth. "I thought I was going to fall out of my chair when she said she was doing away with the Santa visit and the holiday food drive."

"And don't forget the caroling," Dixie reminded via her first complete sentence in over an hour. "Why, there are people who come from two or three towns over to be part of that tradition every year. I can't imagine just stopping it, can you?"

"I can't imagine any of the things she suggested," Leona snapped. "Aluminum trees around the square? A holiday gift snatch? Christmas Eve ring and runs?"

Dixie snorted. "We should have just left. Let her figure out how to execute her insanity all on her—"

"No, we shouldn't have left." Rose extricated her hands from each other just long enough to push her glasses back into position, affording the matriarch a better view of the women seated around her. "That woman is a wolf in sheep's clothing."

"I didn't see anything even resembling a sheep except

when Avery came to pick her up." Leona pulled her plate back to her spot and stared down at the block of fudge. "Why did I order this? I don't eat chocolate."

"I do." Reaching across the table, Tori stilled her hand just shy of Leona's plate before addressing Rose's statement. "Leona, the way she was when Avery showed up is exactly what Rose means by sheep's clothing. She's showing him a different side."

"If Avery is stupid enough to fall for one of the oldest tricks in the book, he's got what's coming to him."

Rose glowered at Leona. "*He* might, but that little boy of his certainly doesn't."

Avery's son.

Kyle.

The epitome of an honest, sweet, loving child . . .

"Rose is right." Tori forked up an even bigger piece of brownie and paused it mere inches from her mouth.

"Maybe she is," Leona conceded grudgingly. "But what does that have to do with us working with that insufferable woman on her Let's Destroy All of Sweet Briar's Traditions Committee?"

Steadying her trembling hands inside her lap, Rose met and held Leona's eyes. "People like Maime Wellington can wear multiple faces for a while. They can even be quite gifted at it. But somewhere along the line they will mess up, showing their true colors. It's only a matter of time. It always is. By staying on that committee, three things will happen."

"And those are . . ."

"First, we're privy to things. What she plans to change, what she's up to, et cetera. Second, we get the opportunity to see what makes her tick, thereby enabling us to know what buttons push her over the edge."

Leona perked up. "Push her over the edge?"

The faintest hint of a smile twitched at the very corner of Rose's mouth, yet she continued on. "And third, armed with that information, we can make sure the true face shows when it matters most."

"Hmmmm. Very diabolical for an old goat," Leona mused, not unkindly. "I'm impressed."

"Then drive me home, will you?" Rose slid her way off the lattice-back bakery stool. "Maybe you can bring Paris inside for a quick little mother-son reunion before you have to get home to Annabelle."

Leona peered down at her wrist and nodded. "Margaret Louise is staying with Mama until I get home, but you're right, I probably should call it a night." Pulling Paris closer, Leona stood, her voice dropping to a near whisper as she addressed the still sleeping animal. "If Rose doesn't shuffle her feet too much between here and the car, Paris, you'll get to see your little boy off to sleep tonight."

Before Rose could protest the thinly disguised barb, Dixie slid off her stool as well, her purse held tightly in her hands. "Leona? Can I get a ride home, too? I'm ready to climb in bed myself and dream of the many ways in which I'd like to rid Sweet Briar of that smug little Grinch we had the grave misfortune of meeting tonight."

A chorus of agreement gave way to cheek kisses and embraces as Tori walked with her friends to the door of Debbie's Bakery, their impending departure perpetuating an all-too-familiar sense of disappointment. And she knew why.

Rose, Leona, Dixie, and the rest of her sewing sisters had become her family—people who cheered her on from the sidelines, rolled up their sleeves when she needed an extra pair of hands, held her when she was sad, and most important, stayed by her side no matter what came over the horizon. Watching a part of that walk away—even temporarily—was always worthy of a deep swallow and a momentary pang.

"I'm too late, aren't I?"

Tori turned, a smile lifting her mouth upward. "Debbie, I didn't know you were here." Leaning forward, she brushed a kiss across the bakery owner's cheek.

"Because I wasn't. I heard you were all here when I called and checked in with Emma." Debbie gathered her sandy blonde hair into a ponytail and secured it with a tie from her wrist.

Sensing an unfamiliar twinge in her friend's voice, Tori rushed to remove any possible misunderstanding. "It wasn't everyone. Just Rose, Dixie, Leona, and me for what could best be described as dessert therapy."

Debbie pointed over her shoulder to Tori's table. "Then why do three of your four plates look as if they haven't even been touched?"

There was no need to confirm Debbie's assessment. "Um, because three of the four prefer the kind of therapy that allows them to . . . *talk*?"

"So how was your brownie, Victoria?"

Knowing denial was futile, she laughed instead. "Really, *really* good."

Debbie gestured toward the table and the uneaten treats left behind. "I've been curious about that apple pie. Think Rose will mind?"

"I'd ask how you know it was Rose's pie, but I won't bother." Rising up on tiptoe, Tori reclaimed her stool. "You're a favorite in this town for a reason."

"So what was wrong?" Debbie asked before forking up a bite of pie and slipping it into her mouth.

Tori shook her head in amusement as Debbie reached across the table and helped herself to a bite of Dixie's scone, too. "Wrong?"

"With the four of you."

"Oh." Reaching onto Leona's plate, Tori liberated the block of fudge she'd been trying to resist all evening, stopping every few bites to bring Debbie up to speed on Maime Wellington and the changes in store for Sweet Briar in the weeks ahead.

When she was done, Debbie could only release a disbelieving sigh. "We can't let this happen."

"I'm not so sure we have a say," Tori said. "But whatever say we *can* have, the four of us will most certainly voice."

"Good." Debbie pushed the pie plate beside the one containing the half-eaten scone and propped up her chin with her hand. "I can't imagine what this town will look like without the garland-wrapped light poles and their great big giant red bows. Suzanna and Jackson equate that with Christmas in Sweet Briar almost as much as they do the big tree in the center of the Green."

She closed her eyes against the mental image of the large pine tree being replaced, instead, by a dozen or more aluminum trees and opted not to share that change with Debbie. Her friend would find out soon enough, as would the rest of the town.

"Makes me wonder if maybe Charlotte Devereaux

drew any pictures of Sweet Briar at Christmastime. You know, just so we can remember the way it was . . ." Her words trailed off as she thought back to the photographs she'd seen in the background of the deceased woman's sketch, the pristine detail and care still mind-boggling twenty-four hours later.

Debbie sat up tall, any hint of melancholy being shoved to the side by one of her megawatt smiles. "Oooh, did Georgina find you?"

"Georgina?" she asked. "No. Why?"

"Frieda wants you to have that framed sketch of the library that was on Charlotte's mantel!"

Tori felt the crackle of excitement as it skittered up her spine. "She does?"

Debbie nodded. "You'll probably want to double-check the details with Georgina, but apparently, Frieda wants you to come by Charlotte's tomorrow so she can give it to you in person."

And just like that, all remaining Maime Wellington–induced stress was gone, in its place the same calming sense of peace she got whenever she thought of the library.

"Maybe, while you're there, you can see some of the other sketches that were in that book Frieda gave her," Debbie continued. "Then you can tell us."

Surprised by the unchecked curiosity in her friend's voice, Tori drew back a little. "Why is everyone so curious about Charlotte's sketches?"

A hint of crimson rose in Debbie's cheeks. "I can't speak for Margaret Louise or Georgina or any of the others. Their reasons might be different. But for me? Well, I guess I was shocked by just how untouched Charlotte's ability to draw was despite her Alzheimer's. My great-aunt died of that when I was a teenager. Most of the time, at the end, she was out of it. She didn't know my name, didn't know her husband's name, didn't know her own name. But one day, when I stopped by for a visit, she was able to recall every detail of a luncheon she'd had with a friend four years earlier. I tried to tell her husband, my mom, my cousin, and anyone who would listen. But everyone discounted it. Almost as if the Alzheimer's had forever tainted everything that came out of her mouth."

Debbie clasped her hands on the top of the table and shrugged. "That always bothered me. It was like her words meant nothing any longer."

"You could come with me," she suggested. "That way you could see the sketches with your own two eyes."

Despite her best efforts, Debbie's squeal still managed to turn the heads of more than a few of her customers. "Oh, Victoria, thank you. I'd love that."

"Good. Then it's settled." Leaning to her left, Tori retrieved her backpack purse from the floor and hoisted it onto her shoulder. "And maybe, just maybe, Charlotte can rest easy knowing that someone saw what she saw at the end even if she couldn't always put it into words."

Chapter 5

Despite the fact that Charlotte Devereaux's address had them standing mere blocks from the town square, Tori couldn't help feeling as if she were standing somewhere a lot closer to Beverly Hills, California, than Sweet Briar, South Carolina. The home itself was southern in so far as it was more plantation than modern mansion, but regardless, it was huge.

The front columns that seemingly rose from the ground to support the two-story overhang were pristine white, gleaming against the brick exterior of a house more suitable for a family of ten than the four that had lived here for the better part of five decades.

Yet as breathtaking as the home and the spacious grounds were, Tori couldn't help feeling a sense of sadness for the woman who had died inside these walls, held captive until the end by a brain that had become traitorous.

Tori lifted her finger toward the doorbell, only to let it drift back to her side without pushing the button. "Did she live here alone at the end?" she asked, turning to look at Debbie.

"No. Both boys still live here from what I gather. Brian lives in one wing with an array of staff assigned to meet his needs, and Ethan pretty much rules the rest of the roost."

Inhaling a measure of comfort into her lungs at the news, Tori looked out at the line of oak trees that bordered the driveway and commanded the sight to memory so she could share it with Milo later that evening. "At least she wasn't alone in this huge house."

"Mizz Devereaux may as well have been alone for as much time as those boys spent with her at the end." Tori and Debbie looked to the left in time to see Frieda ascending onto the porch from a side staircase not more than ten feet from where they stood. Holding a bouquet of wildflowers to her nose, the nurse took in their fragrance before offering a sniff to Tori and Debbie. "Brian did what he could, but his mother's condition tended to leave him agitated and out of sorts, prompting his caregivers to earmark his visits for those times when his schedule matched with Mizz Devereaux's periods of lucidity."

"And Ethan?" Debbie asked as she handed the flowers back to Frieda. "He didn't spend time with his mother?"

A low, mirthless laugh escaped through Frieda's expansive mouth. "His version of spending time with Mizz Devereaux extended to asking for larger and larger handouts. Only he timed *his* visits for the times when she *was* foggy and confused. That way she wouldn't ask questions and he could get away with what he wanted."

"And that was different . . . how?" As soon as the words were out, Debbie held up her palms in surrender. "I'm sorry. I shouldn't have said that. It was out of line."

Frieda shifted the bouquet to her left hand and touched Debbie with her right. "It was also the truth. Mizz Devereaux had a weak spot for Ethan, and he took advantage of it every chance he could. Funny thing was, she knew it. But with Brian the way he is and her husband gone, I think she was just too tired to try and change the way she'd done things for so long. It wasn't worth wasting her rare bursts of energy. Besides, he avoided her at those times."

"Do you think she knew what was happening to her?" It was a question that had been circulating in Tori's thoughts ever since the viewing but wasn't one she necessarily planned to voice aloud. As she stood there, however, on Charlotte's front porch, listening to how alone the woman must have felt, it was all Tori could think about, let alone ask.

A dark cloud passed across Frieda's face, sparking an inexplicable chill down Tori's spine. "In the beginning, I didn't think so. But as time went on, I began to suspect maybe she did." Then, with a quick glance from side to side, the nurse took a step closer and lowered her voice to a near whisper. "I even felt like she was trying to tell me something. Something important. But the harder she tried, the less I understood and the more frustrated Mizz Devereaux seemed to become."

"What kinds of things would she say?" Tori finally asked.

The tips of Frieda's fingers paled as she pushed her hand to her mouth. "It wasn't one single thing, but rather more of a bunch of little things that always made me feel as if there was something she was trying to get off her chest. I'd reassure her that she was a good person when she got like that, but it never seemed to help. That's when I got the sketchbook. That seemed to help for a while. And then, one day, the fervor she drew with began to feel more like"—Frieda craned her neck toward the empty driveway to the side of the porch—"*fear*. Like she was in a race of some sort."

Debbie gripped Frieda's hands and held them until they stopped trembling. "Fear about what?"

Frieda closed her eyes and sucked in a deep breath before releasing it into the clear November day. "I don't know. At first I thought she was simply afraid of dying. But I think it was more than that. She seemed more desperate for me to understand whatever it was she was trying to say. And then it was too late. She—and whatever she was trying to tell me—was . . . *gone*."

With a shake of her head, Frieda brought the bouquet of flowers to her nose once again and inhaled slowly, deliberately, before meeting Tori's gaze. "I'm sorry. I—I didn't ask you to come so I could unleash my regrets on you. I asked you to come because I thought you'd like to have Mizz Devereaux's sketch of the library. I noticed how much you enjoyed the miniature version in her sketchbook last night, and I want it to go to someone who will appreciate it."

Pivoting on her soft-soled shoes, Frieda motioned for them to follow her into the house. Once inside, she bypassed the center hallway in all its gleaming glory and led the way down a side one instead, her footsteps nearly silent against the lush carpet. "Despite the fact that virtually every room in this home looks like something out of a high-end decorating magazine, Mizz Devereaux preferred to spend her days in her husband's study. She said it was where she felt closest to him."

Tori felt the catch in her throat as their feet left carpet in favor of wood as they stepped into the room she'd seen through Charlotte's eyes just the night before. In fact, the woman's drawing had been so accurate, it took Tori all of about a second to locate the chair that had been the vantage point.

She ran her hand along the back of the upholstered recliner, the pull to sit far stronger than her will to resist. "May I?" she finally asked.

Frieda nodded. "Of course." Then, without missing a beat, the woman pulled Charlotte's sketchbook from a desk drawer and opened it to the first page before setting it in Tori's lap. "It's amazing, isn't it?"

And it was.

Because as skillful as the picture was when observed out of context, it was mind-blowing when given the bird's-eye view from which it had been executed. "Wow." Slowly, she looked from the book to the room and back again, a series she repeated over and over as she compared the two. "Look at this," she called to Debbie, who was making the rounds of the room on foot. "Look here, at the fireplace"—her finger tapped the sketch, drawing her friend's eye to the spot in question—"do you see that crack in that brick right there? Now remember where it is in the drawing—third row of bricks from the bottom, fourth brick in from the opening of the hearth, right?" At Debbie's nod, Tori pulled her finger from the book and pointed it toward the correlating brick in the actual fireplace. "She not only put it in, she got it exactly right. And look at the clock. It must be broken because it shows the same time now as it does in the picture."

"It's been broken for as long as I've been here," Frieda volunteered from her spot in the rocking chair forward and to the side of where Tori sat. "Mentioned it a time or two to Ethan, but he didn't care. He had an array of Rolexes he'd gotten from Mizz Devereaux and his father over the years, so he wasn't too concerned about the clock in here."

She heard Frieda, even registered what the woman was saying on some level, but her focus was on the picture and the extraordinary detail that had come from the mind of an Alzheimer's patient. Charlotte was present in the room every time she drew a picture.

"I mean, look at this." Tori held the sketchbook out for Frieda to see. "Charlotte even put a piece of scrap paper on the mantel and made it look as if it was going to fall off."

"Because it was. Sticking things in places where they didn't belong was always Ethan's way of cleaning up."

"I thought you said he didn't come in here often," Debbie reminded her from somewhere behind Tori.

"He didn't. Not unless he wanted something. And even then, it didn't matter how she was feeling or what she was working on in her book, he just wanted to ask whatever he wanted to ask and hightail it out of here as quickly as possible." Frieda sighed in disgust. "Right after I gave her that book, she drew a picture for him. Even ripped it out of her book so he could keep it. But he barely even looked at it, opting instead to shove it on the mantel like you see in that picture."

Tori looked again at the picture, at the scrap paper dangerously close to the edge of the mantel, and realized Frieda was right. "Wow, if you look close, you can actually see the torn edges of the paper," she mused in an awed whisper before Frieda's words hit home. "But how could he do that to her? She *made* him something."

"Now you understand the talk about him at our circle meeting on Monday night." Debbie came around the back of the chairs and perched on the edge of a leather ottoman at Frieda's feet. "I think giving Charlotte that sketchbook was such a gift, Frieda. It's obvious she enjoyed it."

Tori half listened as she turned the page, the next picture in the book nearly identical to the first with a few minor exceptions . . .

"I have to admit part of the reason I gave Mizz Devereaux that book was to help me understand her. But it didn't work." Frieda craned her head around the edge of the chair to get a better view of Tori's lap. "And now you see why."

Tori stared down at the new sketch, her mind registering the absence of Frieda's stethoscope from the side table and its food tray replacement complete with a steaming cup of tea. "It's the same picture," she mumbled.

"As is the one after that . . . and the one after that . . . and the one after that." Frieda's shoulders rose and fell in frustration. "Any hope I had of figuring out what was bothering her via pictures was short lived."

Debbie leaned forward, tugging the corner of the sketchbook into her field of vision before Tori could flip ahead. "The shadows in the room are different."

Frieda agreed. "That one was drawn later in the evening—at suppertime."

Sadness turned to anger as Tori took a closer look, Charlotte's drawing for Ethan still lying precariously on the mantel. Still unwanted. Still unnoticed.

Picture after picture was essentially the same, with only slight variations depending on things like the time of day or visitors in the room. But the vantage point was always the same. Charlotte's chair. Looking toward the mantel.

"I hope you don't think I was lazy looking at those sketches because I wasn't. I tried to move that picture Ethan stuck on the mantel many, many times. But every time I did, Mizz Devereaux got upset."

Tori pulled her focus from the sketchbook and fixed it, instead, on Frieda. "Upset? Upset how?"

"She'd start rocking in her chair. Sometimes she'd make noises, but most of the time it was just the rocking. Like a little kid who'd gotten in trouble . . . or was afraid she would." Frieda pushed off the chair and wandered over to the mantel, her dark hand gliding its way across the edge. "I hated to see her like that so I just left it."

Tori nodded and then looked back at the book, her fingers continuing to flip from sketch to sketch.

"And then, one day, it was gone." Frieda dropped her hand to her waist and turned to face them, her eyes wide. "And so was Mizz Devereaux."

"Gone?" Tori and Debbie echoed in unison.

Frieda worried her lower lip into her mouth. "That's the day she passed. In her sleep."

"Did you know it was coming?" Debbie asked as Tori flipped to the last picture in the book.

"Mizz Devereaux's death? Of course. I knew it was a matter of time. I just thought we had more of it."

She opened her mouth to ask Frieda a question but slammed it shut as Charlotte's final picture came into view. The sketch itself was the same as all the others with the mantel, the framed sketches of Sweet Briar landmarks, the crack in the brick, the end table with its variation of the day, and the broken clock. Only this time, the picture Charlotte had given Ethan was faceup on the hearth, the victim of a swift autumn breeze . . .

Pulling the book closer, Tori stared down at Ethan's picture, the chosen setting bringing an instant flash of recognition.

"She drew him a picture of the library?" she whispered.

Debbie and Frieda rushed to see the picture that had been hidden from view for nearly two dozen pages while she took in the near-perfect copy of the framed sketch showcased on the mantel less than three yards from where she sat.

"She liked to duplicate drawings, didn't she?"

Debbie's words broke through Tori's woolgathering. "I—I guess."

"Well, let's see." Frieda made her way back to the mantel, only to return to Tori's side once again, the framed sketch in her outstretched hand. "Is it the same?"

Tori took the frame and held it next to the sketchbook, her eyes cataloging every detail at warp speed.

"She drew the same trees, the same fine cracks in the front steps . . ."

She followed Debbie's verbal tour around the picture until they reached the last spot. Squinting at the sketch in front of her, she felt her stomach flop, once. Twice.

"Mizz Sinclair? Is there something wrong?"

She stared down at the sticks lying crisscross beside a familiar tree and then up at Debbie, the confusion she saw in her sewing sister's face quickly pushed aside by the horror Tori knew was mirrored in her own.

Chapter 6

If she weren't so worried about what they might find, Tori would have been hunting around for a camera, determined to have photographic evidence of Leona Elkin in galoshes and rubber gloves. But she was, so she wasn't.

Instead, she worked to steady her breath amid the growing complaints taking place just on the other side of her desk.

"These—these boots are horrid," Leona groused as she untucked her pant leg from her left boot, only to retuck it once again.

"You don't have to wear boots at all, Twin."

Leona pinned Margaret Louise with a glare to end all glares. "Then what do you propose?"

"Wear your fancy heels and resign yourself to gettin' 'em dirty while we dig, or stay here and wait for us to tell you what happened." Margaret Louise pulled her work gloves higher on her thick wrists and grabbed the series of shovels she'd propped against the wall of Tori's office. "Tori . . . here's your shovel. Jake says it's a good one."

She swallowed against the lump that had taken up residence in her throat since the moment she saw Charlotte's sketch, the possible implication of the crisscrossed sticks making her more than a little nauseous. "Did you tell Jake why you needed them?"

"No. I figured there'd be time 'nough for that if we find somethin'." Margaret Louise grabbed hold of her own shovel and gestured toward Leona. "So what's it gonna be, Twin? You in or you out?"

Leona hijacked her sister's shovel and made her way toward the door, her shoulders squared beneath her teal-colored cardigan. "I'm just glad Paris is with Rose and Patches this evening. Something like this could give my sweet baby nightmares."

"We don't know that we're even going to find anything, Leona." But even as she spoke the words aloud, she knew they were wrong. Charlotte Devereaux was the queen of details. If a brick was cracked, she drew it. If a window was broken, she included it. And while there were no actual sticks beside the tree when she returned to the library that afternoon, the likelihood they'd be there from one day to the next was essentially nil.

The picnic tables outside the library were used by visiting school groups, reading senior citizens, and hungry library employees determined to get a little fresh air. The tree in question was beside the tables.

"I don't mean nightmares over what we'll find," Leona snapped. "I mean nightmares over seeing her mama dressed like this." Leona motioned toward her getup with her non-shovel-holding hand. "I haven't worn something like this since . . . since *never*."

Margaret Louise's hearty laugh bounced off the walls of Tori's office. "No one told you to wear a trench coat, Twin. Or a hat with a flashlight, either."

"I'm being prepared," Leona protested.

"Prepared for what exactly? A landslide?"

"Oh, shut up, Margaret Louise!"

It felt good to laugh even if the moment was short lived. "Ladies, ladies. Really. However you want to dress is fine." Tori made her way over to the door and flicked off the overhead light. "With any luck, we'll dig and find nothing."

She led the troops down the hallway and toward the library's back door, the shovel from Margaret Louise's son in one hand, Charlotte's sketchbook in the other. She knew the marked spot well. In fact, the picnic table that resided beside it had been the sight of lunches with everyone from Margaret Louise and her granddaughter Lulu, to Milo and his mother. Its location provided shade in the summer as well as a bit of privacy from the curious eyes of passing pedestrians.

"Maybe some kid put those sticks under the tree as part of some game right before Charlotte sat down to sketch. Did you ever think of that?" Leona posed as they exited the library and walked around the west side of the building.

"I did. And I hope that's the case." She shone her handheld flashlight at the ground beneath their feet and continued on. "But I need to know for sure. Especially since the sticks are drawn quite differently than everything else in the picture, almost as if they were an afterthought added for effect."

"Does Milo know about this?"

She winced as first Leona, and then Margaret Louise, ran into her from behind. "Victoria! Why did you stop?" Leona hissed. "You made me chip a nail."

Turning, she shone the flashlight onto Leona's chin. "In answer to your question, Leona, Milo does *not* know. There's nothing *to* know until we dig. Which, as you'll notice, we haven't done yet because . . ." Aware of the tension building in her shoulders, Tori let her words trail off as she began walking once again.

"What she's too polite to say, Twin, is butt out." Margaret Louise huffed and puffed across the library grounds until they came to the spot featured in Charlotte's drawing. "If Victoria chooses to keep secrets from Milo, that's her choice, not yours."

She stopped again. "I'm not keeping secrets, Margaret Louise. Milo left right after school today to visit an old friend in North Carolina. I'll tell him when he calls tonight."

"Men want to hear what you're wearing when they call. They want to hear that you miss them. They want to hear what you'll do when they return," Leona spouted in full lecture mode. "They don't want to hear that you've been traipsing around in the dark, digging. It's not the least bit enticing."

"Neither is the cricket that just landed on your sleeve, Leona."

She knew she shouldn't have said it, but the sight of the always regal Leona Elkin hopping around in galoshes and a flashlight-mounted hat was simply too good to pass up. So, too, was the sound of Margaret Louise's ensuing belly laugh.

"Now, can we do what we need to do and be done with

it, please?" Without waiting for an answer, Tori resumed her stride, the tree in question no more than thirty feet away.

When they reached their digging spot, she propped her shovel against the trunk of the tree and set the sketchbook on the picnic table before addressing the sturdier of her cohorts. "Margaret Louise? Can you give me a hand with this table?"

"You're darn tootin' I can."

"If Charlotte was so detailed with her pictures, why isn't the table in it?" Leona challenged.

It was a point Tori hadn't considered and it gave her pause. "It's not in the framed drawing Frieda gave me, either."

"It wasn't in your picture, Victoria, because there wasn't a picnic table here then," Margaret Louise interjected. "As for the one in the book, my guess is she used your framed sketch as her guide, seein' as how she ain't been out of her home in years."

On the count of three, they moved the picnic table a solid six feet to their left then grabbed hold of their shovels once again. "Are you ready, ladies?" she asked over the sudden roar in her ears.

"Ready." Margaret Louise glanced right. "Twin?"

Leona merely nodded, her chin still jutted forward in protest of the cricket incident.

"Okay, let's go." Tori pushed the shovel into the ground, the rain-moistened earth giving way easily beneath her foot. Shovelful by shovelful they dug, each new scoop of dirt revealing nothing more than an occasional earthworm.

Despite being firmly in her sixties, Margaret Louise

was a veritable workhorse, her contribution to the growing mound of dirt behind them every bit as large as Tori's. Leona, on the other hand, stopped every few seconds to offer an "eww" and an occasional "ick."

But still they dug.

And dug.

And dug.

"Are we hoping to get to China?" Leona whined. "Because if so, might I suggest a wonderful little restaurant in the middle of a darling little Chinese town I visited about ten years ago?"

Tori stuck the end of her shovel into the ground and leaned against the handle as all of the tension and all of the fear she'd been harboring throughout the afternoon and evening drained out of her psyche. "How about we stay right here in Sweet Briar? No restaurant anywhere can beat Margaret Louise's cooking anyway." She turned to Leona's sister. "You can stop digging now. There's nothing here."

As if Tori hadn't uttered a word, Margaret Louise continued, the pace of her task increasing with each noticeable rise of her eyebrows.

"Margaret Louise? Is something wrong—"

The grandmother of seven stopped digging and bent down, her pudgy hand sifting through the dirt to retrieve something small, flat, and rectangular.

"Margaret Louise? What is that?"

"I'm not sure . . ." The woman's words petered off as she flipped the item over. "Good heavens, what on earth is this doin' here?"

Moving in, Tori craned her neck around Margaret Louise's shoulder to find a decades-old wedding photograph that had been laminated for safekeeping. "A wedding picture?"

Margaret Louise relinquished custody of the picture and resumed the task of digging, her voice peppered with huffs and puffs. "You realize who that is, don't you?"

Tori looked again at the photo, the identity of the bride and groom a complete mystery.

Leona picked her way around the outer edge of the hole and plucked the picture from Tori's hands, only to make a face at the dirt it contained. "That's Charlotte. Looking rather plump for someone so young and in a wedding dress, I might add."

Tori stared at Leona. *"Charlotte?"*

Leona pushed the picture back in Tori's hands then wiped her own on her trench coat. "Yes, Charlotte. You know, the woman responsible for us being out here in the first place."

A strangled cry made her turn in time to see Margaret Louise jump backward in their makeshift hole, the woman's moonlit eyes wide with fear.

"Margaret Louise? What's wrong?"

"I—I think I found somethin'."

Leona rolled her eyes. "It's probably just Papa Earthworm getting ready to seek revenge if we don't quit annihilating his children."

"I—I think it's somethin' else. Somethin' bigger."

Shaking off the sudden onslaught of trepidation, Tori moved in with her shovel, the color variation Margaret Louise had unearthed both beckoning and shooing at the same time.

"M-Maybe we should call Chief Dallas," the grandmother of seven suggested by way of raspy whispering.

"It's not worth bothering him until we know there's even something worth bothering him over." Slowly, carefully, Tori moved the tip of her shovel out eight inches and carefully pushed inward, her hand lifting the dirt upward to reveal the sole of a shoe.

A *dark brown* leather shoe.

They sat side by side across the library's stone steps, watching as volunteers from the Sweet Briar Fire Department uncovered more items from the hole, the crew's progress illuminated by a large portable light that had been brought in for the occasion.

"Did you give Chief Dallas the photograph?" Leona asked from her spot between Tori and Margaret Louise.

Tori nodded.

"And the shoe? What did they say about the shoe?"

"He got men out here to dig, didn't he?" Margaret Louise hooked her right arm behind her head and stretched then repeated the same maneuver with her left arm. "Obviously he thinks we found a grave."

A grave . . .

Shivering, Tori squinted against the near-blinding effects of the high-powered light and watched as one man signaled to the others to stop. Then, moving as one, they all stepped forward and looked down. "Uh-oh," she whispered.

Margaret Louise dropped her hands back to her lap and bobbed her head to the side to afford a better view. "Sure looks like they found somethin' else, huh?"

Again Tori nodded.

And swallowed.

"You know," Leona remarked, "finding that wedding picture isn't really so surprising. The one and only time I allowed myself to get hurt by a man, I took every picture I had of the two of us together and tossed them in the fireplace. Watching them burn was . . . cleansing. Freeing." Leona reached up, switched off her hat-mounted flashlight, and set the contraption on the step below her feet. "I imagine burying some of his things would have worked, too."

"Oh. Oh. Fred's bendin' over. He—he's pickin' somethin' up." Margaret Louise paused her play-by-play just long enough to lean forward and groan. "You wouldn't happen to have binoculars in your office or anything, would you, Victoria?"

Keeping her full attention on the Sweet Briar fire chief, Tori matched Leona's lean and raised it with a stand. "It looks like some sort of metal plate and"—she rose up on tiptoes—"rod."

"I bet Charlotte shoved some of Parker's favorite things in a box and buried them where she wouldn't have to think about them," Leona declared. "It makes all the sense in the world."

"Buryin' 'em outside the library makes sense, Twin?"

Leona's chin jutted upward. "Burying them on her own property would have been bad for her home's feng shui."

"Dixie *did* say that Parker loved the library. Assuming that's true, maybe Charlotte decided to bury his stuff here as a sort of retaliation." But even as she posed the possibility, Tori found the notion to be a stretch. Granted, she had never met Charlotte Devereaux, but the one commonality between everything she'd heard was that the woman had adored her husband to the very end.

Adoring wives, whether scorned or not, didn't bury their husband's things in the ground. They kept them close, along with the never-ending hope that the object of their affection would one day rise from the dead or find his way home again after his meandering ways.

"I'll be right back," she mumbled into the night. Slowly, she descended the steps and headed toward the diggers.

As she approached, Chief Granderson broke free of the men and climbed out of the hole, holding her at bay some ten feet out. "So what made you start digging tonight?"

She considered telling him about Charlotte Devereaux's sketch but knew it wasn't the time. That would come later. "A hunch."

Fred swiped the back of his hand across the sweat-dampened dirt on his brow. "Heckuva hunch."

She met his gaze and held it a beat. "There's a body, isn't there?" she finally asked.

"Shallow grave. No casket. South Carolina temperatures and rain." Fred shrugged. "I wouldn't expect anything resembling a body to be left after five years."

Five years.

"Five—but wait." Choosing her words carefully, Tori posed the only question that made sense in light of what Fred himself had just said. "If there's nothing resembling a body in that hole, what makes you think there was one?"

"Doesn't matter how shallow the grave or how hot the climate, metal doesn't go anywhere."

"Metal?" she echoed.

Fred took a second swipe of his face, following it up with a slow, distracted nod. "That's the thing about an artificial hip. It doesn't go anywhere."

Chapter 7

Somehow Tori moved through the next five days, dotting her *i*'s and crossing her *t*'s on all final preparations for the First Annual Holiday Book Extravaganza, spending time with Milo, and fielding have-you-heard-anything-yet phone calls from nearly every member of the sewing circle at some point or the other. But the waiting was killing her.

It didn't matter that Rose, Dixie, Margaret Louise, and Georgina had all confirmed that Parker Devereaux had an artificial hip. And it didn't matter that Melissa, Beatrice, Debbie, and Leona all shared stories about the man's favorite brown leather shoes. She still wanted official confirmation of what everyone was saying across Sweet Briar's dinner tables, park benches, and picket fences.

"Pink and silver? Since when are pink and silver considered Christmas colors?"

Tori glanced up from the library's main computer and smiled. "Good morning to you, too, Dixie. Don't you look festive in your harvest sweater."

Dixie made her way around the information desk and tucked her purse on the bottom shelf, her normal brisk efficiency emitting an air of irritation that, for once, didn't seem to be aimed in Tori's direction. Sure, the ice had more than thawed where her predecessor was concerned, but Dixie was Dixie and she tended to be irritated with just about everyone at some point or another.

"I really thought Georgina would pull rank and put a stop to this woman's shenanigans, but she didn't. And I'm fit to be tied, Victoria. Fit. To. Be. Tied."

Pausing her hands atop the keyboard, Tori did her best to decipher the bubbling tirade but came up short. "Dixie, I'm sorry, I'm not following."

Dixie straightened up and grabbed hold of a nearby stack of returned books. Seconds later, they were sorted into piles based on their shelf position around the room. "That—that woman. That Maime Wellington. She's hammered the first nail into the coffin that is about to hold Sweet Briar's long-standing and long-celebrated Christmas traditions."

She pressed Save on the name card she was making for the festival's visiting author and swiveled her stool around to face Dixie head on. "What are you talking about?"

The irritation that had somehow escaped Tori during Dixie's entrance was missing no more. Hands on hips, eyes narrowed, Dixie stared at her. "Are you going to sit there and tell me you didn't notice the pink bows and the garland of silver stars inching down every single light pole from Town Hall to here?"

"Pink bows and garland of silver stars?" Confused, Tori slipped off her stool and out from behind the confines of the information desk en route to the front door. "No, I drove this morning and I came in the back way . . ." Her words trailed off as she peered through the glass, the object of Dixie's ire impossible to miss.

"Before you stole my job, I used to come to work on the day before Thanksgiving with a sense of childlike anticipation. Because I knew the decorating fairies would have come while Sweet Briar was sleeping and transformed our beautiful little town into something *magical*. And then, after I was tossed to the curb by the library board, it came to hold even more importance for me. As a symbol of tradition and . . . *loyalty*."

Tori leaned her forehead against the cool glass in the hopes it would shield her eye roll as Dixie continued pontificating off to her right. "So today, I came to town, hoping things would be the way they're supposed to be, and instead, I see *that*."

She followed the border of light poles as it surrounded the town square and searched for something, anything, that would soften the harsh reality of Dixie's assertions.

"I—I don't think I'd call it pink exactly," she offered. "I'd say it's more of a dusty rose."

"Dusty rose . . . pink . . . what does it matter? Christmas is green and red. Vegas stages are pink and silver."

Realizing it wasn't the time for playful quips, Tori resisted the urge to ask Dixie about her Vegas knowledge and instead said the only thing worthy of the occasion. "Wow."

"Wow is right," Dixie countered by way of a huff. "Wow that Councilman Jordan could be so . . . so blind. Wow that Georgina would sit back and allow Margaret

Louise's committee to get hijacked away from her. Wow that this Maime person could be so self-absorbed. Wow that—never mind." Spinning around, Dixie fast-stepped it back to the information desk, grabbing three of her sorted piles at one time. "I refuse to let that—that person rob this town of its Christmas spirit!"

Leaving her bird's-eye view, Tori returned to the information desk and grabbed the fourth stack of books. With a quick left and a right she found herself in the self-help section. "So what do you propose?" she asked the woman who was one aisle over.

"That woman may be able to hornswoggle that buffoon she's living with, and the entire town council while she's at it, but she's got no say over the Sweet Briar Ladies Society Sewing Circle."

Tori skimmed the shelf that largely contained authors in the E–L range and popped the top book into its correct spot. "True . . ."

"Well, since Santa is probably making a wide berth around Sweet Briar thanks to you-know-who this year, I say we find someone to wear his suit and pass out homemade stockings to all the children."

"Homemade stockings?" Tori asked through twitching lips.

"That's right, homemade stockings. And I bet if we ask, Fred Granderson would probably allow us to have a meet and greet with Santa inside the fire station." The sound of Dixie's footsteps grew closer, only to fade again as the woman traveled into a section on Tori's other side. "I mean, who says we have to run everything Christmas-related through Georgina and her cronies anyway? We pay taxes. We support that fire station."

Tori left self-help and ventured into local history, the placement of the next return necessitating a bend. "Dixie, I really don't think you can fault Georgina for this Maime stuff. She might be mayor but she still has to work with this council member for the next year or so. I'm sure she'll step in if she needs to."

A snort rang out from the mystery section. "She needed to step in two weeks ago when Margaret Louise was removed from her spot as committee chair."

Tori searched for an argument but came up empty. "So tell me about these stockings."

Dixie's voice remained in the mystery aisle for several minutes, the edge it held giving way to the faintest hint of smile. "Margaret Louise was making one at our last circle meeting. It was simple enough that if we make the stockings as a circle-wide project, we could get them done in no time. And if we pool our resources and buy smartly, we might even be able to fill them with candy canes and inexpensive little trinkets."

No matter what angle she looked at the idea from, it all came back to one place. "I love it, Dixie. It's a wonderful idea. And I'm quite sure the others will agree, as well."

"Then it's settled." Dixie emerged from the mystery aisle to meet Tori at the information desk. "I'll make a sample or two during the day tomorrow and bring them to our meeting on Monday night."

"You mean you'll make a sample or two on Friday, don't you?" Winding her way around Dixie, Tori returned to her stool and the task she'd abandoned in favor of gawking at the spectacle that was Maime Wellington.

"No. I mean tomorrow."

"But tomorrow is Thanksgiving," she protested.

Reaching for the pencil basket and the stack of scrap paper, Dixie rearranged everything so the paper was neat and the eraser ends of the pencils uniform with one another. "So?"

"Aren't you eating turkey?"

Dixie shook her head.

"Ham?"

Again, Dixie shook her head.

"Chicken?"

Dixie replaced the basket and paper in their correct spots and turned to face Tori. "I won't be celebrating Thanksgiving this year."

She drew back. "Why not?"

"I don't have anyone to celebrate it with."

The pain that flickered across Dixie's face at the confession pricked Tori's eyes with an unmistakable burn. "What about Rose?"

Dixie shrugged. "We decided a long time ago that sitting across from each other at the Thanksgiving table was depressing. So we quit."

"So Rose isn't going to celebrate it, either?"

"You can't tell her I told you, or she'll have my head."

"Why?" she asked.

"Because she doesn't like pity invitations." Tori followed Dixie's gaze around the empty library until it came to mingle with hers. "It makes you feel like a bother."

"A bother? You and Rose aren't bothers. You're friends. *My* friends."

Dixie turned and cleared her throat but not before Tori caught the play of emotion across her gently lined face.

Her mind made up, Tori spoke the words that needed to be said. "Milo laughed at me the other day when he saw the turkey I bought. He said it was so big we should be cooking for a small army instead of just his mom. So you and Rose? You're now part of our army."

"I can't impose like that." But even as the words left Dixie's mouth, Tori could see the hope flashing behind the woman's eyes.

"The only reason I didn't invite you sooner is because I didn't realize you were free." And it was true. For as rocky a start as she and Dixie had had in the beginning, their common love for the library had forged a bond between them. "Please, Dixie. I want you to come. I want Rose to come. I'd want everyone from our circle to come if they could."

Dixie shifted from foot to foot, her trouser socks pulled high beneath the hem of her simple housedress. "But Thanksgiving is for families, Victoria. You know that as well as I do."

"You're right. It is." Slipping off her stool once again, Tori closed the gap between the computer and the former head librarian with several easy steps. When they were face-to-face, she took Dixie's hands in hers and gave them a reassuring squeeze. "And that's why I want you and Rose to spend it *with* Milo and me. Because you guys *are* my family."

Chapter 8

One by one, Tori transferred the piping hot rolls from the cookie sheet to the bread basket, the sound of Milo's voice just inside the living room solidifying one of the many things she would give thanks for at the table that night.

Her late great-grandmother had always told her the right man was worth waiting for, and she'd been right.

Milo Wentworth was the perfect man. He was patient and kind, creative and loving, and accepting in a way she never could have imagined.

And he was night-and-day different from her late former fiancé, Jeff—the man she'd once thought was right, only to discover he was wrong with a capital *C*. For cheater.

But she'd been fresh out of college when she'd accepted Jeff's proposal and, thus, rather inexperienced when it came to the warning signs associated with the wrong person.

His painful blind side and her subsequent broken heart had obliterated that naiveté and replaced it with a wariness where the opposite gender was concerned.

Milo, however, had broken through that wariness by being exactly who he was, and exactly who she was blessed to find.

"It's a shame your great-grandmother didn't get a chance to meet him."

The truth behind Rose's words pricked at the corners of her eyes and made her grateful for the last two rolls waiting their turn to be plucked off the sheet.

She felt the weight of her friend's eyes as she filled the basket and then covered it with a cloth, her emotions still too close to the surface to respond.

"I can't imagine many thirty-four-year-old men being terribly thrilled at the notion of four stragglers invading his Thanksgiving dinner."

Pushing the basket to the side of the kitchen table, Tori reached for the pot of gravy and poured its newly warmed contents into the appropriate china piece. When she was confident she could speak without crying, she gave it a go. "You and Dixie and Georgina and Beatrice aren't stragglers. You're my family. He knows this."

"You still miss her, don't you?"

If it were anyone else, she might have gotten away with changing the subject or denying full understanding of the question, but it was Rose.

And Rose knew better.

She felt her grip on the pot begin to give way and opted instead to set it back down on the stove. "Not a day goes by that I don't miss her, Rose. I think about her every morning when I put my feet in my slippers because they're one of the last things she ever gave me. I think about her when I'm at work and I'm standing in the middle of the library looking at all of the books—books she taught me to love. I think about her every time I pick up my needle and thread, knowing the lifelong gift she gave me by teaching me to sew. I think about her every time my mother calls and I hear the growing similarity in their voices. I think about her every night when I lay my head down on the pillow and I glance over at her picture on my nightstand. And"—she paused to steady her breathing, to say the last few words before the growing lump in her throat prevented her from speaking at all—"I think about her every time I see you, Rose."

Surprise widened the elderly woman's eyes behind bifocal glasses. "Me?"

Blinking against the tears that threatened to make her eyes puffy and her nose run, Tori merely nodded before resuming the last few tasks necessary before calling everyone to the dining room table. She added more gravy to the gravy boat, she filled one of the serving bowls with stuffing and the other with the homemade mashed potatoes, and she added a serving fork to the platter of freshly carved turkey.

Quietly, Rose moved in beside her, readying the green beans and the winter squash for their place at the table alongside the plate of cranberry sauce. When everything was ready, Rose took hold of Tori's hands and brought them just shy of her wrinkled cheek. "When you get old, like me, you tend to think you've had your moment in the sun. You've lived your life, accomplished your dreams, and received all your blessings. You start to sit back and wait until it's your time to go. But your coming into my life while I was sitting back, waiting, proved me wrong. At least on the blessing part."

Tori nibbled her lower lip inward and met Rose's gaze through tear-dappled lashes. "Are you trying to make me look all red and swollen at the dinner table?"

With a quick shake of her head and a soft kiss on Tori's hand, Rose grabbed hold of the cranberry sauce and headed into the dining room, her careful steps and momentary hesitations betraying her earlier statements about feeling good. For a moment, Tori simply watched her, all too aware of the passage of time and the need to savor every moment you have with loved ones.

Savor . . .

Inhaling deeply, Tori scooped up the stuffing and mashed potatoes and fell in line behind Rose, her gaze moving beyond the dining table and into the living room, where Beatrice, Dixie, Georgina, Milo, and his mother were seated. "Everything is ready."

And just like that, five additional pairs of hands swooped into the kitchen, only to return carrying the rest of the Thanksgiving meal. When the various dishes were in place, they each took their seat.

"Everything looks amazing, Tori." Milo leaned over the corner of the table and planted a kiss on Tori's cheek. "I've been looking forward to this all week."

She smiled back into his warm brown eyes, marveling at the way their amber flecks seemed to dance in the glow of the candlelight she'd chosen for the meal. "I'm glad." Turning her attention to include everyone assembled around the table, she took a deep breath then released it slowly. "Every Thanksgiving for as far back as I can remember, my great-grandmother would ask us to hold hands around the table and take turns sharing something we were thankful for that year."

Before she could continue, Milo grabbed hold of her with his right hand and his mother with his left, prompting a domino of hand holding to move around the table until Rose took hold of Tori's right hand.

Blinking against a sudden threat of tears, Tori looked across the table at Milo's mother. "Rita? Would you like to go first?"

Rita Wentworth nodded. "I'm thankful for you, Victoria. For the chance to have a daughter again."

Tori felt Milo's squeeze on her hand, knew that the reference to Milo's late wife, Celia, was just that—a reference. Celia's death over a decade earlier had been tragic and sad, but as Tori had come to realize, life went on. It didn't forget. It just moved on.

Dixie was next. "I'm thankful for friends, like Victoria, who make me feel wanted—at the library and at a Thanksgiving meal."

Always shy, Beatrice kept her contribution short, giving thanks for all of God's blessings before her silence paved the way for Georgina to speak.

"I'm thankful for—"

The mayor's sentence was cut short by the first few notes of *Hawaii Five-0*, the song alerting Tori and her assembled sewing circle sisters to both the phone's owner and the caller's identity. "I'm so sorry," Georgina said, breaking contact with Beatrice and Rose in order to push back from the table and jog into the living room in search of her purse. "Chief Dallas wouldn't call me on Thanksgiving unless there was good reason."

Tori watched as Georgina located her purse and slipped

her hand inside, only to retrieve the phone just as the ring-
ing stopped. "Oh, darn."

"Give him a minute, maybe he'll leave a voice mail or
call back," Milo suggested from his spot at the head of the
table.

Sure enough, less than thirty seconds later, the phone
chirped, signaling the presence of a voice mail. Flipping
it open, Georgina pressed a few buttons and then held it to
her ear, her eyes closed tightly as she nodded along to the
voice in her ear. When the message was done, Georgina
shut the phone in her hand and slowly opened her eyes,
her voice void of its normal strength and confidence.
"Well, it's official. The apparatus removed from the library
grounds last week was, in fact, Parker Devereaux's."

Tori heard the gasp as it left her mouth, felt the subsequent tightening of Milo's hand on hers, but the sudden
roar in her ears made it nearly impossible to acknowledge
either. On some level, she knew her reaction was silly. The
presence of the man's shoe-of-choice, coupled with an
apparatus Chief Granderson had already deemed an artificial hip, had left her with little explanation other than
the obvious. But still, she'd hoped . . .

Hoped the metal plate and rod had been a contraption
Charlotte's husband had built out of boredom. Hoped the
buried shoe had been what Leona had suggested—an
attempt, by Charlotte, to rid her life of reminders of a
philandering husband. Hoped the woman who'd sketched
such beautifully detailed drawings had been incapable of
taking a life.

Chief Dallas's phone call removed that hope.

A gentle shaking of Tori's hand inside Milo's broke
through her woolgathering and forced her attention back

to the here and now. A here and now that had her sitting at the Thanksgiving table, surrounded by her loved ones, all of whom were casting worried looks in her direction.

She could try to explain what she was feeling, but then again, maybe she couldn't.

Trying to explain your feelings to other people when you weren't even sure what, exactly, those feelings were, wasn't easy.

"Don't mind me. I'm fine. Really. Truly." Forcing the corners of her mouth into something resembling a smile, Tori nodded her head at Georgina, who'd just returned to the table. "Georgina? You were saying . . ."

Georgina replaced her napkin in her lap and took hold of Beatrice and Rose's hands once again. "I'm thankful for the opportunity to serve the residents of Sweet Briar—people I consider dear friends."

Rose was next, her age-weakened voice bringing a catch to Tori's throat. "I'm thankful for . . . for this. This moment. Right now."

As all eyes turned back toward Tori, Milo spoke, his request to go next followed by his heartfelt words, making them all blink in rapid succession. "Tori, I'm thankful for many things in my life. My mom, memories of my dad, good friends, good health, and the innocence of the kids I teach every day. But having you in my life and knowing that I will share the rest of my days hand in hand with you is what I'm most thankful for."

That did it. Her repeated attempts to ward off tears finally failed, leaving her reaching for her napkin to fend them off. When she had stopped their flow, she took her turn, her own words only serving to undermine her efforts.

"Three years ago, I thought my life was over. I'd lost

my beloved great-grandmother, and what I thought was my future. But it all turned around. I moved here. I got my dream job. I found the friends my great-grandmother always knew I'd find—people who have kept her spirit alive in my heart." Slowly, she took in the faces assembled around her—Dixie, Beatrice, Georgina, and Rose— before closing her eyes as the image of four more faces flashed through her thoughts.

Margaret Louise.

Leona.

Debbie.

And Melissa.

Her lashes parted and she turned to Milo, her voice trembling with emotion. "And I found the man I was destined to spend my life with. A man I cherish and adore."

The way Charlotte adored Parker . . .

The thought churned in her stomach as hands released one another around the table and began reaching for platters and bowls.

Beans changed hands.

Stuffing was passed back and forth.

Turkey was scooped onto plates.

Gravy was poured across potatoes.

Pockets of conversation sprang up on both sides of the table.

But none of it mattered except the one question that had been playing peekaboo with Tori for days . . .

Why would Charlotte Devereaux have killed her husband, and who on earth helped her bury his body?

Chapter 9

Tori was waiting on the front porch when Margaret Louise's powder blue station wagon came careening around the corner at a speed more in keeping with a race car driver than a grandmother of seven. And like Pavlov's dog, she smiled at the sight.

It didn't matter whether Margaret Louise was picking her up for a shopping expedition, a girls' weekend in the mountains, or an emergency chocolate run to the bakery, time spent together in that car was always a treat.

Pulling to a stop at the curb, Margaret Louise reached across the wide bench seat and rolled down the passenger-side window, her rounded cheeks pushed upward by the laugh that wafted onto the sidewalk. "I was just sayin' to Melissa how much I miss our snoopin', when you called. Nearly fell down the front steps tryin' to get over here."

"I didn't mean you had to come this second." Tori

plucked her backpack purse from its spot by her feet and hoisted it onto her shoulder before making her way down the steps and over to the wagon. "I could have waited a little while, you know?"

"And take a chance you'd realize your big book event is tomorrow and back out? Not a chance."

"Oh, trust me, I'm aware it's tomorrow. But I've triple- and quadruple-checked every possible detail, and if I don't stop, I'm going to go insane. Truly."

The back window inched down to reveal their tried-and-true backup, as well as her long-eared sidekick. "Paris was in need of a break, too, dear. All those dirty little hands constantly running along her back have to become tiresome."

Tori yanked open the door and climbed inside just in time to see Margaret Louise turn to her sister in the backseat. "My grandbabies don't have dirty hands."

Leona and Paris shifted across the backseat, affording Tori a much better view of the eye roll that accompanied the dramatic sigh. "You might find a house full of kids running here, there, and everywhere to be relaxing, dear sister of mine, but I don't. And neither does my precious Paris."

Margaret Louise's eyebrow arched upward. "Oh? Then why does Paris wiggle out of your arms every time you drop by Jake's?"

"To borrow a phrase from Jake Junior—D'uh . . . Because my precious angel is desperate to secure a hiding spot until I remove her from that circus." A second eye roll gave way to a defiant glimpse out the window.

"So she hides by hoppin' straight into Lulu's arms?" With a celebratory glance at Tori, Margaret Louise swiveled her body around until her hands were on the steering wheel once again. "So? Where to, Victoria?"

Where to . . .

That was the million-dollar question.

Only problem was, she didn't really have an answer. Not a concrete one anyway.

"I guess I want to learn as much as I can about Parker Devereaux."

"He's dead, dear. What more is there to know?" Leona drawled. "He had no imagination where footwear was concerned, and his wife should receive an Oscar posthumously for her role as a loving wife."

She turned back to Leona. "An Oscar? Why?"

Bending her non-Paris-holding fingers inward, Leona inspected her latest manicure, declaring it a success with a faint nod of her head before meeting Tori's gaze. "Why? Why? Did she not bury the man on library grounds and then tell the world he'd up and left her for another woman? Because if I have my facts wrong, please tell me."

Margaret Louise peered into her rearview mirror and made a face. "Twin, must you always be so—so sarcastic?"

"Yes."

She had to laugh. But at the same time, she couldn't fault the woman in the backseat for her statement, sarcastic or not.

Facts were facts. And the facts staring her in the face were easy.

Charlotte Devereaux had essentially dropped out of sight five years earlier after her husband of fifty years disappeared.

That same woman told everyone in Sweet Briar he left to pursue another woman.

Yet all the while, his body was buried some fifteen or so yards from the Sweet Briar Public Library.

One could argue Charlotte hadn't known if they hadn't seen the sketch she'd drawn marking the spot where her husband's body had been buried.

But Tori had seen the sketch.

So, too, had Margaret Louise, Leona, and Debbie.

Feeling the weight of Margaret Louise's stare, Tori shifted her focus forward and clicked her seat belt into place. "I think we need to take a tour of Parker Devereaux's life. See if maybe we can piece together the why behind Charlotte's crime."

"You got it!" With a tug of her forearm, Margaret Louise shifted the station wagon into drive and pushed down on the gas, the sudden surge of power resulting in a narrow miss with Tori's neighbor's car and a rapid string of prayers from the back seat. "Woo-eee! This is fun . . ."

"So where are we going exactly?" Tori asked as the car turned left and then right before heading toward the main road leading in and out of Sweet Briar.

Margaret Louise tightened her grip on the steering wheel and sped up as a truck tried to pass them on the two-lane rural highway. "To the Devereaux Center in Tom's Creek."

"Devereaux Center?" she echoed.

"Parker was a big supporter of the mentally challenged in the area on account of Brian. He funded the buildin' of a special center where they could meet each other in a social environment as well as interact with counselors trained to meet their individual needs." A peek in the rearview mirror, coupled with Margaret Louise's subsequent laugh, prompted Tori to check her side-view mirror in time to see the truck's proximity increase to nearly six car lengths. "It was really a beautiful thing watchin' the way he accepted that boy and worked to help him and others like him."

She lifted her chin to the speed-induced breeze flowing through the car and mulled over her friend's words. "And Brian was the oldest, right?"

"That's right," Margaret Louise confirmed. "Ethan is the younger, pampered one."

"So tell me about Brian. Who's been looking after him these past few years while his mother was ill?"

"From what I understand, Victoria, there's staff assigned to him—people who cook his favorite meals, attend to his shoppin', and drive him to work and the center."

Turning her head to the left, Tori took in the rounded features of Margaret Louise's face and found herself smiling all over again. "Work?"

"Brian is very high functionin', particularly if there's a strong routine involved. Why, Jerry Lee says he's even been known to help work kinks out of programs they've brought to market." Margaret Louise's eyes shifted toward the rearview mirror briefly. "Hard to imagine when it wasn't too long ago that people like Brian were shoved in institutions and written off as lost causes, ain't it?"

"He worked at his father's company?"

"Don't sound so shocked, Victoria. Parker was smart. He got Brian involved when he wasn't more 'n eighteen. Started him slow, doin' things like sortin' mail and stuff. But Jerry Lee said he was quick *and* curious. Before long, Brian was sittin' at the drawin' table, helpin' programs get off the ground."

"Wow." It was a simple word, yet it fit perfectly.

"As Parker began to travel more," Margaret Louise continued, "Jerry Lee sort of volunteered to look after Brian at the office. Said it was a pleasure."

"For Jerry Lee maybe, but his wife tells a very different story."

Bending her left leg at the knee, Tori lifted it onto the vinyl seat and shifted her whole body to the left to afford a better view of both Margaret Louise and Leona. "Why do you say that, Leona?"

Leona hooked Paris in the crook of her arm, stroking the bunny's head until her eyes began to close. Once she was asleep, Tori's question was addressed. "Sadie Sweeney is one of those picture-perfect women who maintains that picture-perfect image by keeping a tight leash on the people in her life. Her friends pass their time *with her*. The charities she volunteers with *tout her*. Her husband spends his time talking *about her and their picture-perfect life together.*"

"Okay . . ."

"The problem came when Jerry Lee started coming home from work talking about Brian. What strides he was making, what ideas he'd come up with, and what milestones he'd hit that particular day."

"And she was jealous?" She heard the incredulousness in her own voice and rushed to soften it. "I mean, what was the problem?"

Margaret Louise engaged her sister by way of the rearview mirror. "May I, Twin? After all, you only know this story because of me."

Leona flicked her hand in indifference then looked back down at Paris as Margaret Louise took over the story. "Jerry Lee and Sadie were high school sweethearts. She was the prom queen of her graduatin' class, he was the promisin' football star she'd had her sights on since freshman year. And aside from an underclassman who caught his eye midway through their senior year and periodically throughout the next year or so, Jerry Lee was pretty smitten with Sadie."

Palmetto trees whizzed past the driver's-side window as Tori took in everything she was hearing. "So they got married and had kids, right?"

"Accordin' to Dixie, they got engaged 'bout two years after graduatin' from high school," Margaret Louise confirmed, "but they didn't have any kids. She didn't want them. I suspect that's because she didn't want Jerry Lee's attention on nobody but her. Worked for her for a whole lot of years 'fore Parker brought Brian to work."

"He was that taken with Brian?" Tori asked, her curiosity beginning to grow.

"At first, I imagine he took Brian under his wing out of a sense of loyalty to Parker . . . for bringin' him into a company that was startin' to gain attention. But as the company began to earn more and more money and Brian continued to show up and work as hard as he was, Jerry Lee's desire to help Parker out shifted into genuine interest and pride in the boy's accomplishments."

"Which meant the focus came off Sadie, yes?" The pieces were beginning to fall into place, the picture they formed more than a little disturbing.

"Precisely," Leona declared. "It became all she could talk about at society events, charitable drives, and the beauty shop. She found it deplorable that her husband was being used as—and I quote—a well-paid babysitter."

"Do you think he was?" It was a question she hated to ask but one she needed to explore.

Margaret Louise sighed. Loudly. "I think he was a friend. First to Parker and Charlotte, and then to Brian."

"And he stuck with Brian even after Parker allegedly took off?"

"The two of them been runnin' the company ever since, sendin' Charlotte checks like clockwork just so that worthless piece of garbage could pilfer it right out of her pocket." Margaret Louise let up on the gas pedal as the turn for Tom's Creek approached.

"We're talking about Ethan now?" Tori asked.

"Who else?" Margaret Louise piloted the car right, the back end of the wagon kicking up dust as they left pavement in favor of gravel. "Charlotte signed the checks, Frieda deposited them, and Ethan became good friends with the ATM."

Tori rested the back of her head against the window and sifted through everything she'd heard thus far. What it all meant, if anything, was unclear save for one thing . . .

Ethan Devereaux wasn't nice.

He wasn't nice at all.

The car slowed again, this time turning left into a parking lot containing a bright blue half-sized bus and a white four-door sedan.

"Looks like you're about to meet Jerry Lee." Margaret Louise maneuvered the station wagon around the bus and pulled into a vacant spot beside a large green Dumpster, her finger drawing Tori's attention to the sedan parked to the left of the modest building's side entrance. "When Parker left, Jerry Lee stepped in to fill his role here, too."

For a moment, Tori simply sat there, studying the

building's well-maintained grounds, which included a circular walking trail and a few benches. "I wonder if he knows," she mused as her gaze moved from the grounds and the building to Margaret Louise. "About Parker."

"Livin' in a town that thrives on gossip the way Sweet Briar does? Why, I reckon he must. But there's really only one way to find out for sure, and it ain't by sittin' here in the car wonderin' if he does, now is it?"

Chapter 10

The Devereaux Creek Center for the Mentally Challenged was, without a doubt, one of the happiest buildings Tori had ever entered. The sunshine yellow walls that greeted visitors and clients alike created an instant mood lift, as did the happy music wafting out of a nearby room. Artwork ranging in ability from childlike to near professional lined both sides of the front hallway with an accompanying miniature plaque attached to each picture boasting the name and age of its artist. Comfy couches and bean bag chairs were scattered around an open area that might normally be a waiting room in a doctor's office yet presented itself as a family room there at the center.

"Wow, this is really nice," she said, looking around. "The place just makes you feel all warm and happy inside, doesn't it?"

"That's certainly the intention." A tall, lanky man Tori judged to be in his mid-seventies strode into the room with a generous smile that stopped just short of his eyes. "Welcome to our center, is there something we can help you with . . ." His words trailed off as the identity of Tori's friends clicked inside his head. "Oh. Margaret Louise. Leona. What a nice surprise."

Leona lifted her cheek for a kiss then took advantage of her sister's moment in the sun to smooth her skirt, perfect her ankle-cross pose, and give her salon-softened gray hair a playful toss. If the man noticed, though, he didn't let on as his focus left Margaret Louise in favor of Tori. "Hi, I'm Jerry Lee Sweeney. I don't think we've met . . ."

Tori stepped forward, her hand quickly disappearing inside his strong grasp. "Hi, Jerry Lee. I'm Tori Sinclair, a friend of Margaret Louise and Leona." When his grip loosened, she stepped back and swept her hands outward. "This place is amazing."

"And it's only the beginning," Jerry Lee said with obvious pride. "C'mon, let me show you gals what we've done with this place."

Room by room, they made their way from the front of the center to the back, marveling at the care and thought that went into its creation. At the doorway of each splinter room, Jerry Lee would give a little explanation.

"The game room is interactive, as you can see—Ping-Pong table, air hockey, checker area, puzzle table. The idea was to provide our folks with a fun way to engage with one another while working on things like eye-hand coordination, acceptable sportsmanship, and good old-fashioned fun. Since yesterday was Thanksgiving, most of our clients are with family this weekend. But on a normal day, this room is brimming with activity."

"I bet it is," Tori said across Leona's shoulder.

The next room was a reading room, only instead of being lined with bookshelves the way the library was, it held cozy reading nooks with what appeared to be audio equipment attached to each and every chair. Margaret Louise and Leona parted from their shoulder-to-shoulder stance to allow Tori easier access to a room they all knew had piqued her curiosity.

"Are those headphones?" she asked, crossing to the first of six stations lining the room.

"They sure are. While a few of our clients are traditional book readers, many benefit more from audiobooks. These stations allow them to sit comfortably while they listen to whatever adventure they've chosen as their book of choice."

She felt a familiar excitement bubbling up inside her chest at the power of books. "How do they choose the titles they want to hear?"

"Easy." Jerry Lee lifted one of six colorful binders from a small table and handed it to Tori. "They make their selection from one of these."

With eager fingers, Tori opened the binder to reveal the first page of a brilliantly formatted catalog that utilized the most effective way of reaching its intended audience. Page after page depicted the covers of hundreds of books with a one-sentence description written in big, bold type. "Oh, Jerry Lee, this is wonderful . . ."

"Victoria is Sweet Briar's head librarian," Margaret Louise offered by way of explanation. "Nothin' gets this child more excited than books."

"Good thing Milo isn't around to hear you say that," Leona mumbled before glowering at her sister over the elbow to the side she hadn't expected.

"Like the game room, this is a favorite among our folks." Jerry Lee took the closed binder from Tori's outstretched hand and placed it back on the table. "Sometimes I like to just stand in the doorway and watch their expressions as they hit an especially exciting part of whatever story they're listening to. It's like they're there in that make-believe world, living a completely different life for a little while."

"One of the best parts of reading for anyone." Tori took one last look over her shoulder before following Jerry Lee and her friends back out into the hallway and on to the next stop in their tour.

A quick flick of his hand bathed the next room in fluorescent overhead light and solicited a near ear-piercing squeal from Margaret Louise. And it wasn't hard to see why. The state-of-the-art kitchen sprawled out in front of them boasted endless counter space, multiple ovens, and a baker's rack with an all-too-enticing supply of mixing bowls and pans.

"Oh, Jerry Lee, do they get to bake by themselves?" Margaret Louise whispered in an almost childlike voice.

"They do, with supervision from one of our volunteers to make sure there aren't any mishaps. But all in all, our folks do a really nice job." Jerry Lee pointed toward a long bulletin board across a side wall then down at the bulge beneath his shirt. "These are some of the recipes that are responsible for me looking like this."

Margaret Louise moved in for a closer look. "Oooh, teddy bear bread. That's one I need to make with Lulu and Sally over the holidays . . . Oh, and look at the cup-cakes, they're darlin'."

"There's something about making an edible treat that makes our folks come alive. It gives them such a sense of pride and accomplishment when they make something that can be enjoyed by others."

"Could you use another volunteer from time to time?"

The hope in Margaret Louise's voice was unmistak-able as was the resulting surprise and cautious optimism in Jerry Lee's.

"We'd be honored," Jerry Lee said before leading them back out into the hallway and toward the next room in the center—one outfitted with a desk and chair, a cash register and conveyer belt, a restaurant-style table, and a computer terminal.

Tori turned to Jerry Lee. "What's all this?"

The man's chest lifted beneath his gray button-down shirt. "This is what I call the Career Role Play Room. Very often people with these types of obstacles find their way into very specific jobs—baggers, busboys, greeters, those sorts of things. And by providing a snippet of those environments here, we're allowing our folks an opportu-nity to practice the skills they'll need to secure such jobs."

"What kind of things can they do on the computer?" Leona slid the tips of her fingers over the terminal.

"Depends on the person and their abilities. Some can't get past turning the machine on, while others can put a trained computer tech to shame." Jerry Lee stood in the center of the room with his arms crossed. "Unfortu-nately, the first group is seen by the working world as not worth the effort, while the second group can't seem to achieve the respect they deserve."

"What you're doing here is really very special." Margaret Louise and Leona nodded along with Tori's words. "I had no idea a center like this even existed."

A flash of something ignited behind Jerry Lee's eyes, only to extinguish just as quickly. "That's because Parker wasn't about doing this for glory or accolades. He did it for Brian and for kids *like* Brian. Though what's going to happen to this place now remains to be seen."

"So then you've heard?" Margaret Louise prompted.

Lines Tori hadn't paid much attention to until that point deepened beside the man's eyes and mouth, aging him beyond his seventy-plus years. "Yeah. I heard. Though I have to admit, I'm having a mighty hard time digesting it all."

Reaching out, Tori placed a gentle hand on Jerry Lee's arm. "Margaret Louise said you were friends with Parker Devereaux for a long time."

Jerry Lee nodded. "I can't really remember a time Parker wasn't part of my life. But it's more than that. I was there when he met Charlotte. I was the best man in their wedding party. I was there when they learned of the challenges Brian would face in life. I was there when Ethan came along twelve years later as the son with no problems. And I was with them when"—the man gestured around the room—"they dreamed up this place. Now I'm supposed to be able to accept the fact that a woman I grew to cherish every bit as much as Parker *murdered* him?"

She hadn't considered that aspect of their grim discovery. And judging by the way Margaret Louise and Leona looked to the floor at the man's admission, she wasn't the only one.

"I think we're all havin' a hard time wrappin' our brains 'round that one," Margaret Louise mused. "And an even harder time tryin' to imagine *why*."

"Or *how*."

Three sets of eyes turned to stare at Leona with Margaret Louise putting words to what was surely in all of their minds. "Do you mean how she killed him?"

"That's certainly of interest but not something we'll probably ever know when all that was left was a shoe, a picture, and an artificial hip."

Jerry Lee dropped his hands to his sides. "Picture? What picture?"

"A laminated photograph of Parker and Charlotte on their wedding day." Leona's shoes made soft clicking sounds against the linoleum flooring en route to the desk on which she, eventually, perched. "I was referring more to how she got his body into town and buried him on the library grounds."

"Maybe that's where she killed him," Margaret Louise suggested.

"Maybe. But that doesn't answer the other how."

Tori felt her eyebrow rise. "The other how?"

Keenly aware of her position in the spotlight, Leona took a moment to check her nails, smooth her hair, and perfect her already perfect posture. Then just before everyone's undivided attention turned to irritation, she gave the explanation they were seeking. "Five years ago, Charlotte was what? Sixty-seven, sixty-eight years old, right?"

"She was sixty-nine," Jerry Lee confirmed.

"So she was sixty-nine. Five years ago, you were fifty-eight, Twin. What's that got to do with anything—"

Leona's gasp echoed off the walls, calling even more

attention to the instant red of her cheeks. "I'm not sixty-three!"

"The hell you ain't." Margaret Louise made a face before addressing Jerry Lee. "My sister lives in a bit of a dream world if you can't tell . . ."

Mouths continued to move around the room as the true meaning behind Leona's words hit Tori with a one-two punch. "Oh, my gosh . . . that's it! That's what's been bugging me this past week!"

Margaret Louise held her hand up in front of Leona's face, successfully thwarting any further discussion on their shared age. "What's it, Victoria?"

"Charlotte was *sixty-nine*, Margaret Louise. Most sixty-nine-year-old women aren't strong enough to dig a grave on their own. They're just not."

"*I* will be," Margaret Louise boasted with her hands still splayed in front of her sister's face.

"But"—Tori pointed to Leona—"*she* won't. Not for that kind of menial labor, anyway."

Leona shoved her sister's hand out of the way but not before giving Margaret Louise an evil eye to end all evil eyes. "Which was exactly my point had I been *allowed* to make it."

"And it's a good one." Tori wandered around the room, passing the makeshift grocery checkout and the single-station restaurant setting, only to turn back when she reached Leona. "Which means someone helped her dig that hole."

Jerry Lee staggered backward into the door frame. "But who would help her do that?"

"Someone who was tryin' to protect her?" Margaret Louise suggested.

Leona waved her sister off, her anger over the outing of her true age still alive and well. "I think we need to focus on the why first. Having that will make figuring out the who a whole lot easier."

"I couldn't agree more." Tori retraced her steps back toward the open doorway. "Jerry Lee, I want to thank you for giving us a tour of the center. Seeing the thought and care that went into making this place has been an honor. Truly."

The heartache-induced lines softened momentarily to reveal a face lit with pride. "Watching your ideas become reality is incredible all on its own. Watching them impact others and knowing you're responsible for that impact takes it to an entirely different level. Suddenly, all the mistakes you made in life don't seem so overwhelming."

Tori thought back to the library—to the children's room born in her imagination, realized through passion and hard work, and cherished by many. Jerry Lee was right. Making a difference in another person's life by way of a dream was something worthy of pride. It made all the stress, all the expense, and all the second-guessing worth it.

Jerry Lee walked them to the door, his footsteps slowing every few steps to make sure the lights were off in each and every room they passed. "If there's any hope of saving this place, I need to make sure all unnecessary costs are at a minimum."

"Save it? Save it from whom?" Leona questioned as Tori and Margaret Louise stopped to hear the man's answer.

"Parker saw the center as important and, thus, worthy of whatever expenses it incurred. The Prince, however, doesn't share those feelings." When they reached the front room with its cozy couches and colorful bean bag chairs, he took a moment to shake their hands. "Margaret Louise, anytime you'd like to volunteer in one of our cooking classes, give us a shout. I'm sure you'd be a hit.

"And Tori, if you ever think you could use one of our folks at the library—shelving books or reading to kids— let me know. They're hard workers, every single one of them. And I'd sure like to help as many of them as possible before The Prince takes his throne."

Tori slipped her hand from the man's grasp and shifted her purse from one shoulder to the other, a burst of curiosity preventing her feet from walking through the door Jerry Lee held open. "Prince?"

"Prince Ethan. Parker's son."

Chapter 11

"It's going great, Victoria."

Tori pulled her gaze from the crowd and fixed it on the source of the whispered voice at her elbow, the smile she'd finally allowed herself to enjoy stretching still wider. "Melissa, you came."

"Came? Are you kidding me?" Margaret Louise's daughter-in-law joked as Tori leaned forward and kissed the strawberry blonde perched on her hip. "The kids circled this day on my kitchen calendar weeks ago and put twenty little stars around it just to make sure it wouldn't get overlooked." Lifting her right index finger into the air, Melissa guided Tori's focus toward six familiar heads moving up and down each makeshift aisle in search of literary treasures. "So far, Jake Junior, Julia, Tommy, and Kate have found their allotted three books each. Technically Lulu has, too, but now she's searching for books for Molly Sue so you and I can chat."

At just under two years old, Molly Sue Davis was the youngest of Melissa and Jake's brood, a title she'd be relinquishing come spring when the couple's eighth child made his or her debut. And just like her two brothers and four sisters, Molly was sweet, good-natured, and a loyal member of Tori's personal fan club based on her outstretched arms.

"Remind me to get them all an extra special something this year for Christmas," Tori quipped as she took hold of Molly and brought the toddler in for a cuddle.

"Christmas . . ." Melissa mumbled. "I have to tell you, Victoria, as much as I love seeing the kids excited about all the books, it was also a treat to see their faces when they walked in here and saw the holiday decorations. Now, if only the town would take notes before they ruin the fun for all of us . . ."

Tori touched her forehead to Molly's and closed her eyes, inhaling the sweet smells of talcum powder and recently eaten sugar cookie before addressing the topic that seemed to have everyone in Sweet Briar talking. "I take it you've driven around the town square?"

"After Thanksgiving dinner at Margaret Louise's, Jake and I got all of the kids into their jammies and out to the car for our annual Let's Get Ready for Christmas drive. We started it when Jake Junior was only a year and far too young to even know what he was looking at." Melissa glanced toward the book section, her lips moving along with her mental count. When she hit six, she continued on. "Year after year, we make the same drive on the same night, knowing that all of the decorations around the Green will be in full force. It gets the kids excited and, in turn, makes the whole season even more fun for Jake and me.

"Anyway, we figured it might be a *little* different with Margaret Louise not running things this year, but, Victoria, it was downright awful. The wreaths and garland and big red bows the kids have come to associate with the season were gone! Even the nativity scene that's been outside Sweet Briar Town Hall since *I* was a little girl was gone. And do you know what they had in its place? A bench! Painted to look as if it's covered in snow . . . in *Sweet Briar*!" An uncharacteristic frown took up temporary residence on Melissa's finely featured face. "By the time we pulled back into our driveway, the kids' disappointment was palpable. Even Molly Sue seemed sad."

Tori rested her chin atop Molly's smooth hair and skimmed the room with a different purpose—bypassing the book browsers, the autograph line for visiting author Felicia Donovan, and the promising expressions on her volunteers' faces in favor of the holiday magic she'd tried to sprinkle around the empty warehouse loaned to the Friends of the Library for its First Annual Holiday Book Extravaganza. The Christmas trees, while artificial, looked grand with their ropes of silver garland, bursts of multicolored lights, and array of book-themed ornaments. Poinsettias and sprigs of holly arranged atop the book tables were a festive touch, as was the presence of Santa's elves moving their way through the crowd with candy canes for the children.

"I just wanted everything to be nice." The fact that it helped offset some of the disappointment over the changes in town was a benefit she hadn't anticipated.

"It's better than nice." Melissa swept her hand in the direction of the book tables. "Even the volume of books is better than I expected. And they were all donated, right?"

"People drop off books for us all year long. Sometimes the books are in really bad shape and other times they're practically new. Either way, they're generally donated in conjunction with a thorough house cleaning, a garage sale, an upcoming move, and/or a death."

Melissa drew back. "Death?"

Tori nodded, the motion receiving assistance from Molly's dimpled hands. "When someone dies, their loved ones go through their belongings in an effort to sell their home, or vacate their room at the assisted living facility, or whatever. Goodwill gets their clothes, shelters get their food, and libraries get their books. It happens all the time.

"In the past, the Friends of the Library held their book sale in the spring, selling off the donated books and giving the proceeds to us for programs and events. It's been successful, but the thought was that by doing it in conjunction with the holidays and making a daylong event out of it with a visiting author and programs for the kids, it would be even more successful." Molly Sue released her face long enough to allow Tori to take in the room yet again. "And from what I can see so far, it is."

Molly Sue retrieved Tori's face long enough to shower it with kisses before reaching for the safety of her mother's arms. Melissa obliged. "I've been to the fair in the spring every year for as long as I can remember. It was always good, but this is a million times better."

Tori couldn't agree more. The decorations, the visiting author, the food, and the assorted craft stations for kids had transformed the annual book sale into a can't-miss event for all ages. The fact that folks could take care of the book lovers on their holiday lists at the same time was simply an added bonus.

"Mama?"

Tori and Melissa looked down simultaneously to find Lulu, the fifth child in the ever-growing Davis family, peering up at them with a picture book in her outstretched hands and an impossible-to-miss question in her dark brown eyes.

"What did you find, Lulu?" Melissa lowered Molly Sue to the ground and squatted beside her, bypassing the book in her older daughter's hand in favor of a loving nose tap. "Did you find something good for Molly Sue?"

At the sound of her name, Molly Sue did a little dance in place, earning her a smile from Tori and her mom as well as several elderly event goers seated at a nearby table.

A brief hesitation was followed by a slight nod. "It's a book about a little boy who makes messes everywhere he goes."

Melissa scrunched her eyebrows and settled her hands on her hips in dramatic play. "Are you saying Molly Sue is messy?"

Turning her head ever so slightly, Lulu addressed Tori, the question in her eyes finding its way through her mouth. "I was looking at all the pages, Miss Sinclair. Making sure it was a good book for Molly Sue. But when I got to the second-to-last page, I found this." Lulu flipped open the book from the backside and pointed at a folded piece of paper wedged inside the binding. "It's a drawing."

"A drawing?" Melissa echoed.

"A real good one, Mama," Lulu said. Then, with sturdy

hands, the ten-year-old retrieved the picture and handed the book to an overjoyed Molly Sue. "Do you wanna see it, Miss Sinclair?"

There was something about Lulu Davis that jettisoned Tori into the past while simultaneously making her long for the future. And it had been that way from the moment they met during a third grade outing to the library. Somehow, the dark-haired child had reminded her of the best parts of her own childhood—sewing lessons and trips to the library with her late great-grandmother and reading away the hours in her room. At the same time, Lulu's genuine sweetness and priceless innocence touched something maternal in Tori, as did the accompanying images of the little girl she hoped to have one day.

A little girl who was a lot like Lulu Davis.

"Of course, I'd like to see it, Lulu." She took the offered piece of paper from the child's hand and unfolded it bit by bit, the quick glimpses of a pencil sketch building to a complete picture that set Tori's heart pounding. "What on earth . . ."

Melissa shot upright. "Victoria? What's wrong?"

She stared down at the sketch, her focus bouncing from the broken clock on the wall to the row of framed photographs and the discarded piece of paper intended for Ethan that adorned the mantel below. It was the same drawing. The same exact drawing as the dozen or so others Charlotte Devereaux had sketched while confined to a chair in her late husband's study. And like the final drawing that had led to the discovery of Parker Devereaux's body a week earlier, the page in Tori's hand showed signs of tearing along the left side, too.

"I—I don't understand."

Ever so gently, Melissa turned the paper in Tori's hands to afford a closer look. "What is this?"

"It's exactly like all the others," she whispered, overriding her head's refusal to accept what her eyes were seeing. "I mean, every last detail is the same."

"All the others?" Melissa parroted.

"All the other pictures Charlotte drew before she died."

"Charlotte Devereaux?" At Tori's silent nod, Melissa's eyes widened. "Then how did it end up here? In a *children's picture book*?"

Melissa's questions broke through her cloud of disbelief and forced her to focus. How indeed.

With a shaky smile, Tori accepted the book from Molly Sue's tentative grasp and positioned it right side up in her own hands. The whimsical title, the author's name, and the beautifully illustrated cover barely registered as she flipped it open in favor of the inside front cover and the inscription that brought a strangled gasp from somewhere deep inside her throat.

My dearest Brian,

I love the you that you are—the you that you are because of a father's love.
Forever and Always.

Love,
Mommy

No. It didn't mean anything. It couldn't . . .

"Okay, well, I guess it makes sense why one of Charlotte's pictures was in there, but still . . . Brian is like what?

Fifty?" Melissa posed. "How would a picture she recently drew end up in a picture book from his childhood?"

Her friend was right. So the familial connection was there, big deal. That didn't mean there was some big dark meaning behind the picture's presence in the book.

Yet even as her mind did everything in its power to convince her heart of the coincidence theory, Tori's experience over the past two years told her otherwise. The sketch had been folded into quarters and placed inside a decades-old storybook. The chance of that meaning nothing was next to nil.

Which meant she needed answers. Answers that would only come if she asked questions.

The problem was figuring out whom to ask.

Melissa closed the book in Tori's hands and passed it to Lulu, her happy-go-lucky smile back where it belonged. "Thank you for bringing this to us, sweetheart."

Lulu looked down at the book and then at her baby sister. "Mama, can it still be one of Molly Sue's books? It's a really good story."

"Of course it can, Lulu." Swooping her arms close to the ground, Melissa lifted Molly Sue back into her arms. "Now why don't you round up your brothers and sisters and ask them if they'd like a little treat before we head home, okay?"

At the mention of the word *treat*, Lulu's eyes danced. Yet even with that pull, the little girl still took the time to wrap her arms around Tori's middle before going off in pursuit of her siblings. "I love you, Miss Sinclair."

Blinking against the sudden burn in her eyes, Tori leaned down and whispered a kiss across Lulu's soft mane. "I love you, too, Lulu."

And with that, the child was gone, skipping her way back toward her brothers and sisters with Molly Sue's new books tucked safely under her arm. "She really is a very special little girl, Melissa."

"I think so, too."

"Miss Sinclair? Ms. Donovan only has a few people left in her line."

"Thank you, Sarah." Shifting her gaze from one side of the warehouse to the other, Tori confirmed the event volunteer's words. Break time was over. It was time to reengage herself as host. "I guess I better get back to it, Melissa. Felicia Donovan has been amazing today and I need to make sure I thank her properly."

"I understand." With a protective arm on Molly Sue's back, Melissa brushed a quick parting kiss on Tori's cheek before lowering her voice to a near whisper. "When Ms. Donovan is gone and all of this is over, you need to find out how Brian Devereaux's book ended up here."

"I imagine it was donated like all of the other books on those tables."

"Okay . . . But when? And by whom?"

She let the questions swirl in her thoughts for all of about two seconds. Melissa was right. The when and the who were the perfect place to start.

Chapter 12

It didn't matter how many Internet articles Maime Wellington referenced, or how many magazine pictures she shoved in front of their faces, the notion of a greenery-free Christmas just wasn't sitting well with Sweet Briar's ragtag holiday committee. Not that it mattered, really.

Maime Wellington had made up her mind. If she hadn't, her ideas would have been formed as questions, not statements. But they weren't.

Rose could stamp her feet—and she did. It didn't matter.

Dixie could snort and flail her arms and even smack her hand on the table—and she did, numerous times. It didn't matter.

All that *did* matter was Maime and her single-minded and oh-so-transparent pursuit of destroying all customs and memories that transpired before her. Yet knowing that and accepting it were two very different things. Especially when the vocal elimination of each treasured tradition was met with a palpable hurt from the little boy at the far end of the conference table.

"How can you even propose doing away with the annual tree-lighting ceremony?" Rose hissed through clenched teeth. "It's—it's unconscionable."

Tori saw Maime's mouth move, knew the words being formed were stinging in nature, but her thoughts, her empathy, her worry was on Councilman Jordan's son, Kyle, whose crayon hadn't moved across his coloring book in nearly thirty minutes despite the near death grip with which he held it to the paper.

The sound of Rose's foot, stamping on the ground next to hers, forced her attention back to Maime in time to hear the second part of her biting rant. "Cutting down a Christmas tree simply to string it with lights and stand around singing songs is what's unconscionable. My idea would cost the town less money overall, jettison this dinky little town into the twenty-first century, and position us to be more green."

Dixie's hand shot into the air like a crossing guard halting traffic. "You truly think sitting on the ground in front of a projection screen and waiting for the computerized image of a Christmas tree to glow with lights will give the same warm and fuzzies as the real thing?"

Maime's catlike eyes narrowed as if Dixie were a mouse that had just made the mistake of peeking out its hole in plain view. "I'm not about warm and fuzzies."

"Really? I wouldn't have guessed," Rose grumbled.

Ignoring the elderly woman's sarcasm, Maime continued, her detailed description of Sweet Briar's cyber-tree-lighting ceremony bringing a strangled sob from the opposite end of the table.

"Kyle?" Tori pushed back in her chair and stood, her feet leading her to the little boy's chair. Crouching down beside him, she pushed a scrap of auburn hair from his forehead in time to see a tear fall from his freckled cheek and onto his coloring book. "Hey, sweetie . . . What's wrong? Are you feeling sick?"

The eight-year-old shook his head, hard.

Tori peeked under the table. "Did you bump your leg or something?"

Again, the boy shook his head, yet said nothing.

She let her hand slip from his head to his back, where she moved it in slow, even circles. "Are you upset about the tree-lighting ceremony?"

Burying his head in his hands, Kyle began to sob, his shoulders shaking and trembling beneath an invisible weight far too heavy for a child to carry alone. "Hey . . . Kyle . . . talk to me."

After several long moments, the child popped up his head, his red-rimmed eyes moving from Tori to Maime and back again. "I—I don't want the tree to go away," he said during breaks in his crying. "I want it to stay."

"Oh, quit your stupid crying!' Maime gathered her articles and magazines together into a pile. "It's a tree. Who cares?"

"I—I care. M-My m-mom h-helped pick out its ornaments." Kyle's breath hitched once, twice, three times. "It—it m-makes us think of her."

Maime picked up the pile, only to slam it back down on the table. "Us? Who's us, Kyle?"

"M-Me and—and B-Billy and—-and Daddy."

The pain in the child's voice grabbed hold of Tori's heart and twisted. "Oh, sweetie, I can see why it's important to you—"

"Enough! Your daddy doesn't *need* to remember," Maime thundered, her anger and her meanness leaving Rose and Dixie utterly speechless. "And I've seen those ornaments she bought and they're sappy and pathetic."

Kyle's lips trembled with a mixture of hurt and rage. "Stop it! Leave my mom out of this."

"That's exactly what I'm trying to do, young man." Glancing at her watch, Maime grabbed hold of her stack of papers once again. "Let's go, Kyle. Your dad should be done at his council meeting by now, and I need to be at the house when he gets home."

With shaking hands, Kyle wiped the last of his tears from his face. "Daddy and me used to go for ice cream sometimes after his meetings."

"Not anymore you don't. Not unless I'm there, too." Maime made her way over to the door and snapped her fingers at Kyle. "Let's go."

Slowly but surely, Rose pushed her own chair back from the table and struggled to her feet, her eyes wide and angry behind her bifocal lenses. "I don't know who you think you are, Ms. Wellington, but Avery is a bloody fool for giving you the time of day."

"Oh?" Maime taunted before every last shred of irritation disappeared from her voice in favor of a sugary-sweet tone reminiscent of a preschool teacher. "Avery thinks everything about me is wonderful—the way I dress, the way I look, the way I care for his son, and the ideas I have for improving Sweet Briar. In fact, he says I was made for him."

Tori wasn't sure how long they sat there, staring at the empty doorway in disbelief. Ten minutes? Maybe twenty?

But either way, nothing changed.

In fact, no amount of blinking, eye rubbing, or disgusted moans could change the scene that had just unfolded in front of them like some sort of poorly written horror movie. Yet true to form, they still blinked . . . and rubbed . . . and moaned, hoping against hope someone would walk through the doorway and tell them it was all a joke—that Maime Wellington was a figment of their nightmares.

Rose was the first to break the weighted silence. "Someone has to tell Avery. That woman is going to destroy that little boy if she isn't stopped."

"But you saw her, Rose," Dixie protested. "You saw the way she transformed herself from a witch to a princess right in front of our eyes. He'll think we're causing trouble simply because we're angry about Margaret Louise being ousted from her job as chairman of the Chirstmas Decorating Committee."

"We are. But that has nothing to do with the simple matter of what's right and what's wrong."

"You're right, Rose. But so is Dixie." Tori planted her elbows on the table and propped her chin up with her hands. "Right now, Avery wants, maybe even *needs* Maime to be this perfect little angel that found her way into his life. Hearing anything to the contrary from us is only going to make him defensive and even more protective of her."

"But if Kyle tells him the things she says, that should be enough to wake him up."

She tried Dixie's words on for size but they didn't fit. Not with the reality they'd witnessed less than thirty minutes earlier. "But when would Kyle be able to say anything? I mean, you heard that woman. She won't even let the kid have ice cream alone with his dad."

"I almost wish Leona had made tonight's meeting because we need to do something," Rose insisted, her voice barely more than a trembled whisper. "We can't stand by and let this woman talk to that child that way. It's not healthy!"

Rose was right. The key, though, was how. Finding opportunities to talk to a third grader that wasn't your own wasn't always easy.

A third grader . . .

"Wait!" The word shot from her lips with a crack of excitement. "I'm pretty sure Kyle Jordan is in Milo's class this year. Which means maybe Milo can help!"

Dixie and Rose exchanged glances and then shrugs. "Maybe. But if he can't, Victoria, I will," Rose declared before pulling the cotton flaps of her sweater close to her body as she shuffled her way toward the door. "I will see you ladies tomorrow. It's eight o'clock, which means it's time for this old decrepit body to go home and get its beauty sleep."

When Rose had disappeared into the hallway, Dixie turned to Tori and mustered a genuine smile. "Victoria, I have to say, the holiday book fair was outstanding. Can you believe how much money we raised for programming and updates?"

It was hard not to meet and raise Dixie's smile with one of her own. The First Annual Holiday Book Extravaganza had been a smashing success. The dedicated crew of volunteers, the timing of the event, and the generous book donations they had received over the past six months had all culminated in a success they were already eager to duplicate again next year.

Before Tori could respond, Dixie pushed a folder at her from across the table. "I got a hold of that log you asked me about, Victoria. Though what you're trying to figure out is beyond me. All that really matters is the bottom line, right?"

She studied the stout woman closely. "Log? What log . . ." And then she remembered.

Flipping open the folder, Tori glanced down at the donation log listing the name of every book donated to the library over the past six months. The computerized list identified the title and genre of each book as well as the name of the person who made the donation.

"The Friends of the Library are already writing out thank-you notes as we speak," Dixie continued. "People were very generous this year."

"Yes, they were. But that's not why I wanted this." Slowly, she worked her way through the log, passing pages devoted to mysteries, romances, thrillers, science fiction, women's fiction, and historical biographies before stopping on those devoted to the hundreds of children's titles that had been dropped off at the library in the hope of finding new homes.

She allowed her eyes to guide her index finger down

the column on the far right side, the same donor often responsible for dozens of donated titles. Name by name she made her way from one page to the next until she found what she'd been seeking when she asked to see the log in the first place.

There, beside a single children's book title, was a handwritten notation by a member of the Friends of the Library . . .

November 18th—Donated by Frieda Taylor in Charlotte Devereaux's Memory.

Melissa's questions had been answered.

The book had been donated within days of Charlotte's death by the woman's full-time nurse.

But instead of putting an end to the questions, the information only served to spark one more.

"Now what?" she whispered.

Chapter 13

Two years earlier, when she'd attended her first-ever Sweet Briar tree-lighting ceremony, Tori had been all too aware of the non-Christmas-like climate and the absence of anything resembling the kind of weather Bing Crosby had sung about on her great-grandmother's record player growing up. Yet thirty minutes later, after the tree had been lit and the first round of carols sung, she'd quickly realized how unimportant the outside temperatures were compared to the heart and spirit of a decades-old tradition.

She'd learned a lot that night about preconceived notions and the benefits of being open minded, the town's age-old tradition quickly claiming a spot on her own annual holiday must-do list before the night had even officially come to a close. But even knowing that, and having experienced that, she still couldn't manage to muster up so much as a shred of excitement for this year's event.

And it wasn't hard to see why.

Seeing families huddled together on picnic blankets and beach towels as they stared at a darkened projection screen on the other side of the Green just didn't have the same feel as standing shoulder to shoulder around a tree with people of all ages—waiting. There was no magic, no sense of wide-eyed anticipation, no impatient squeals.

There was just sitting.

And yawning.

And a fair amount of whining and complaining from both children and adults alike.

"I tried to get the kids excited for this at school but I wasn't terribly convincing." Milo's chin moved against the top of her head as he spoke. "It's like they knew it wouldn't be the same—and these are kids! They're used to virtual sports and virtual drawing and all sorts of computerized things."

Tori closed her eyes briefly, savoring the feel of her back against his chest and his arms around her midsection as they waited for Maime Wellington's version of Christmas in the millennium. "I know. It's why I almost called you tonight and asked if we could go to a movie or take a walk instead of coming here for *this*. But I couldn't."

"You could have persuaded me," Milo joked. "And pretty easily, too, I might add."

"At the moment Maime told us about this, Dixie, Rose, and I were ready to get up and walk out, boycott all of these changes on principle . . ." she mused, her words disappearing into the night as she thought back to the last committee meeting.

"What stopped you?"

It was a question she knew he'd ask and, thus, a topic she'd avoided until that very moment, when she was as certain as she could be that she could talk without crying.

"Kyle Jordan stopped me."

She felt Milo's chin leave the top of her hair, felt the way his head bobbed to the left in an effort to see her face. "*My* Kyle Jordan?"

She allowed herself to draw some much-needed strength from the smile his words created. Milo Wentworth was the kind of teacher that parents adored. He was motivating and creative in the way good teachers were, but he also truly loved each and every student in his classroom. "Yes, your Kyle Jordan."

"How, may I ask, did Kyle stop the three of you from boycotting this debacle?"

Reluctantly, she wiggled out from the warmth of his arms and turned around on the blanket to face him, the amber flecks of his eyes nearly impossible to see in the faint glow of the streetlamps that bordered the green. "Of all the people sitting around us tonight, no one is sadder about the changes taking place than Kyle. Margaret Louise might be upset that her hard work over the past decade or two has been tossed aside, but Kyle? His heart is breaking."

Despite the low lighting, the worry in Milo's eyes was unmistakable. "Breaking? Why?"

"Because doing away with the tree-lighting ceremony as it was is just one more way his mother is disappearing from his life." Sure enough, despite her best intentions, her voice cracked, the passage of time since seeing Kyle's face and hearing his sobs doing little against the very real emotion invoked by the mere memory.

Milo's brows furrowed. "How so?"

"He remembers his mother picking out some of the ornaments for the town's tree." It was a simple statement but one Tori knew he'd understand. And he didn't disappoint.

He raked his hand down his face, releasing a sigh as it passed his mouth. "Wow. I didn't realize."

"What I don't understand is how Kyle can remember that, *treasure* that, yet his father can be so clueless as to its significance for his child." She drew her knees upward and rested her forearms across them. "I mean, the kid's mother died, right?"

"My guess is he's only aware of himself right now." Milo sat up straight on their blanket and canvassed the crowd between them and the projection screen. "He's feeling hope with this new woman because he sees it as a new beginning. Unfortunately, he's obviously so focused on that, he's forgetting the fact that his son wants the memories . . . even *needs* the memories. Especially during the holidays."

She nodded, yet said nothing, her gaze joining Milo's in what she suspected was a shared pursuit.

"Maybe I could say something to Avery the next time I see him, though in all fairness, the girlfriend seems to have taken over the task of bringing Kyle his lunch whenever he forgets it at home. Maybe I should mention something to her. Perhaps she just doesn't understand."

Three blankets shy of the projection screen she found Kyle and his brother huddled together while Maime commanded their father's full attention. "I don't think it'll do any good," Tori mumbled. "Besides, it's not like she doesn't know how Kyle feels . . ."

Milo stared down at her. "She knows?"

"She knows," Tori repeated. "Kyle told her outright."

"And . . ."

Waving her hand toward the projection screen, she managed to speak around the lump of emotion lodged in her throat. "You don't see a tree any longer, do you?"

"Mizz Victoria, is that you?"

Tori glanced up, Frieda Taylor's narrow face barely discernible in the growing darkness. "Oh. Frieda. Hi." She turned to Milo and held her hand up in the nurse's direction. "Milo, this is Frieda Taylor, Charlotte Devereaux's nurse. Frieda, this is my fiancé—Milo Wentworth."

After a handshake and a few pleasantries, Frieda focused in on Tori once again. "I hope all those books I dropped off last week made it in time to be part of your library's Christmas book fair, Mizz Victoria."

And just like that, Tori's focus shifted to the other worry nagging at her heart.

"They most certainly did, Frieda . . . and thank you. Charlotte's books found good homes, and the money raised will certainly help to fund many of our programs throughout the coming year."

Frieda's smile grew. "I'm so glad. Mizz Charlotte . . . she loved her books right up until the very end. Why, during some of her clear spells, I could read two or three chapters to her while she sat in her chair and drew. Sometimes, she'd even lay her pencil down long enough to comment on something I'd just read."

She took in the woman's words and let them process

for a moment. "And the picture book? Was there a particular reason she liked you to read that one when all of the other donated titles were adult books?"

"Picture book?" Frieda echoed in surprise. "I didn't read no picture book to Mizz Charlotte. We read stories about women who accomplished great things."

"But what about Messy Mikey?" she asked.

"I don't know a book called—"

Her hand shot up as the cover of Molly Sue's new book flashed before her eyes. "Wait. No. It was called, *It's Not Mikey's Mess.*"

Frieda's shoulders sagged ever so slightly. "I didn't read that to Mizz Charlotte. Mizz Charlotte used to read that to Brian every day when he'd come into her room for a goodnight kiss. At least she did up until about six weeks ago."

"What happened six weeks ago?"

"I guess he could sense a change in his mama. Because one evening he came in and held the book in his hands and began reciting the story—page by page—to *her.* I had to walk out of the room that night to keep my blubbering from ruining his story. But he did it again the next night . . . and the next night . . . and every night thereafter until Mizz Charlotte left this earth. And every night, after he'd finished the book and had given her a kiss, she'd sit there in her chair and just hold that book for hours."

It all made sense now—the inscription, the lone children's book in a large donation of adult titles, and even the presence of one of Charlotte's sketches. Tori slumped against Milo's chest once again, although her gaze, her focus, remained on Frieda. "I'll let my friend Melissa know just how special that book was to Charlotte. I'm sure that'll only make reading it to her daughter all the more special."

Frieda's left brow hiked upward. "That's an old book. Where did your friend find it?"

"Well, actually, her daughter, Lulu, found it while searching for the best trio of picture books for her baby sister at the festival yesterday. When she showed me the inscription inside the front cover, I figured it must have come from Charlotte's collection."

Slowly, the nurse's mouth dropped open. "Brian's book? I didn't donate that."

She sat upright again as the shock in Frieda's tone registered in the forefront of her mind. "It was checked off and initialed by one of our volunteers. It came in on the same day you donated the rest of Charlotte's books."

Several long beats of silence gave way to a burst of anger that skittered across Frieda's face. "You know, I told Ethan to leave that book alone. I told him it was something his mother would have wanted Brian to have. Shame on me for thinking he'd leave his jealousy at the door and heed his mother's wishes . . . shame on me."

"Jealousy?" she parroted. "What was Ethan jealous of?"

Milo looked from Tori to Frieda and back again. "I don't think Ethan was jealous of a what so much as a who." At Frieda's nod, he continued, filling in a little backstory. "Despite all of the advantages Ethan Devereaux has had in life—good looks, a comfortable upbringing, his parents' obvious adoration, and good health—he seemed to be bothered by the attention his mentally challenged older brother got from his father."

She looked to Frieda for confirmation of Milo's words, the nurse's follow-up delivering so much more than she could have imagined. "I tell you, Mizz Victoria, this town and its police have it all wrong. Mizz Charlotte wouldn't have hurt her husband if her life depended on it. No way. No how. But Mr. Ethan? He wouldn't think twice if he thought it could benefit him somehow."

Tori heard the sharp intake of air through her lips, felt Milo's hand on her arm, but it paled in comparison to the sudden roar in her ears.

"Tori? Are you okay?"

Could Frieda be right? Could Ethan Devereaux have killed his own father?

"Hey . . . Baby. Are you okay?"

And if he did, how would Charlotte have known where to find the body?

"Tori?"

The sound of her name brought her back into the moment to find Milo's face mere inches from her own. "I'm sorry, Milo, I guess I was just caught off guard by all this talk of . . ." Her words petered out as she looked up. "Wait. Where's Frieda?"

Milo rocked back on his feet. "I don't know. I was so busy looking at you, I didn't notice she'd walked away until she was already gone."

Tori rose up on her knees and looked around the crowd but to no avail. "Ugh. I hope she wasn't mad that I zoned out like that."

"I suspect she just wanted to get a seat for"—Milo nudged his chin toward the projection screen that was suddenly illuminated—"the show."

Sure enough, a large cartoon-like tree appeared on the screen along with a talking magic wand tasked with taking the crowd through the process of a virtual tree

trimming—one animated lightbulb and one singing ornament after the other until the entire tree was decked out in
all its virtual finery.

Five minutes later, amid a prolonged bout of stunned
silence, blankets were folded and carried off by one dis-
appointed family after the other.

"I can't believe we just sat here for over an hour waiting
for . . . that." Milo blew out a whoosh of frustration and
then helped Tori to her feet. "I—I'm speechless. Truly."

Tori stepped off the blanket and reached for the two
corners closest to her feet, folding them toward one
another and then again toward Milo before finding some
semblance of a response. "I am, too."

"All we can say is how glad I am my mama refrained
from coming."

Pulling the folded blanket against her chest, Tori spun
around. "Melissa . . . Jake . . . hi!"

Milo sidled up beside Tori and offered his hand to
Margaret Louise's son and a warm embrace to the man's
wife. "You know something? I was actually hoping against
hope your mom wasn't here tonight. She'd have been
heartbroken."

Tori followed the path made by Jake's eyes as he took
in the couple's seven children sitting quietly on a blanket
of their own. "She's already heartbroken, bein' here would've
just made it worse. Much worse."

Melissa hooked her hands around her husband's forearm. "Today wasn't all bad for your mom, Jake. She was
bubbling with excitement when she stopped by after
Molly Sue's nap."

The image Melissa's words evoked brought a smile to
Tori's lips. "Oh?"

"She went back to that center she took you and Aunt Leona to the other day, Victoria. Signed up as a volunteer."

Tori's smile widened still further. "She's going to teach some cooking classes?"

"First one will be next week."

"Mee Maw's not plannin' on teachin' them folks how to make sweet potato pie, is she? 'Cause a recipe like that might get her in a little trouble," Jake teased before shooting his hand into the air and gesturing for the Davis Seven to gather up their blanket in preparation for the drive home.

"Nooo," Melissa chided. "She's going to make Christmas cookies with them." Lowering her voice, Melissa peeked around Jake's arm toward the virtual tree still posted on the screen despite nary a straggler left on the Green. "And by the time she was done telling me all the cookies they're going to make and decorate at the center, that sadness in her eyes was almost all gone. In fact, she said if Sweet Briar doesn't need her, maybe Tom's Creek does."

Chapter 14

Tori was waiting at her desk with two to-go cups of hot chocolate, a bag of Debbie's homemade truffles, and a foolproof plan when Margaret Louise barreled around the corner and into the room, huffing and puffing from the brisk walk through the parking lot.

"There you are, Victoria. If I'd known you were in your office, I could've saved my tootsies a few extra steps by comin' in the back door instead of the front." Margaret Louise peeked her head back into the hallway and looked both ways before claiming the chair across from Tori with an audible oomph. "I know my sister would say the extra walkin' is good for the waistline or some such foolhardy thing like that, but the truth is it just makes you hungry faster."

"Which is why I have truffles . . . and hot chocolate."

Tori slid the baby blue bakery bag in the woman's direction and grinned.

"Because you knew I'd be hungry from walkin'?"

Heat spread through her cheeks like wildfire through a prairie. "Um. Uh, well not exactly. I just figured you might like a treat."

"Don't you pee on my leg and tell me it's rainin', Victoria. Besides, you're not any good at it anyway." Margaret Louise folded her arms across her chest. "So quit goin' 'round the barn and just get to it, will you?"

She choked out a laugh. "There's no fooling you, is there? Okay, I got this stuff as bribery."

Margaret Louise's lips twitched as she looked from the bag of truffles to Tori and back again. "Who are you tryin' to bribe? Me . . . or *you*?"

"You."

"Hmmm. 'Cause from where I'm sittin', this looks like a bribe that would work on you."

There were times when Tori was touched to find out how much her Sweet Briar friends knew about her—her likes, her dislikes, et cetera. But sometimes the transparency wasn't such a good thing.

"I thought it would look like less of a bribe if they were things I liked?" she asked before remembering to bat her eyelashes for added innocence the way Leona was always after her to do.

"Don't you go battin' your eyes like my sister, neither."

Tori closed her eyes and forced a sigh. The first act was going better than she'd hoped. Just a little longer and her performance would be complete . . .

Her lashes parted to reveal a look of amused curiosity on Margaret Louise's face. "Okay. The bribery was intended for you but purchased with the notion we could enjoy it together. And the reason for the bribery is because I need a favor. A great big huge favor."

The curiosity retreated to make way for Margaret Louise's infamous face-splitting smile. "I don't need no bribery to help you with somethin', Victoria. You should know that by now. Just tell me what you need and it's yours."

Inhaling deeply, Tori plowed through the rest of her performance. "Since the firehouse won't be doing its annual Santa fire truck ride this year—"

"On account of a certain Grinch," Margaret Louise interjected through lips that were no longer smiling.

She nodded, then added the should-have-seen proviso to her line. "Since the firehouse won't be doing its annual Santa fire truck ride this year on account of a certain Grinch, I—along with Dixie—have decided to roll out a slightly tweaked version . . . here at the library."

"At the library?"

"That's right. Dixie first suggested the firehouse, though I think this particular idea lends itself better to the library."

The curiosity was back. In spades. "Tell me."

"I was thinking something along the lines of Cookies and Books with Mrs. Claus."

The faintest hint of a smile resurrected itself on Margaret Louise's face. "On the same weekend as the fire truck ride should have been?"

"Same weekend. Same time."

"Can Mrs. Claus make it?"

She paused, letting her eyes do most of the talking. And then, "I sure hope she can . . ."

Margaret Louise's cheeks rose nearly to her brow

line. "Think Mrs. Claus can make all of the cookies herself?"

"I think the kids would love that." Tori rested her elbows on the top of her desk and allowed her mind to veer off script momentarily. "And if we get everyone in the sewing circle on board with this plan, Mrs. Claus might even have enough homemade stockings in her bag to hand one out to everyone."

"With some homemade treats inside?"

"If Mrs. Claus wouldn't be too tired from making all those cookies . . ."

"Oh, she won't be!" Margaret Louise's brown eyes danced with excitement. "She'll be . . . tickled."

"I'm counting on that." Tori allowed herself a momentary mental pat on the back before forging ahead for the closing number. "I'm also hoping that Debbie and Beatrice can help us get the word out around town and that maybe *you* might help me transform the children's room into something very Mrs. Claus-ish for the day."

For a moment, Margaret Louise said nothing, opting instead to do a little nonverbal speaking of her own before haphazardly swiping their remnants from her cheeks. "Don't think I don't see through what you're doin', Victoria. 'Cause I do. But that don't mean I'm not touched just the same."

"Doing? What am I doing?" she asked, employing Leona's angelically innocent tactics once again.

"Givin' me a Christmas project so I can forget about The Grinch."

Harnessing all of the remaining theatrical ability she could possibly muster, Tori allowed her shoulders to fall. "I guess I'm not as convincing as I'd hoped."

Margaret Louise waved a pudgy hand in the air. "Don't you worry none. It's the thought that matters. Especially if we can get Debbie to make a sign announcin' the event and stick it right on Maime Wellington's front lawn."

Just as long as it's not a For Sale sign on yours, my dear friend . . .

For most folks, the holiday season was most often equated with a flurry of shopping and wrapping tucked around decorating and party going. For librarians, the holiday season also meant an influx of high-school-aged patrons racing to locate research books for the barrage of midyear term papers rapidly closing in on their due dates.

Some of the faces were familiar, of course, as their after-school visits were merely an extension of those they'd been paying since they were old enough to sit still for story time. But others were completely new, their discomfort in a library setting as tangible as the books they seemed almost reluctant to touch.

Yet for the first time since Tori's arrival, the ranks of the utterly clueless were beginning to thin thanks to the teen book club her assistant, Nina Morgan, had dreamed up and executed with the help of her husband, Duwayne. Both avid proponents of reading, the couple had advertised the club on posters throughout Sweet Briar High School, luring potential members with cool titles, cool discussions, and the kinds of snack foods that spoke to teenagers. Within a matter of months, they'd built the club to ten regular members and as many as twenty drop-ins depending on the book being read.

And while there were inarguably more students *not* in

the club than *were*, somehow word seemed to have gotten out that the library wasn't such a bad place, much to Tori and Dixie's delight.

"That Nina should get a raise when she returns from maternity leave," Dixie spouted as she moved from computer to computer, shutting each machine off for the night. "I've never seen the kind of cooperation we got from those kids today. Why, they were almost *appreciative* this year."

"I noticed it, too. And I actually had a few of them inquire about next month's book club, which will please Nina and Duwayne to no end." Tori grabbed the last stack of books from the research table and carried them to their appropriate aisles, the promise of impending sewing circle treats providing a spring to her end-of-the-workday step. "But that said, I'm so ready to just flop on Rose's sofa and lose myself in my sewing."

"You're real good with those teenagers, Victoria. Real good. They respond to you in a way they don't respond to me." Dixie shuffled over to the information desk. "They just seem to see me as old. Like the library board did when they decided to retire me two years ago."

Tori popped the last book into its spot and joined the seventy-something at the desk. "They respond to Nina more than they do me. And as for seeing you as old, I didn't get that today. Those two boys—the tall ones— seemed to take to you immediately, hanging on every word you said about the Vietnam era."

Dixie laughed. "Because I was the only one in the library who was alive at that time!"

Tori pulled her coworker's purse from the bottom shelf of the semicircular counter and held it outward. "Maybe. Or maybe they just found you to be cute."

A flash of crimson rose in Dixie's cheeks just before she snatched her purse from Tori's hands. "Oh, stop it, Victoria! Talk like that won't get me preening the way it does Leona."

"I know. I'm just playing." Tori backed herself against the counter and looked around the empty room, the break in activity providing not only a moment to breathe but one to remember with as well. "Dixie? Can I ask you something?"

Dixie stilled her hand inside her purse and gave Tori a once-over. "Of course . . ."

"You've lived in this town your whole adult life just like Charlotte and Parker Devereaux did, right?"

Pulling her hand from her purse, Dixie made her way over to the stool and sat down, the nod of her head answering Tori's initial question while her mouth began filling in the details. "My late husband, Tucker, and I got married about the same time as Charlotte and Parker. We were only a few years older than they were, so we gravitated toward each other fairly quickly. Why, we'd invite each other over for supper and games, and spend the whole evening hootin' and hollerin' as Margaret Louise might say. Sometimes, Parker would even invite his friend Jerry Lee and his wife, Sadie, to join us, but Sadie was always a bit highfalutin for my taste. Liked being the center of attention all the time."

Tori crossed to the other side of the counter and brushed at a speck of dirt before finding her next set of questions. "So you were friends when the Devereauxes had their children, yes? First Brian and then Ethan?"

"We were." Dixie's eyes gravitated upward, their expression a giveaway to the mental journey the woman was taking right there in the middle of the library. "I remember the initial shock poor Charlotte had when Brian arrived with the problems he has. She blamed herself for everything."

She spun around. "Blamed herself? Why?"

"That's what we did back then, Victoria. If something wasn't perfect, we naturally assumed we'd done something wrong to make it so. Ate the wrong foods, wore the wrong clothes, drank the wrong tea, were being punished for some lie we'd told as a child. We blamed ourselves for everything. Charlotte, I know, blamed Brian's problems on her one big blemish."

"Blemish?" she asked.

"Brian's arrival came six months after her wedding. Not nine."

So Leona had been right about the mound under Charlotte's wedding dress . . .

"Charlotte didn't dwell there for long, though," Dixie explained. "Why, she treasured that little boy with everything she had. Parker, too, embraced that little boy as the wonder she was determined he would be.

"Charlotte always had help, of course, that's what money enables you to do . . . but she always kept that little boy home with her rather than sending him off to a special school or living facility as others in her financial circle often did when faced with a similar trial."

Tori took a moment to process everything Dixie said before moving on to the son who had plagued her thoughts off and on since Frieda's comment at the virtual tree-lighting ceremony the previous night. "And Ethan? What was it like when he was born?"

Dixie slid off the stool and wandered out from behind

the confines of the information desk, her sensibly clad feet taking her halfway across the room before doubling back once again. "Ethan came along about twelve years later and he was Charlotte's vindication."

"In what way?" she asked.

"I always suspected she saw Ethan as her gift to Parker. He was the son that he could play ball with in the yard, the son he could coach through life, the son that would carry on the family name and one day take the company's reins."

"Did Parker share that feeling?"

"He did. Which is why that young man could do no wrong. Ever." Once again, the faraway look was back in Dixie's eyes, only this time it was accompanied by a hint of anger and disgust. "And when he did, they'd swoop in and clean up his mess as if it had been one of them who had made it, rather than Ethan."

Tori was just about to comment when Dixie barreled on, the words pouring from the former librarian's pencil-thin lips. "Rose dealt with it when she had Ethan in class, I dealt with it when he was here at the library, and people all over this town dealt with it whenever that young man was within a stone's throw. But by then, Ethan had grown so accustomed to the routine that Charlotte seemed to think it was her duty to carry on the status quo."

"Parker, too, I imagine?"

Dixie returned to the counter and the purse she'd left open. "Actually, no. As time went on and Parker began to travel, I think he began to see the monster they'd created in Ethan. The willfulness, the sense of entitlement, the lack of remorse, all of it. By then, Jerry Lee was working with the company, too, and he started letting Brian assist him with different tasks. After a decade or so of watching the results, Parker began to see that it wasn't Ethan to hold out with pride but, rather, Brian."

She watched Dixie reach into the purse once again, hunting, she suspected, for car keys. "Is that when he opened the center out in Tom's Creek?"

Sure enough, the woman's hand emerged from the purse with a cat-shaped key chain and an assortment of keys. "As sweet as they'd always known Brian to be, I don't think Parker ever really believed Brian could learn much beyond simple daily tasks. But Jerry Lee proved otherwise. I think it woke Parker up to the notion that people like Brian could do a lot if they were exposed to more things. So he funded the opening of the center and turned over the creative side of the venture to Jerry Lee, who, from what I've been told, has done incredible things with it over the last few years."

Tori thought back to the center and its various rooms and offerings, her head automatically nodding as she did. "Margaret Louise, Leona, and I took a tour of it not too long ago. It really is something special. You should drive out there one day and see for yourself. The audiobook room Jerry Lee set up is absolutely amazing."

With a quick zip of her purse, Dixie collected the rest of her belongings and pushed the stool into its proper position beneath the keyboard tray of the branch's main computer. "Then I guess I better get out there soon. Before the audiobook room and everything else disappears."

"Disappears?" Tori echoed.

"Now that Parker and Charlotte are both dead, the Prince will be taking the throne any day now. And if there was one thing Ethan despised more than being wrong, it was watching his father put more faith in Brian than in him."

"And so he'll strike back by closing down a center that has nothing to do with him?"

"If he owns the company that's backing it, he will," Dixie mused en route to the front door. When she reached it, Dixie turned and offered a smile. "So I'll see you tonight at Rose's, right?"

Tori closed the gap between them in anticipation of bolting the door in the woman's wake. "I'll be there. With our Christmas sewing project."

"The way you're incorporating Margaret Louise into our event is mighty kind, Victoria." Dixie tightened her grip on her car keys. "Mighty kind, indeed."

"I don't know about kind, I just hope it helps make her a little happier. Like volunteering her cooking expertise at the Devereaux Center will."

A cloud passed across Dixie's face. "If Ethan does what I think he's going to do, closing that center is going to hurt a lot of folks besides just Brian and folks like Brian."

"You mean like Margaret Louise?"

"Yes . . . and Frieda, too."

She drew back in surprise. "Frieda?"

Dixie pushed against the metal lever and stepped outside, stopping the answering close of the door with her back. "Now that Charlotte is gone, Frieda no longer has a patient to look after. And if Ethan closes the center without so much as a look backward, she won't be able to go back and volunteer there as an onsite health professional while she waits for work again, either. Which gives him a two-for-one in the revenge department."

"Ethan didn't like Frieda?" she guessed.

"He despised her, quite frankly." Stepping forward, Dixie jangled her keys at Tori in a makeshift wave. "But trust me, the feeling was more than mutual."

Chapter 15

There was something about the sound of women's chatter that had always made Tori smile, whether she was hiding behind a sofa listening as her great-grandmother played pinochle with the ladies from the neighborhood or simply sitting next to a table teeming with old high school chums at a coffee shop in Chicago. She'd always assumed it was the memory of her great-grandfather covering his ears and his refusal to rat her out that had caused the reaction. But the man had been long gone by the time she'd moved to Chicago and he most certainly wasn't winking at her in the middle of Rose Winters's sewing room, either.

Now, looking back, Tori knew it had had nothing to do with anything besides the sound of friendship. It hadn't mattered that she was merely a witness at the time. Happiness was happiness, and it had a way of making a person smile.

Yet now that she was part of the friendship sound, she couldn't help seeing the difference. Her smiles of old had been based on hope, while the smile on her face at that very moment was based on insider knowledge. An insider knowledge that filled her heart and made her whole.

"Would you get a look at Victoria, Mama?" Margaret Louise crowed. "She looks as happy as a clam at high tide, don't she?"

Tori looked to her left in time to see Annabelle Elkin nod her head slowly, the elderly woman's pronounced cheekbones a near perfect match to those of Margaret Louise's twin sister, Leona, and the youngest grandchild bouncing on Melissa's lap in a far corner of the room.

"Happy," Annabelle repeated in a whisper. "Happy as a clam at high tide."

"My sister is right. You're looking even happier than normal, dear," Leona proclaimed from her spot between Georgina and Beatrice on the sofa beneath the plate glass window overlooking Rose's famed garden. "Is there something we should know?"

"No, I'm just—"

"Perhaps you've rethought the color of our bridesmaid gowns to something more flattering?" Leona lowered her travel magazine to her side and rested a hand atop a sleeping Paris, peering at Tori above the rim of her stylish glasses as she did. "If not, may I suggest a royal blue? I look magnificent in royal blue. Or even a hunter green, which would play up the hint of green in Paris's eyes?"

"Victoria is not going to select her wedding colors based on a rabbit," Rose hissed from her cozy armchair beneath the gooseneck lamp. "And you're one of *eight* bridesmaids, Leona. What looks spectacular on you might not look spectacular on me or Beatrice or Debbie or Melissa or Dixie or Georgina or Nina or your sister."

"There's no need to worry about the ones no one will be looking at, you old goat." Leona rolled her eyes skyward before bringing them back down to focus on Tori. "I can see that now is not the time to talk details, so if it's not wedding plans, what has you looking so . . . so *gleeful*."

Tori nibbled back the laugh that would surely land her in hot water with Paris's mother and opted instead to simply finish the answer she'd been trying to give when Leona cut her off in the first place. "I'm just happy to be here. With all of you."

"And the feelin' is mutual, Victoria." Margaret Louise pushed her feet against the hardwood floor and scooted her wheeled chair still closer to the couch Tori shared with Annabelle. "Can we tell 'em?"

Ignoring the eight sets of eyes she felt trained on her face, Tori waited for Margaret Louise to explain her question.

"You know . . . about"—Margaret Louise looked toward Melissa and Molly Sue and lowered her voice a notch—"Mrs. Claus and the cookies and the decorations?"

"And the stockings," Dixie reminded. "Don't forget about the stockings. We only have two weeks to get them all done."

She felt the smile as it spread across her face and knew it matched the one Margaret Louise sported. "Ahhh, yes. The library's very first Cookies and Books with Mrs. Claus event." Pulling her gaze back to the center of the room, Tori took a moment to look at each and every one of her friends before sharing the details of the upcoming family event. When she was done, she pulled Dixie's stocking sample from her tote bag and held it up for all to see. "Margaret Louise and Dixie were thinking that it might be neat to have a little stocking like this to give to each child who comes to the event."

Debbie squealed. "Oooh, can we put things inside it? I think a candy cane or two and maybe a small crayon box would fit in one of those stockings."

"That's what we're thinkin', ain't it, Victoria?"

"If we can get some donations, sure. But first we're going to need to make about fifty of these stockings to be on the safe side. Do we think that's doable?"

"I think we should make closer to a hundred." Rose pointed at the stocking then motioned for Tori to send it around the room for everyone to see. "Better to be safe than sorry when children are involved. If we have extras when it's over, we can decide what to do with the leftovers then."

Rose was right. Too much was always better than too little.

And besides, the stocking pattern was a simple one.

"Looks just like one I made last week." Margaret Louise turned the sample stocking over in her hands before handing it across the circle to her daughter-in-law, Melissa. "We got enough fabric?"

Tori nodded. "I had two full bolts of Christmas fabric in my bin at home, so I brought one of them with me tonight. If we cut carefully, there should be more than enough to make a hundred stockings."

That was all it took for the divvying of tasks to begin. Debbie volunteered to cut appropriately sized sections from the bolt, Rose shuffled off to her personal copier to make copies of the simple pattern, and all remaining members of the circle began searching through their sewing boxes to locate a pair of scissors and the best thread for the project.

For the next hour they pinned and cut and sewed one small stocking after the other, adding those they finished to the ever-growing pile on Rose's coffee table. Ideas for the event were batted around, peppered, of course, with talk about the atrocious decorations springing up around Sweet Briar and the woman behind it all.

"I was at the school the other day, dropping off Luke's lunch, when I saw who I think was this Maime woman." Beatrice's needle-holding hand stilled above the red-and-green-checked stocking in her lap. "She was bringing lunch to the councilman's son and she was rather horrid to him."

"I don't know how that woman can look at herself in the mirror," Rose groused. "Anyone who can be so nasty toward a child is harboring a very cold heart."

"Not much we can do, though, when Councilman Jordan is so blind." Debbie bent atop her latest stocking and knotted off the final stitch. "I just wish there was something we could do to wake him up."

Dixie scooted to the edge of her chair and rested yet another completed stocking on the pile. "That woman is very careful not to show him what the rest of us have seen."

"The key is setting her up so that he sees what she's so cleverly hiding from him." Leona flipped to the next page in her magazine, her voice emerging from behind its glossy cover. "It's easy for him to pretend it's everyone else right now—their jealousy, their reluctance to embrace the new woman in his life, et cetera. But if he can see it with his own two eyes, he can no longer pretend it's everyone else.

Once he does, *her* horrible behavior becomes *his* horrible behavior if he then *knowingly* looks the other way."

It made sense. It really did. But as enticing as the notion of seeing Maime Wellington get her comeuppance was, Tori was much more concerned with the effects on the councilman's son now. She said as much to the group, sharing the hurt and pain Kyle had exhibited over Maime's decision to do away with his mother's ornaments in favor of electronic ones that danced and talked from the branches of a virtual tree.

A round of tsks and a series of snorts made their way through the room until they were silenced by a sharp intake of air from the town's mayor.

"Ms. Wellington may have taken the annual tree-lighting ceremony in a different direction this year, but that doesn't mean she did away with the remnants of previous holidays. Those things belong to the town, not an individual person."

"Well then, maybe the town should allow Kyle to borrow a few of those ornaments for his tree at home this year." Rose ran a trembling hand down the front of one of the freshly cut stocking pieces lying in her lap and sighed. "After all, they seemed mighty important to the lad."

"You honestly think this woman would allow those ornaments on her personal tree if she essentially moved heaven and earth to keep them off one located two blocks from her home?" Leona closed her magazine and tossed it onto the coffee table, narrowly missing the pile of stockings.

"It's not her tree, Leona." Rose narrowed her eyes on her nemesis. "It's the boy's tree."

"Which is in the house she's hell bent on making her own," Leona snipped back.

Reality dawned on Rose's face, pulling her lips into a heart-tugging frown. "Oh."

Margaret Louise pushed off her chair and began pacing the room, the occasional squeak of her Keds against the wood floor signaling the start of yet another lap. Midway through her fourth lap across the sewing room, the woman stopped and turned to Georgina. "So you still have all those ornaments I put on the town tree last year?"

Georgina bobbed her head above her fifth stocking.

"I reckon that means they could be used for somethin' else in town?"

Again, Georgina nodded.

"Mrs. Claus is goin' to need a tree in her winter wonderland, ain't she, Victoria? A really pretty tree with extra special ornaments, wouldn't you say?"

Tori dropped her threaded needle onto her lap and clapped her hands into a tight clasp. "Oh, Margaret Louise, what a great idea."

"And somethin' tells me I'm gonna need some help decoratin' that tree."

"Kyle?" she whispered.

"He'd be the best choice," Margaret Louise dropped back onto her chair. "Think he might be willin' to help me?"

"You are brilliant, Margaret Louise. Absolutely brilliant, you know that?" She glanced back down at the stocking taking shape atop her thighs and laughed softly. "Can't you just see Kyle's face when we ask him?"

"And can't you just see Maime's when she finds out?" Leona drawled.

Rose stamped her foot on the floor. "Must you always try to dampen everything, Leona?"

Leona's eyes widened. "I'm not—"

"Oh, put a sock in it, would you?" Dixie stretched her arms over her head and held them there long enough to earn a crack that echoed around the room. "No one is concerned about Maime's feelings because she has none, Leona. This is about a little boy."

"I'm well aware of that," Leona said through clenched teeth. "If the ever-charming Rose Winters had let me finish, I'd have—"

"So what's going on with the whole Parker Devereaux thing?" Scooting forward ever so slightly on her chair, Rose turned her body away from Leona and toward Georgina. "Will there be an investigation?"

"There's nothing to investigate."

Tori drew back in her spot. "But you have a dead body that didn't bury itself."

"A five-year-old dead body found based on a drawing done by a woman who's no longer with us, Victoria." Georgina lifted the pile of stockings from the table to her lap and began counting, each number easy to recite along with the woman's lips. When she reached thirty-six, she put them back. "Not bad for"—Georgina glanced down at her watch—"a little less than ninety minutes."

"I say it's time for desserts," Debbie proclaimed around a yawn. "I brought a new pie I've been thinking about selling at the bakery."

"But wait. What happens if someone else killed Parker?"

All eyes turned toward Tori.

"Someone else?" Georgina questioned.

"Yeah." Now that her mouth was moving, she couldn't

stop the flow of words that came out. Not even for the promise of chocolate or one of Debbie's new pies. "If someone else did it and you shut the case, that person will get away with murder."

"Who else could have done it, Victoria?"

She looked from Georgina to Rose and back again, her internal wheels turning so fast she could barely keep up. "I—I don't know. Maybe Ethan?"

"Ethan?" Dixie gasped.

"I—I don't know. I'm just throwing him out as a possibility. I mean, think about it, Dixie. Even you said Ethan is selfish. And Charlotte's nurse, Frieda . . . she seems to think Ethan is more than capable of having killed his dad if he thought it would benefit him somehow."

Georgina lifted her hands in the air and waved them back and forth. "First things first. There is no love lost between Frieda Taylor and Ethan Devereaux. We know this. So one of her fingers being pointed in Ethan's direction doesn't really surprise me. But regardless of all that, there's one major factor we can't ignore. Charlotte's drawing took you to the spot where her husband was buried. A husband she told everyone had up and left her in favor of some pretty young thing he'd met while traveling. She made everyone believe Parker Devereaux was a cad. And all the while she was making us believe that, she knew exactly where she'd buried his body. That's about as cut-and-dried as it's going to get, Victoria."

She knew Georgina was right. There was really no other explanation. Charlotte's drawing had led them to Parker Devereaux's body.

Slowly but surely, each member of the sewing circle added their final stocking of the night onto the pile on the coffee table and filed into Rose's hallway, the promise of food leading all but one down the hallway and away from Tori.

"Victoria? Aren't you coming?" Melissa asked as she held her arms out toward Molly Sue.

"Book!"

"Mommy has read that to you ten times already today. We'll read it again in a little while, sweetheart. I promise."

Molly Sue's bottom lip quivered. "Book?"

"After we have a treat."

"No treat," Molly Sue replied. "Book!"

Tori watched as Melissa looked from the hallway to Molly Sue and back again, the gurgle from her ever-growing stomach echoing around the room. "Sweetie, Mommy is hungry."

Shifting her stocking onto the empty cushion beside her, Tori stood and crossed the room to sit beside the youngest Davis child. "I'm with Molly Sue. I'd rather read a book than eat right now, too. So go on . . . get something to eat. I'll stay here with her until you get back."

"Are you sure?" Melissa asked despite the hope in her eyes.

"Positive. Now go." When her friend was gone, Tori lifted Molly Sue onto her lap, pausing briefly to take in the title and cover illustration she'd seen in Lulu's hands just two days earlier. Only this time, instead of stopping on Charlotte's loving inscription to her older son, Tori kept going, turning the very same pages Charlotte had turned night after night until Brian had been forced to take over.

Clearly the story had been a favorite for the mother and son just as it seemed to be for Molly Sue. And as the story progressed, it wasn't hard for Tori to see why.

The concept of making messes was something even a child of Molly Sue's age could understand. It was a part of their daily life. But what touched Tori as an adult was the notion that sometimes, when someone makes a lot of messes, they're often blamed for ones they don't make as well. Because it's easier to assume, even for adults.

"I know it's awful, but I can't look at that last page and not think about Charlotte's drawing being wedged inside."

Tori looked up from the book in time to see Melissa slowly lower herself onto the ottoman at Tori's feet.

"I guess it's because I keep wondering why she stuck it in there."

Tori felt Molly Sue's head stirring beneath her chin and glanced back at the space dividing the final two pages of the book. "The drawing was here?"

"That's what Lulu said." Melissa let her hands fall to the growing mound beneath the maternity shirt that had seen her through seven pregnancies thus far. "Which is kind of sad if you think about it."

Tori's head snapped up. "Sad?"

Melissa nodded. "Yeah. I mean, look at the way that story ends . . . with the mom and dad realizing they'd been blaming little Peter for something he hadn't done."

"I don't get what you're saying, Melissa."

"If you think about it, Charlotte's drawing was kind of her way of telling everyone the truth about Parker. Even if it was just to clear her conscience before she passed."

Chapter 16

Tori could feel Milo watching her as she made her way back and forth between the living room and the kitchen carrying drinks and munchies for their Tuesday night movie date. He'd offered to help several times, yet she'd declined in the hope that the flurry of activity would quiet her thoughts for the first time in nearly twenty-four hours.

In the beginning, after she'd gotten home from Rose's house, Melissa's comment about Charlotte's note had still been fresh in her mind, making it easy to figure out why she'd revisited it while brushing her teeth and getting ready for bed. But when it came time to close her eyes and go to sleep, the thoughts had still been there, driving her from bed before dawn.

Work had been no different, only instead of staring at a ceiling while Melissa's words looped through her head again and again, she'd been shelving books and helping patrons and making more than her fair share of stupid mistakes.

Dixie had asked her what was wrong the third time Tori pointed a patron toward the front door rather than the bathroom.

Rose had asked her what was wrong when she stopped by the library with a question about a particular book and was given the ingredients for a gooey butter cake instead.

Debbie had asked her what was wrong when Tori showed up at the bakery after work and left without ordering anything chocolate.

She hadn't answered because she didn't know what to say about her weird obsession with Parker Devereaux's death.

Everyone around her thought it was cut-and-dried. Charlotte had stashed her husband's body and simply told everyone around her that he'd left their marriage. But it didn't sit right. Not with her anyway.

"So how many more bowls of popcorn are you going to pop before you think we've got enough? Because I'm thinking a fourth bag might be a bit much . . ."

Tori stopped midway across the room and glanced over her shoulder at the coffee table. Sure enough, there were three bowls of popcorn lined up in front of Milo with the telltale aroma of a fourth wafting its way out of the kitchen. Shaking her head, she slumped into a dining room chair. "I'm sorry. I've been like this all day. If you want to take a rain check until next week, I understand."

"I don't want a rain check." Milo closed the gap between the couch and the dining room chairs in several easy strides. "I just want to know what you're thinking."

She couldn't help laughing at yet another example of her transparency. "Who says I'm thinking?"

"Am I wrong?" he challenged.

"No."

Reaching outward, he took hold of her hands and pulled her to a stand, wrapping his arms around her as she did. "So lay it on me. What's going on in that head of yours?"

"Stuff that doesn't make any sense," she whispered with her cheek pressed against his chest. "Stuff that's gonna make me sound like a nut if I say it out loud."

"I don't mind nuts."

"This might change your mind."

"I doubt it, but why don't you let me be the judge." He released her from his arms and took hold of her hand. "C'mon. Come sit with me on the couch and fill me in. If it gets really interesting, we've got popcorn, right?"

"True." Step by step, she followed him back to the couch, snuggling into the crook of his arm with very little coaxing. "Just remember, I warned you."

"I consider myself warned. Now talk."

She twisted her body so as to afford a view of the ceiling while still taking advantage of the courage Milo's body warmth instilled. "Okay, so everyone thinks Charlotte Devereaux dug a hole on the library grounds five years ago and tossed her husband's body inside. Yet no one seems to wonder why? Or how? I mean, don't they seem like important questions to you?"

His body tensed ever so slightly beneath her head. "What do you mean?"

"All I've ever heard from anyone in this town is that

Charlotte Devereaux was head over heels in love with her husband."

"As he was with her," Milo said.

Tori sat up and spun around on the sofa until they were face-to-face. "Exactly. So what could possibly have happened to make her kill him? And how could a woman who was sixty-nine dig a hole all by herself and get a grown man's body inside?"

A flash of something Tori couldn't quite identify made its way across Milo's face. "I'll be honest, that last question has mulled itself over in my own head more than a few times since I heard the news about Parker's death and Charlotte's drawing."

Somehow, the notion that someone besides herself found a few oddities in everyone else's thinking buoyed Tori's spirits and encouraged her to continue. "See? It doesn't make sense. Someone else had to have done it."

"Whoa. Slow down a minute. I said I've wondered how she could have dug the hole and gotten him inside it, but that doesn't mean I think someone else did it."

Her mouth gaped open for the briefest of moments. "But then—"

"I mean, I've thought of my own mom, who's only a year or so younger than Charlotte was when Parker was killed, and I'm not sure she could dig a hole like that too easily. In a private setting with less chance of being spotted . . . maybe. But on the grounds of the library when time isn't on her side . . . a bit more doubtful."

"So why is the notion of another killer so hard to imagine?" she asked.

Milo pulled his hand down his face and let it linger on

his chin before addressing her question head on. "Because there's no getting around the fact that Charlotte drew a picture showing where her husband's body was buried. How would she know that if she wasn't involved?"

She grabbed hold of his hands and squeezed, hoping that somehow what he said would make him think along the same lines she'd been toying with all day long. "Of course she had to have been involved . . . there's no doubt about that."

He made a face then worked to soften it just as quickly. "Then I don't get where you're going with this."

"She was sixty-nine, Milo. You said yourself that makes the whole situation tough to imagine. But if someone else was involved . . . if someone else dug the hole and put the body in it . . . it's much less of a stretch, don't you think?"

Milo opened his mouth to respond but closed it without saying a word.

"It makes you think, doesn't it?" Leaning to the left, she snatched a bowl of popcorn from the table and pushed it into Milo's hands. "Here, eat."

He did as he was told without taking his eyes off Tori.

"So, at the very least, Charlotte didn't act alone." There, it was out in the open. Glad to finally have voiced her conviction aloud, she retrieved an extra buttery piece of popcorn from the top of the bowl and popped it in her mouth. "If she's the one who even killed Parker in the first place."

Piece by piece Milo crunched his way through the top layer of popcorn before officially weighing in on her theory. "Okay, so let's assume you're right. That someone did help her with the body. And maybe, just maybe, that someone is the one who actually killed Parker. But if that's true, why didn't Charlotte say something? Why did she tell everyone he'd run off?"

"Maybe she was afraid? Maybe whoever did it threatened to do the same to her if she told anyone?" Suddenly, all the fears, all the far-fetched theories she'd been afraid to share, seemed a lot less nutty now that they were coming out of her mouth. "Maybe that's why she finally drew that last picture. Because she knew she was dying anyway and she wanted the truth to be known."

Milo stopped chewing and narrowed his eyes in thought. "If she was going for broke because she knew she was dying anyway, why not just tell someone what happened?"

"Because she had Alzheimer's, Milo. If she'd suddenly blurted out that the husband she'd always said had left her for another woman had actually been murdered . . . and then named a culprit . . . no one would have believed her. They'd have thought it was the bizarre rantings of a sick woman. And who knows? Maybe she *did* try to say something and finally resorted to drawing it when no one would listen to her words."

Burying her head in her hands, Tori tried to imagine such a scenario playing out, the frustration Charlotte would have felt virtually maddening. "Ugh. I wish there was a way to know."

"A way to know if she tried?" Milo asked. At her nod, he shrugged. "It seems to me the best way to find out would be to ask Frieda. Maybe now, with everything we *do* know about Parker's body, something Charlotte might have said along the way can be revisited in a different, more educated light."

"Maybe." She pulled her hands from her face and reached for one of her favorite throw pillows. Hugging it to her chest, she sank against the sofa's back cushion. "And that might work . . ."

Milo cocked his head and studied her closely. "I know that look. Something is still bugging you so spill it, please."

He knew her well, there was no doubt about that. But in order to fill him in on the last of her worries, she had to be able to pinpoint it for herself first.

And she couldn't.

So much of what she'd shared with Milo thus far made sense if each and every point was considered on its own merits. After all, Charlotte hadn't been a young woman when Parker's body was buried on the library grounds. And she had drawn a treasure map of sorts directing them to the exact location of that burial. But if she was trying to clear her conscience or point a finger at someone else for the crime, why didn't she draw the map over and over again instead of sketch after sketch of her husband's study?

That didn't make sense.

She said as much to Milo, then sat back and waited for him to announce he was no longer a fan of nuts. But that didn't happen. Instead, he slipped his hand around her shoulders and guided her back into his arms. "Then I guess you're just going to have to keep digging until it *does* make sense."

"But it's almost Christmas. And we've got a wedding coming up in a little over ten months," she pointed out on his behalf. "Shouldn't you be reminding me that I've got enough on my plate without playing detective once again? Especially when I have no connection to Charlotte or Parker Devereaux to start with?"

Milo's chin bobbed against the top of her head. "I could. But why? You know all of those things already yet you still feel a pull towards this case. And as I see it, the only way you'll be able to truly focus on Christmas and our wedding is if you free your mind of these nagging questions."

"But what happens if I'm wrong?" she asked before closing her eyes and savoring the warmth of his lips on her temple.

"Then you're wrong," he whispered. Dropping his mouth in line with hers, he hovered there long enough to complete his thought, his words enveloping her in a much-needed sense of calm and validation. "But at least you'll *know* you're wrong."

Chapter 17

Tori had learned a lot of things from her friends in the Sweet Briar Ladies Society Sewing Circle over the past two years—life lessons that had made her a wiser person and a better friend. In some cases the lessons had been absorbed by merely watching and observing, as was the case with Debbie and her poster-child status for hard work and determination.

In other cases, lessons learned had come via quiet conversations with Dixie, and moments of immense courage and grace as demonstrated by Rose.

But of all the women who'd impacted her life since leaving Chicago, no one had affected her quite the way Margaret Louise and her twin sister, Leona, had.

With Margaret Louise, it was easy to pinpoint the lessons and how they'd been taught. Loyalty was demonstrated, kindness was exuded, genuine happiness was second nature, and love unconditional.

With Leona, the lessons weren't quite so obvious. In fact, if Tori hadn't dug beyond the antique store owner's surface of narrow-minded, holier-than-thou arrogance, she would have missed out on the gems hidden behind the prickly façade.

On the surface, the sisters were as different as night and day. Where Margaret Louise was humble, Leona was boastful and cocky. Where Leona was poised, refined, and cultured, Margaret Louise was earthy, easygoing, and simple. And where Margaret Louise was endearingly unkempt, Leona was not-a-single-hair-out-of-place-ever perfect.

Underneath all of that stuff, though, the two women weren't all that different. They both treasured their family—even if Leona tried to disguise that fact with eye rolls and dramatic sighs. And they both had a need to be liked—even if Leona's was harder to detect behind her sarcasm and off-putting barbs.

But Tori saw it plain as day. And regularly thanked her lucky stars for their presence in her life even if it meant an occasional near-heart-attack experience when one or—as was the case at that very moment—*both* opted to knock on her office window after hours.

When she was alone.

All alone.

Grabbing hold of the corner of her desk, Tori spun around and then slumped in her chair. "Oh, thank God . . ."

Leona pushed her face against the plate glass window and moved her mouth to simulate their inability to hear a thing Tori was saying while Margaret Louise pointed toward the library's back door.

"You should have knocked there first," Tori mumbled before turning her back to her friends and heading out into the hallway. When she reached the back door, she disengaged the dead bolt and pushed the door open. "Okay, you two, I'm at the door . . ."

The answering rustle of bushes that lined the outside of the library let her know she'd been heard. Seconds later, her eyes solidified that confirmation.

"We didn't knock here first, *dear*, because we knew you were in your office." Leona tightened her grip on a nose-twitching Paris and pushed her way past Tori. "To knock here when you were there would have been point-less, don't you think?"

She let Margaret Louise pass and then followed them both down the hallway and into her office. "I thought you said you couldn't hear me through the window, Leona."

"I can hear attitude, Victoria. And you had attitude when you suggested a better knocking venue," Leona drawled as she stopped just inside Tori's office door and looked around. "You really need to listen to at least one of my many suggestions about sprucing this place up. It's so—so boring."

She nibbled back the urge to laugh out loud at Marga-ret Louise's eye roll and instead gestured toward the empty chair across from her desk for Leona, and toward Nina's chair for Margaret Louise. "If I spent more than a handful of hours a week actually in this room, I might be more inclined to hang a few pictures but I—"

"I never said anything about pictures. I said candles and a tented drape of some sort that would encompass your desk and provide an opportunity for privacy if Milo happened to stop by for a visit."

Tori walked around her desk and claimed the chair she'd vacated in response to her friends' stealthy tapping. "Leona. This is a public library. I am a librarian. The board didn't hire me so I could entertain my fiancé in my office."

"Then perhaps you should consider a different field . . ."

Nina's chair squeaked under the weight of Margaret Louise's plump form. "Don't you pay no mind to my twin, Victoria. She's in a bit of a foul mood."

"Oh?"

"She's still stewin' over puttin' the fat in the fire at Rose's the other night." Margaret Louise dropped an elbow onto Nina's desk and rested her left cheek in the heel of her hand. "You know, when Rose cut her off and started interrogatin' Georgina about Parker's body . . . Why, she's been stickin' to that slight like it's the last pea at the bottom of the pot."

Leona's fist came down on the edge of Tori's desk with a thud. "That's because everyone thought I was worried about Maime's feelings if you use those ornaments you were talking about the other night. Or they think I'm trying to discourage you from asking the councilman's son to help. But I'm not and I wasn't."

"Then why didn't you tell them that?" Tori asked.

"I tried to! But Rose and Dixie wouldn't listen."

Margaret Louise propped her other cheek up with her right hand and yawned. "And why is that, Twin?"

"Because the two of them are like the bullies in the school yard at those circle meetings."

Tori couldn't help it—she laughed.

Leona's left brow rose upward. "You find my plight funny, dear?"

Tori cleared her throat of any residual happy sounds and replaced them with a quick head shake. "No. But calling Rose Winters and Dixie Dunn bullies? Don't you think that's a little over the top?"

"Are you going to tell me Dixie never bullied you? Because I can remember several examples right off the top of my head if your memory needs to be jogged a little."

Touché.

"Tell Victoria what you were tryin' to say, Twin," Margaret Louise encouraged.

Keenly aware of her moment in the spotlight, Leona threw her shoulders back and neatened her already sprayed-to-perfection hairstyle. "I was trying to point out the fact that your using those ornaments and asking the Jordan boy for his assistance isn't going to sit well with Maime—"

"The Grinch." Margaret Louise lifted her face from her hands, matching her sister's posture while bypassing the whole hair thing. "From this day forward, Maime Wellington is to be referred to as The Grinch."

Leona flicked away her sister's interruption yet made the necessary adjustment to her story. "The Grinch isn't going to be happy. And when nasty people aren't happy, they tend to snap . . . as you and I both saw in the conference room during our Decorating Committee meeting, Victoria."

All Tori could do was nod and wait for Leona to fill in the rest.

"Which means one thing. Councilman Jordan needs to

be within earshot when The Grinch reacts to the tree. And if she reacts all over the boy in a public forum, even better."

Margaret Louise beamed with pride at her sister. "Ain't my twin as smart as a tree full of owls figurin' that out?"

"That's what you were trying to say the other night?"

Leona looked down at Paris sitting quietly in her lap and gave her a gentle scratch behind her ears, the animal's eyes closing to half-mast in response. "Yes, it is."

"Then I'm sorry Rose and Dixie didn't give you the chance." And she was. "But do you think it will really work?"

"If the councilman has half a brain in that noggin of his, he'll realize The Grinch is as cold as a cast-iron toilet seat and get back to being a man. If not, then his shirt is missin' a few buttons and he don't deserve the respect of that young boy."

Leona's hand paused mid-scratch as she met Tori's eye. "I agree with my sister, although I wouldn't have put it in exactly those same words."

"Oh no?" Tori teased before grabbing a pencil from the wooden holder on her desk and slowly turning it over and over between her fingers. "I hate to say it, but I hope it works. Maime Well—"

Margaret Louise cleared her throat loudly and decisively before pinning Tori with an expectant stare.

"What?" And then she remembered. "Oh. Sorry. The Grinch is just not a nice person. It's like she lives to be contrary for the simple sake of being contrary." Tori slid her fingers down the barrel of the pencil, only to turn it over and repeat the process when she reached the bottom. "Kyle came into the library today after school to find a book for an upcoming travel project he's doing in his social studies class." Her hand slowed as she recalled the incident that had left her both shocked and saddened, and more determined than ever to include the boy in the decorating plans for the Christmas cookies and book event. "So he disappears into an aisle filled with travel books to see what interests him. Less than five minutes later he comes out with a book on Florida and saying he wants to do something on Disney World because it's one of his favorite childhood memories. The words were barely out of his mouth when Ma—I mean, The Grinch starts mocking him for wanting to do a project about a place she insisted was for babies."

"Babies?" Margaret Louise parroted. "Is she serious?"

Leona gave Paris one final scratch and then put him on the floor at her feet, her mouth and her face set in rigid lines. "That woman is threatened by Avery's past with his first wife, plain and simple. And it's become her mission in life to eradicate every memory she can and taint those she can't regardless of whether they're Avery's memories or Kyle's."

Pausing her thumb and index finger halfway down the pencil, Tori gave Leona a once-over. "Why does it seem as if you understand Kyle's predicament on a personal level?"

Leona uncrossed her ankles and rose from the chair. "Because my best girlfriend in the sixth grade went through this same thing when we were kids. Her father remarried a woman who was nothing short of hateful to my friend. She tried to talk to her dad to tell him how she felt . . . but he either refused to believe it or simply didn't care. Eventually, he just stopped talking to her unless the new wife was around. When my friend turned eighteen, she simply gave up on him."

Margaret Louise clapped her hands together. "Well, that's 'bout enough of that, I think. Christmas is comin', and as long as the Lord is willin' and the creek don't rise, we've got a hoot'nanny to plan for the kids in this town. So let's quit flappin' our jaws over the weeds in the garden and pluck 'em when the time comes."

Tori laughed.

Leona rolled her eyes.

When she'd gathered herself together, Tori pulled her leather-bound organizer from the top drawer of her desk and opened it to a clean page. "So let's talk details. I'm thinking maybe we could transform the children's room into our temporary winter wonderland. With a little help from some of the guys, we could move the bookshelves into here and open up the space a little bit." She jotted her thoughts down on the paper and then glanced up at Margaret Louise. "What do you think? Will that work?"

"Maybe you could put the tree in that area where the stage normally is," Leona suggested, earning herself a nod from both Margaret Louise and Tori. "And there's going to be cookies at this thing, right?"

"You're darn tootin' there's gonna be cookies. And they're gonna be just like the ones I made with them sweet little things out at the Devereaux Center this mornin'. Snowflake cookies lightly dusted with sugar and maybe some snickerdoodles, too."

Tori pushed her notebook to the side and focused her attention on Margaret Louise. "You worked with the kids out at the center today?"

"It was my first day volunteerin'," Margaret Louise

boasted. "Only they ain't kids. They're older—like my Jake's age. They come to the center so they can be with others like them and have a little fun. And whoo-wee, did we have some fun."

"I'm so glad," Tori said, looking back down at her notebook and considering the details they still needed to discuss. "Was Jerry Lee out there again today?"

"No. But Frieda was."

Her head snapped up. "Frieda? Why?"

Shrugging, Margaret Louise scooted her chair away from Nina's desk and reached her arms toward Paris. "She was volunteerin' the same as me. Only instead of runnin' a cookin' class, she was talkin' to a few of the folks 'bout keepin' healthy."

"How is she doing?"

Margaret Louise lifted the bunny into her arms and gave it a gentle squeeze. "She seems sad. Like she's fallen on stony ground. But she'll be smilin' again soon, just you wait and see. Helpin' folks like she does has a way of erasin' your cares away. Long as she has that, she'll be okay."

Chapter 18

Tori pulled her finger back and listened as her presence on the front porch was announced via a series of chimes discernible through the large mahogany door. Room by room the sound reverberated around the large plantation-style home before staging an encore through the front hallway.

Seconds gave way to minutes before the faintest hint of approaching footsteps reversed her own back to the welcome mat in anticipation of a familiar face that didn't materialize. Instead, Tori found herself staring up, up, up into the greenest eyes she'd ever seen.

"Yes?"

Her gaze moved still higher, taking in the silky smooth hair that framed a classically handsome face with its flawless nose, chiseled jawline, and perfectly proportioned mouth of pristine white teeth. "Uh . . . hi. You must be Ethan Devereaux, yes?"

"I am. And you are?"

"Victoria. Victoria Sinclair." She extended her hand toward the man, only to retract it when it went unacknowledged in favor of a slow, head-to-toe visual inspection she found herself copying.

Ethan Devereaux was tall. Very tall. Six foot three, at least. His workout shirt, pulled taut across his chest, silently boasted the benefits of daily weight training while the toned muscles in his thighs spoke to a regimen that surely included time on a track as well.

"Victoria . . ." Faint lines appeared at the outer corners of his eyes at the sound of her name. "Wait. You're not the girl from the other night, are you?'

She shook her head at his inquiry but not before her cheeks warmed to the point she was grateful for the outside air. "N-No. I'm here because I was hoping to have a moment with Frieda?"

Any hint of ease disappeared from Ethan's stance. "My mother is dead. So why on earth would you think Frieda Taylor would still be here? She was an *employee*. My *mother's* employee. And unlike my mother, who actually believed Frieda gave two hoots about her, I'm not blind to that woman's dishonesty and greed."

Tori felt her jaw start to slacken but did her best to rein it in before Ethan could register the reaction as shocked disagreement. To give him that window into her thoughts would most certainly result in the door being slammed in her face before any snooping opportunities could be realized.

"Wow. I'm sorry. I didn't know. I"—she glanced down at her purse long enough to concoct a workable story that could be backed up by the leather-bound notebook it housed—"I just saw her name alongside your address and, well, here I am. To say thank you."

Ethan's shoulders dipped ever so slightly as the bubble of tension began to ease. "You're thanking me? For what?"

"For the very generous book donation that was made to the Sweet Briar Public Library in memory of your mother." Again, she extended her hand, this time sensing at least a flash of hesitation before he shrugged it away sans shake. Letting it fall to her side once again, she continued on, the need for answers winning out over the desire to walk away in disgust. "I'm the head librarian there and the donation came in just in time to be part of our First Annual Holiday Book Extravaganza last weekend."

"Oh, yeah. I saw those books." A twitch in the left corner of Ethan's mouth gave way to a mischievous smile that spread from one side to the other. "Even added one to the pile myself."

Digging the tips of her fingers into the palms of her hands, she resisted the urge to call him on the motivation behind his particular donation selection and opted instead to keep him talking.

"I guess your mother was quite the reader," she mused.

"Well, when you don't do anything except spend your dead husband's money all day long, what else is there to do?"

Tori cast about for something, anything, to say. "I— I'm sorry about your dad."

"Yeah. Me, too. Had I known my mother offed him five years ago, I wouldn't have had to keep asking her for money when I wanted to buy something. *She'd* have been asking *me*."

"I don't understand—"

"And I can tell you right now I'd have put the kibosh on her hiring Frieda as her nurse these last few years. Nope, Frieda would have been out on her keister long before my mother got sick and came up with the idiotic notion to give that woman even *more* of our money."

This time when her jaw went slack, she let it go. Though, if he noticed, he gave no indication, proceeding ahead with his rant. "Between my mother and my father and the way they tossed money around, it's a wonder there was even enough money for me to get my Corvette and my sailboat at all."

"Tossed money around?"

Ethan snorted back a brittle laugh. "Tossed it. Handed it. Threw it. Call it whatever you will. But I stand to get a whole lot less now than I would've if my mom had tossed my father into a hole *before* I inspired his case of the guilts where my older brother is concerned. But I'll tell you this much . . . That was my old man's guilt. It sure as hell isn't going to be mine."

She'd have to be an idiot not to hear the meaning behind Ethan's words, his thinly disguised innuendo all but shoring up speculation over the fate of the Devereaux Center now that Parker Devereaux had been declared dead. All the work, all the time, all the volunteer hours, all the love and care that went into making the lives of people like Brian Devereaux better was about to come to an end. The writing was on the wall, and Ethan's comments and attitude were merely serving as a few extra exclamation points at the end.

"Your older brother's name is Brian, right?" It was a lame question but at least it was something.

"Yeah, Lord Brian . . . Creator of All Delusion. He actually managed to make *my* father believe he could run . . . no, wait. You know what? I'm not gonna go there. He obviously wasn't persuasive enough, thank God." Ethan crossed his arms and leaned his shoulder against the door jam, Tori's presence on his front porch obviously seeping back into his conscious thought. "So, what about you? Don't you think a package of thank-you notes and a couple of stamps would be an easier way to pat your book donors on the back?"

Uh-oh.

She tried to make her laugh sound natural, her efforts falling short to her own ears. "Normally, a note would suffice, but for a donation as large as your mother's—and particularly one that was such a huge part of an event like last weekend's—it seemed to me as if a personal visit was appropriate. Especially in light of the fact that the books were given in memory of such a well-respected member of our community."

For a moment, Ethan said nothing, his gaze playing down her body in slow, even intervals. When he reached her heeled boots, he skipped back to her face. "So how much did you pay her for the books?" he asked.

She stared at him. "Excuse me?"

Dropping his arms to his sides, he left the confines of the open doorway and stepped onto the porch, his sudden nearness making her swallow. "How much money did you give Frieda for all those books?"

"I didn't. We didn't." She heard the incredulousness in her voice but could do little to soften it. "They were donated . . . like all the other books we get each year from people in this town."

"You didn't grease her palms a little bit on account of the *volume* of books she dropped off or the fact that my mother was so meticulous with them over the years? I mean, did you see most of them? They looked brand new."

"Mr. Devereaux!" Tori spat through clenched teeth. "While we certainly appreciated the fine condition of your mother's books, we didn't treat your donation any differently than we did anyone else's. To do so would be dishonest."

His left eyebrow rose upward. "So you're sticking with the notion that you didn't pay Frieda for the books?"

"You bet I am." Turning on her heels, Tori began pacing back and forth across the length of the porch, the gentle and rhythmic clacking of her boots against the wooden slats doing little to calm her nerves. Who did this guy think he was?

When she reached the eastern side of the porch for the third time, she stopped and faced Ethan Devereaux once again. "Where on earth would you get the notion that the library would have paid Frieda for those books? I just don't get it."

He strode to the edge of the porch and perched himself on the top rail, hooking his foot around one of the uprights. "It came from experience, that's where."

She narrowed her eyes in a near mirror image of his. "You're telling me the Sweet Briar Public Library has given money for donated books in the past? I don't believe that. Not for one second."

He flashed a devilish grin. "Anyone ever told you how sexy you are when you're angry?"

Tori splayed her hands in the air. "You know what? I'm done here. The woman who cared for your mother until her last breath didn't get a dime for the books she donated to the library. Believe what you want."

She spun around and made her way toward the front walkway, anger propelling her feet off the porch and onto the circular driveway.

"I was referring to my experience with Frieda."

Pausing beside her car, she simply looked at Ethan and waited.

"Frieda Taylor plays the part of the giving soul, constantly spouting off about the importance of volunteering and donating. Help the less fortunate, she says. If you don't have money, give of your time, she says. But between you and me . . . she's a hypocrite."

For the briefest of moments Tori considered asking him for specifics but opted to let it go instead, yanking her door open and settling herself behind the wheel.

"Did you hear what I said?" Ethan called.

She gave him the nod he was after and the response she was craving. "I can't say whether Frieda Taylor is a hypocrite or not. But I *can* say that *you*, Ethan Devereaux, are a *jerk*."

Chapter 19

Tori dropped her chin onto the heels of her hands and watched as Margaret Louise moved between the refrigerator, the countertop, and the stove with the ease of someone who not only knew their way around the kitchen but also savored the experience as well. Egg after egg was cracked over a large metal mixing bowl then stirred into the flour mixture with a practiced hand.

"I really think these cookies will be perfect for Mrs. Claus to have with all those youngins at the Christmas party. And just to be sure I was right, I tried them out on Lulu and Sally day before last." When the mixture was at the desired consistency, Margaret Louise set it to the side to make way for the Santa cookie jar Tori had been eyeing over the past thirty minutes or so. "They ooh'd over 'em the whole time they were eatin' 'em and darn near emptied the jar before they went home."

Her ears perked.

Darn near?

Buoyed by the promise of a cookie, she leaned forward on the stool and peered inside the jar, it's sparkling clean ceramic interior dashing her hope with a one-two punch.

"What they didn't eat, I wrapped up and sent home with them for their brothers and sisters."

"Oh," Tori mumbled.

"But don't you worry your head none, Victoria. Because by the time we're finished here, that jar will be filled to the top once more."

She peered around Margaret Louise and noted the time. "What time is everyone expected to be here?"

"I reckon the first of 'em will show up on the porch in 'bout twenty minutes, but don't you worry none about havin' to share with the circle. I'm makin' two batches. One for the circle and one just for you, Victoria. Think *that'll* put a smile on your face?"

She forced her lips to turn upward but couldn't maintain it convincingly enough to chase the worried creases from her friend's forehead. "I'm sorry, Margaret Louise. I really am. I guess I'm just tired. I didn't sleep all that well last night."

And it was true. She hadn't. But if she was honest with herself as well as Margaret Louise, it was the *reason* she hadn't slept that was on her mind at that moment, not the fact that she was tired.

"You must think I'm dumber than a box of rocks, don't you?"

Tori gasped. "No! Of course I don't think that!"

"Then why else would you be tryin' to tell me those eyes are tired. Anyone with half a brain knows those are sad eyes." Margaret Louise grabbed a tiny scooper from a nearby drawer and dipped it into the mixing bowl, retrieving a perfectly rounded ball of dough and transferring it to a waiting cookie tray.

She considered her friend's assessment and realized it didn't quite match reality. "I'm not sad. Not really anyway. Just worried a bit more than I thought I'd be."

Then again, if she'd thought *at all*, she wouldn't be sitting there in Margaret Louise's kitchen, awaiting an emergency sewing circle meeting with anything other than the usual anticipation.

No, this one was on her.

And her failure to keep her mouth closed.

Scoop by scoop she watched Margaret Louise empty the bowl in favor of filling the metal trays awaiting their turn in the preheated oven.

"You ain't gonna tell me, are you?"

Tori swallowed against the lump that formed in her throat at the hurt in the woman's voice. Knowing she'd been the one to put it there only made her feel worse. "No, it's just that I said something I probably shouldn't have said today and I did it while under the guise of library business."

Margaret Louise slid the trays into the oven and set the time for nine minutes. When she was done, she hoisted herself onto the stool across the countertop from Tori. "We all put our fat feet in our mouths at some point, Victoria. Why, look at Leona . . . she—"

"Yes, look at me. Don't I look stunning in this dress?" Leona pranced into the middle of her sister's kitchen and struck a runway-style pose—complete with a garden-variety bunny tucked under her arm. "I found it at a one-of-a-kind dress shop in Lawry last week. When I tried it on, the salesclerk said it looked as if it had been made for me."

She saw Margaret Louise's mouth open, knew an explanation of her dilemma was about to be shared, and rushed to head her off at the pass with a pointed look and a throwaway comment tossed in Leona's direction. "That shade of red is really pretty on you, Leona."

"It's wine, dear, not red," Leona corrected before retrieving a carrot from Margaret Louise's refrigerator and offering it to Paris. After several nibbles, Leona pointed an accusing finger in their direction. "What's going on between the two of you?"

"I've been knocking and knocking for the past five minutes and not a one of you came to answer the door," Rose groused as she shuffled into the kitchen and stopped short at the sight of Leona. "What are you doing here?"

Leona's chin rose, ready to do battle. "There's an emergency sewing circle meeting tonight, isn't there, you old goat?"

"There is," Rose sparred. "But unless you were able to fit your sewing needles and thread inside that too-tight dress you're wearing, I don't think you have any intention of sewing."

"I don't."

"Then why on earth are you here?"

"Because I'm a member of this group just the same as you are," Leona spat through teeth that were suddenly clenched.

"Oh. That's right." When Leona's mouth gaped open, Rose flashed a knowing smile at Tori and Margaret Louise. "Good Lord, she's fun to poke at, isn't she?" Then, without waiting for a response, the matriarch of the group continued on, the mischievous sparkle leaving her eyes in short order. "Have you talked to Debbie yet today? Did you hear what that Maime Wellington is trying to do now?"

"You mean, The Grinch . . ." Leona, Margaret Louise, and Tori clarified in unison.

Rose rolled her eyes and sighed. "Well, did you?"

"No, Rose." Tori slid off her stool and offered it to Rose. "What's going on?"

"She's trying to put a limit on the number of decorations a person can put on their lawn during the holidays."

"She's w-what?" Margaret Louise stammered. "But she can't. We just said four years ago that we weren't goin' to do that here in Sweet Briar the way them uppity folks did in Lawry."

Leona's brows rose. "We?"

"Yes—*we*. The Christmas Decorating Committee . . ." Margaret Louise's mouth pinched together.

Leona crossed behind Rose's stool and grabbed a pot holder from its hook beside the oven just as the numbers on the clock moved into single digits. Wrapping her hand around the Christmas-colored square, the self-declared anticook opened the oven door and proceeded to pull out each of the three cookie trays with nary a word to her sister or anyone else.

Tori blinked, once, twice, three times, yet said nothing. Now was not the time to call attention to Leona's odd behavior.

Once the trays had been set on the counter to cool, Leona returned to her spot at the head of the counter and cast a pointed look in her sister's direction. "Ahhh. Now tell everyone who was on the Christmas Decorating Committee four years ago when that recommendation was made."

Margaret Louise's head dropped to her hands, muffling the names so that Rose and Tori had to lean forward to hear. "Me, Sally Mae from Town Hall, and Kelly Sue Jordan."

Tori leaned forward still farther. "Kelly Sue Jordan? Who's that?"

"Councilman Jordan's late wife," Rose explained.

"Who was, of course, the drivin' force behind that recommendation." Margaret Louise's head snapped up to reveal eyes that were as close to steely as Tori had ever seen. "Why—why, that Grinch is as crooked as a hound dog's leg and twice as dirty, ain't she?"

Rose's head bobbed along with Tori's. "My daddy used to say folks like her were so crooked, no one could tell from their tracks whether they were coming or going."

"Or crooked as a barrel full of snakes," Margaret Louise retorted before Leona shot her hand in the air.

"Why use so many words to say what needs to be said? Maime Wellington is a witch. And I think it's high time we put her back on her broomstick and sent her on her merry way. In style."

The mischievous sparkle resurrected itself in Rose's eyes. "In style, you say?"

Leona met her glint and raised it with one of her own. "Of course. Is there any other way?"

Margaret Louise jumped back into the mix with a twinkle all her own. "It's like I always say—two wrongs don't make a right, but they sure do make it even."

"Amen, Twin. A-men." Leona bent over, plucked Paris from the ground, and tucked her safely inside the crook of her arm once again. "If it's okay with all of you, I'd like to do the planning on this one as my contribution to the event with Mrs. Claus."

"I'd like to help . . . if you'll have me."

Leona's hand paused atop Paris's fur. "What was that, Rose?"

"I said I'd like to help . . . if you'll have me."

"*You* want to help *me*?" Leona asked, stunned.

Rose grabbed hold of Tori's arm and slowly lowered herself off the stool. "Is your hearing starting to go, Leona?"

"Of course not!"

"Then you heard what I said." Rose shuffled over to the nearly cooled cookies and slowly inhaled, a sweet smile playing across her lips. "You want the help or don't you?"

Leona remained glued in her tracks. "Will you be nice?"

"Nice as I always am." Rose glanced toward Margaret Louise then plucked a cookie from the tray at her nod.

"Are you going to tell me I'm getting old?" Leona asked.

Rose paused the cookie mere centimeters from her mouth and shrugged. "Depends on my mood, I guess."

Tori stood frozen in her spot beside the counter, unsure of what, if anything, she should say. Conversations between the two battle-weary opponents were rare, offers to lay down their weapons—even temporarily—still rarer.

Leona glanced down at Paris and then back up at Rose. "Will you bring Patches to all strategy sessions?"

Rose chewed quietly for a moment or two and then offered a simple nod.

"Then Paris and I accept your offer, you old goat."

Even with Leona and Rose holed up in the kitchen collaborating over the best way to rid Sweet Briar and Kyle Jordan of The Grinch once and for all, the pile of homemade Christmas stockings was almost complete. Cut by cut and stitch by stitch, they'd managed to make nearly a hundred of the holiday goodie bags Mrs. Claus would give to the children at the library.

"These are really very precious," Debbie declared when she'd knotted off the final stitch of her final stocking. "They're not too little so they're a why-bother, and they're not so big they'll look silly with just a candy cane or two inside."

Melissa opened her last stocking and peeked inside. "I talked to Jake after Monday night's meeting, and he said we could donate a few boxes of candy canes to the cause."

Tori poked her needle through the front of her stocking and pulled it out the other side. "That's great, Melissa. Thank you. And please thank Jake for me, too."

"Count me in for ten boxes," Georgina offered from her spot on Margaret Louise's well-worn sofa. "You might talk to Chief Granderson, too. I know he tended to buy candy canes in advance of Santa's fire truck ride, and since that won't be happening this year, he might be willing to share."

Melissa pulled her hand out of her stocking and slumped back against the recliner she'd inhabited at her mother-in-law's urging. "I can't believe anyone would want to do away with that tradition. The kids in this town look forward to that every year."

"Don't you worry none, Melissa. Santa might not be ridin' into Sweet Briar on one of them shiny red trucks this year, but I reckon that won't be the case next year."

"Yeah, it'll probably be worse if that—that woman has anything to say about it," Beatrice mumbled from atop her seat on Melissa's ottoman.

"My money is on my sister and Rose," Margaret Louise boasted with pride. "In the meantime, it's 'bout time the youngins in this town get to meet Mrs. Claus. After all, without her bakin', Santa would be skinny as a rail."

"And Mrs. Claus? What about her?" Georgina teased.

"Mrs. Claus must taste-test all her recipes before givin' 'em to Santa, of course." Margaret Louise transferred her final stocking onto the pile and reached for the plate of cookies she'd set on the oversized toy trunk that doubled as a coffee table. Slipping a cookie into her mouth, she chewed her way around the edges, smiling between every bite. When she was done, she scooted to the edge of her sofa cushion and gave her hands a little clap. "Did I tell you them stockings are goin' to have a small book inside 'em, too?"

Tori stilled her needle mid-stitch. "A small book?"

"That's right."

"But—"

"I was out at the center in Tom's Creek again today and I was tellin' Jerry Lee 'bout our event. By the time I was done yappin', he was offerin' to donate a box of them little tiny look-and-find books some company donated to the center a while back."

"Aren't they for the folks at the center?" Georgina inquired.

"They were s'posed to be, but Jerry said they were given more 'n they needed and that we could have the rest if we wanted." Margaret Louise plucked a second cookie from the plate and then passed it to Beatrice. "I told him we did.

"After all, the way I figure it, all them donations the center has gotten will be findin' their way into a Dumpster before long so we might as well take what's offered."

"Who would throw something like that away?" Beatrice asked before securing a second cookie from the plate and passing it on to Georgina.

Margaret Louise's smile disappeared along with any attempt at eating slowly. "The same person that would throw somethin' as special as that center away, that's who."

Reaching forward, Beatrice grabbed a napkin from the top of the trunk and wrapped her own cookie inside it, saving it, no doubt, for her young charge, Luke. "But who would do that?"

"Ethan Devereaux," Tori snapped.

Six sets of eyes turned in her direction, each depicting a varying form of shock at the tone with which she'd spoken.

Uh-oh.

"I take it you finally met?" Georgina drawled between bites of cookie.

"Oh, yes. We've met."

"And?" Margaret Louise prodded.

She considered downplaying her meeting with the handsome yet arrogant-beyond-belief man, but in the end, she couldn't. These women were her friends. Her lifeline.

Inhaling every semblance of courage she could find, Tori finally put into words the fear she'd been harboring all day.

"*And* if Ethan Devereaux has anything to say about it, it's very likely the board will be looking for a new head librarian before the week is out."

Chapter 20

For the second time in as many weeks, Tori found herself traveling down the narrow two-lane highway that linked Sweet Briar with its neighboring Tom's Creek. Only this time, instead of making the drive from the passenger seat of Margaret Louise's powder blue station wagon, she was playing the part of pilot from behind the wheel of her own car.

Each curve she took, each mile she drove, brought her closer to being able to ask the questions that had made sleeping nearly impossible since finding Parker Devereaux's body. The list had changed, of course, since then, with certain questions elbowing their way to the top while others underwent a complete overhaul, yet they were all still there. Waiting. Begging to be asked and answered.

Had Charlotte even tried to tell Frieda about her husband's body?

What was it like when Ethan came to visit Charlotte? Was there tension? Did it seem as if they shared a secret?

And finally, what had transpired between Frieda and Ethan to make them hate each other so much?

Yes, they were all good questions. Important ones, in fact.

She let up on the gas pedal as she reached the turnoff for Tom's Creek and again when she approached the parking lot for the center, the list of questions quickly prioritizing themselves as she came to a stop next to a familiar four-door white sedan that served only to make her visit more plausible if not a bit more nerve-racking.

"This time, just stick to the thank-you, Tori," she chastised herself on the brisk walk from her car to the center. "And whatever you do, don't call anyone a jerk."

"Do you always talk to yourself like that, Miss Sinclair?"

She stopped as she neared the corner of the building and looked to her right to find Jerry Lee Sweeney returning from the Dumpster in back. "Oh, Mr. Sweeney, I didn't see you there. How are you?"

With a little hop, he left the pathway that led to the Dumpster and joined her on the sidewalk. "I'm good. But you, my dear, look troubled. Is everything okay?"

Keenly aware of the fact that the true reason for her visit was most likely *inside* the center, she cast about for something to say that would buy her time until she was where she needed to be. "I'm fine. I think you just caught me talking through the trouble spots on my holiday shopping list is all."

"Ah, yes . . . been there, done that many times. My wife, Sadie, is a tricky one to shop for. Hit the jackpot last year when I bought her a pair of clip-on pearl earrings, although she's bound to lose one of them these days. She has a habit of taking them off every time she drinks a glass of wine. Says they make her ears itch, if you can believe it. Then again, if she loses them, I guess I can hit the jackpot again."

She laughed. "Then you understand where I'm at."

"I do, indeed." He stepped around her as they reached the door and pulled it open to allow her entrance. "But you've come to the right place."

"Oh?" she quipped when they stopped inside the front sitting room, which was alive with talking and laughter this time around.

Jerry Lee gestured toward a petite woman with reddish brown hair and large brown eyes. "Deidre, honey? Would you get Miss Sinclair one of those special cookies you made with Ms. Davis yesterday afternoon? I think she would love one."

Deidre bowed her head but not before the shy smile gave away her pride at being asked to secure a cookie for the unfamiliar visitor.

"Do you know that Ms. Davis is my friend?" Tori asked as the young woman peered up at her.

"Really?" Deidre gasped. "Wow, she's my friend, too."

"Then we're both very lucky, aren't we, Deidre?"

"Yes. We. Are!" Deidre declared before disappearing down the hallway and into the kitchen.

"She liked you." Jerry Lee motioned Tori to follow him down the very same hallway Deidre had taken. "And she—along with everyone else here—loves Margaret Louise. Wow, getting her on board as a volunteer here was quite a coup for us, I'll tell you."

"And in a roundabout way, for us at the Sweet Briar Public Library, too." Tori peeked into each room they passed en route to the kitchen, hoping and praying to see the one face that had inspired her to drive to Tom's Creek in the first place. At Jerry Lee's quizzical look, she filled in the blanks. "Margaret Louise told me about the look-and-find books you're donating to the library for our Cookies and Books with Mrs. Claus event next week."

His broad shoulders rose and fell beneath his thin khaki V-neck sweater. "I'd rather see them being used than sitting in a closet gathering dust."

She looked to the left mid-nod and stopped short at the sight of the woman seated behind a desk flipping through a pile of charts.

Bingo . . .

"Frieda? Is that you?"

Charlotte Devereaux's devoted nurse looked up from the chart in her hand, recognition lifting the corners of her mouth upward. "Mizz Sinclair, what are you doing here?"

Veering from the course set by Jerry Lee, Tori stepped into the health room and extended a hand in Frieda's direction, the warmth of the woman's touch bringing a smile to her face as well. "I came out to thank Mr. Swee-ney for something and, well, here I am."

She poked her head back into the hallway and waved at Jerry Lee. "If it's okay, I'm going to visit with Frieda for a little while."

"Of course, it's fine. I'll have Deidre hold on to your cookie until you're done."

When he disappeared into the kitchen, she popped back into Frieda's office and dropped into the closest chair. "So how are you doing?"

The smile that failed to reach Frieda's eyes told her everything the woman's words didn't say. "I'm doing good. Keeping busy. Hoping to get a call on another job as soon as possible."

Tori waved her hand around the room, happily decorated in colorful posters trumpeting things like healthy eating and good personal hygiene. "You don't want to work here anymore?"

"Oh, I love it here, Miss Sinclair. I always have. But this is volunteer. I need a job that will keep a roof over my head and food in my stomach." Frieda closed the file she'd been studying when Tori arrived and placed it on the smaller of two piles. "Fortunately for me, Mizz Devereaux was a very generous woman and she made sure I'd have enough to tide me over for a few months after her passing. We just never counted on it happening so quickly."

She considered the woman's words, a question forming on their heels. "But you knew she was dying, right?"

Frieda pushed back in her chair and stood, her soft-soled shoes nearly silent as she made her way over to the small window that looked out on the major thoroughfare through Tom's Creek. "I knew it would happen . . . eventually. But not as fast as it did. She had more declining to do, or at least I *thought* she did. God saw fit to prove me wrong, I reckon."

The hurt in Frieda's voice was rivaled only by the defeated droop of the woman's shoulders. For a moment, Tori thought better of voicing the questions she'd come to ask, but her heart won out over her head and forced her to press on.

"Do you think Charlotte knew what was happening to

her?" It wasn't the first question she'd intended to ask, but it set the scene well enough.

Frieda turned from the window, her eyes wide in pain. "I don't *think* she did, I *know* she did."

She worked to hold down her reaction, hoped the relatively calm feeling in the room would keep the conversation going as long as possible. "You mean, she knew she was dying?"

"Yes. That's how she was able to set aside a severance of sorts for me for when she was gone and I was between jobs." Frieda slowly breathed in through her nose then leaned her back to the window. "But I also mean she knew she was fading in and out of reality. It's why she tried so hard to seize those precious moments."

"I bet she shared a lot of special memories during those times," Tori said. "Happy times spent with her husband and sons . . ."

Frieda swiped a trembling hand across her brow. "Sometimes. But then there were times she seemed to be upset about something that happened in the past. And for the longest time, I thought those were her foggy times, making me hush away her panic with soothing words and promises of clarity coming real soon. Only now, looking back, I have to wonder if those *were* the clear times."

Tori tried to tamp down her excitement, to show respect for the hurt Frieda obviously felt, but it was hard. What she was looking for was finally within her grasp.

"So you're saying Charlotte was panicked?" she prodded.

"At first she wasn't. It was more like something was skipping in her brain. Like an old record. She'd just say the same something every single time."

"What did she say?"

Frieda clamped the bridge of her nose with the thumb and index finger of her right hand and closed her eyes. "She'd say . . . 'I couldn't tell. I couldn't stand to lose them both.'"

Tori stared at the woman on the other side of the room, her own thoughts running round and round. "She couldn't tell? She couldn't stand to lose them both? But what did that mean?"

With great effort, Frieda dropped her hand to her side and shook her head. "I don't know. But it was the same thing all the time. Maybe, if I'd been a better nurse and a better friend, I wouldn't have hushed her words away until so close to the end."

Tori's heart broke as tears made matching paths down both sides of Frieda's dark face.

"But Mizz Charlotte, she said the same thing over and over and over again. I figured she was just confused. You know, lost in her own mind the way Alzheimer's patients get. So that's why I got her that notebook. I thought maybe she could draw her way out of wherever she was stuck." Frieda brushed first at the left and then the right side of her face, only to have a new crop of tears prove her efforts futile. "And it worked for a time. At least I thought it did anyway. But after that first picture, everything was the same—from the perspective of her chair, day after day. Repeating herself in pictures the way she did when she spoke."

Tears turned to sobs as Frieda hunched her shoulders forward and cried into her chest.

Unable to maintain a respectful distance any longer, Tori rose from her chair and walked to the woman, pulling her into an embrace and holding her until the sobbing subsided. "Maybe she really was trapped in one place," she offered.

"But she wasn't. She was trying to tell me something, and I failed to hear her." Frieda stepped from her arms and pulled a tissue from the box on top of a nearby filing cabinet. "I think she was trying to tell me something the one day her verbal mantra changed, just the way she was trying to tell Ethan something with that one picture that was different than all the rest."

Her breath hitched. "What do you mean?"

Frieda wiped at both eyes with her tissue then quickly blew her nose. When she was done, she took a deep, calming breath. "Remember how I said she said the same thing all the time?"

" 'I couldn't tell. I couldn't stand to lose them both,' " Tori recited from memory. "Right?"

"Yes. But the day before I bought her that notebook, she added one more sentence. And that's when her demeanor changed to seeming almost panicked. And that's when I came up with the idea of giving her a notebook to draw her way out of the issue. She drew that one picture and then the record skipping started again, this time with her drawing."

Tori fisted her hands at her sides and worked to keep her voice steady. "What was the new sentence? The one she added to the two others?"

Frieda tightened her hand around the crumbled-up tissue as her eyes took on an unfocused, almost dazed quality. "She said . . . 'but I was wrong.' "

"Wrong?" Tori asked with a voice that was quickly approaching shrill. "What was Charlotte wrong about?"

"I wish I could answer that, Mizz Sinclair. It's all I can

think about. And then, when she drew that first picture for Ethan, I didn't know what I was looking at. I don't really know Sweet Briar all that well, so I didn't realize it was a real place. So I stuck it on the mantel on the off chance Ethan would actually come by to spend some time with his mother."

Tori recoiled at the name. "How did you know it was for him? Did she say that?"

"When she insisted I rip it out of the book, she looked me in the eye and said his name." Frieda shook herself back into the room and tossed the tissue into a small rectangular wastebasket just below the window. "When I asked her if she wanted me to give it to him, she nodded. Hard."

"I take it he never came?" She heard the disgust in her voice and did nothing to try to rein it in. There was no need. Because as strong as the disgust was in her voice, it was a million times stronger on Frieda's face.

"No, and I knew he wouldn't. He was busy with whatever toy he'd just gotten, which is the way it always worked. He'd show up, ask his mother for money for whatever it was he wanted at the time, and then, once she gave it to him, he wouldn't come back until he was ready for the next big-ticket toy or trip. I knew this. I'd watched it for nearly a year. Yet I still stupidly put that picture on the mantel where Mizz Charlotte had to see it every day . . . reminding her again and again that Ethan hadn't cared enough to come."

Tori closed her eyes against the countless pictures Charlotte had drawn of that rolled-up picture on the mantel and the pain the woman must have felt knowing that, once again, her words were being dismissed.

"I think that picture being there day after day caused her undue stress. Why else would she have kept drawing that same picture again and again?" Frieda continued. "At the time, I didn't see the connection. I thought she was just repeating her pictures the way she'd repeated her words for so long. But now, knowing what we know about that first picture, I have to believe everything she said, everything she drew, had been intentional."

Slowly Tori opened her eyes and fixed them on Frieda's face, the raw pain she saw there now taking on an entirely different meaning. "I'm sorry, Frieda."

"No more than I am, Mizz Sinclair. It was hard to see her the way she was at the end, but I think it's even harder now, looking back. Because at the time, I kept thinking she'd rebound. That she'd get a burst of clarity that would help bring sense to everything she'd said and everything she'd drawn. But that burst never came. One day she was sitting there drawing that same old picture, and then the next . . . she was gone."

Chapter 21

There was something about holding an animal and stroking its fur that had a way of making a person feel a little less stressed and a lot less alone. It was a quality Tori had always attributed to cats and dogs because that was all she'd ever known.

But sitting there, on Leona's couch, stroking Paris's back while they waited for Leona to emerge from her bedroom for their first-ever sleepover, Tori was more than a little aware of the fact that the tension she'd been harboring since leaving Frieda was finally ebbing enough to become tolerable. And it was because of Paris.

And her sweetly twitching nose.

"The secret I swore you to the last time you caught a glimpse of me in my pajamas is still in effect. You do realize that, don't you, dear?" Leona's voice drifted down the hallway from the partially closed door at the end.

The smile felt good on her lips, as did the feel of Paris's fur beneath her fingertips. "I won't tell, Leona."

"Do you promise?"

"Yes, Leona, I promise."

Her assurance was met by a soft padding sound on the hardwood floor that spanned the length of Leona's town house. As the noise grew closer, though, the padding became more hesitant.

"I'll have you know, dear, I take promises very seriously," Leona reminded her from somewhere just off to Tori's right. "And to break one would result in my warranted denial of the entire matter."

"Duly noted." She lowered her mouth in line with Paris's long ears and lowered her voice to a whisper. "Your mama is very silly, Paris."

"Paris does not find me silly, dear. In fact, she thinks my pajamas are wonderful, don't you, my precious?" Leona stepped into the living room and stopped, holding her freshly manicured hands out to the sides. "They're soft, they're warm, and—"

"They've got footies!" Tori laughed. "Oh my gosh! Leona, you look so . . . *adorable.*"

"And if anyone from the sewing circle saw me in these, I'd never hear the end of it," Leona insisted before dropping onto the upholstered lounge chair across from Tori. "Especially that Rose Winters."

"*That Rose Winters?*" Tori ran her palm along the back of Paris's back, reveling in the sense of peace she emanated through her fur. "Uh-oh. That doesn't sound good. Are you two butting heads again over your plan to expose The Grinch?"

"No. Not exactly." Leona bolted upright on her lounge

chair and looked around. "Wait. I haven't offered you any wine yet. Would you like some wine? Maybe some crackers as well?"

"Leona, please. My being here is supposed to be relaxing . . . for both of us. For me, because it's alone time for the two of us. For you, because Annabelle is spending the night with Margaret Louise. I'm not here to be treated as a guest from out of town."

Leona's bottom lip jutted outward for the briefest of seconds before aligning itself with its counterpart once again. "But it's proper etiquette, dear. And if I don't demonstrate it, how will you ever learn?"

"It'll be our little secret. Like the footy pajamas." She glanced down at Paris in time to see her eyes begin to droop. "She's getting sleepy," she whispered.

"Because she feels warm and safe. . . . which is why I always hold her until she falls asleep." Leona scooted her body along the lounge chair until she was reclining against the back pillow. "Rose, on the other hand, puts Patches in his bunny bed—awake—and shuts off the light. Can you imagine such a thing? Why, I had to cover Paris's ears so she wouldn't hear the cruelty her offspring faces on a nightly basis."

She considered riding to Rose's rescue and citing a few articles she'd read on the importance of children learning to fall asleep on their own, but opted instead to let it go. This was their night. A night for gabbing as the invitation had proclaimed when it arrived in Tori's mailbox six weeks earlier.

At the time, once she'd gotten over the shock of a sleepover at Leona's, Tori had found the linen stationary, calligraphy, and excessive notice to be a bit over the top, but then again, it was an invitation from Leona, a woman who didn't believe in ordinary.

And now that the sleepover was finally there, Tori couldn't help being glad. For as prickly as Leona could be most of the time, she was also an amazing listener with a second-to-none radar where people and their motivations were concerned.

"So tell me, do you need to get a darker shade of foundation or are you really that pale right now, dear?"

"I'm really that pale."

Leona narrowed her gaze on Tori's face. "How come I've never noticed how ghostlike your skin is until tonight?"

"Because it's not really been tanning temperatures these last few weeks?" she offered, although she knew it was futile. Leona Elkin was like a dog with a bone. She didn't give up until she'd sniffed out the prize.

"That's true, but that doesn't explain the darkened circles under your eyes." Leona bobbed her head first left and then right as she gave Tori a more thorough once-over. "Or that tension I felt in your shoulders when you insisted on hugging upon your arrival this evening."

It was no use. She might as well hand her the bone and call it a day. "Any paleness you're detecting is truly just a matter of cooler temperatures and spending every spare second of the last month preparing for last weekend's book fair."

"And the black circles?" Leona drawled.

"Those would be from not sleeping."

A flash of interest propelled Leona forward on her lounge. "Is Milo keeping you awake?"

"No. I'm staring at the ceiling long after we've hung up for the night."

Leona rolled her eyes and sank back in her chair. "Then why aren't you sleeping?"

"Well, until today, I'd say it was due to an overactive imagination and a laundry list of questions that kept nagging at me every time I tried to shut my eyes."

"And now?"

"That laundry list of questions has been replaced by answers."

Leona cocked her head ever so slightly to the left and studied her sleeping Paris. "Then that's good, right? You've got your answers so you should be able to sleep."

If only it were that easy . . .

"But you see, that's the problem. Those answers I got? They just underscored the fact that my overactive imagination isn't so overactive after all. In fact, thanks to those answers, I'm more convinced than ever that things are not as they seem on the surface regarding Parker Devereaux's death."

Leona hoisted her body forward and off the lounge chair. "That's it. I need wine. Are you sure you don't want any?"

She glanced down at Paris, who was watching her mother through partially open eyes. "Um . . . does Paris still have carrots and milk before bed?"

"Of course. It's part of her nighttime ritual—a ritual that Rose Winters thinks is hogwash!"

"Any chance you might be able to substitute one of those crackers you mentioned earlier for a carrot so Paris and I can have our snack together?"

"Of course, dear. I'd have milk, too, except I have a feeling I'm going to need a little alcohol when you tell me about your latest attempt to play detective."

"I didn't set out to get involved in this, Leona, I really didn't. But something just hasn't felt right since we found Parker's body on the library grounds."

"So tell someone else," Leona mumbled as she moved around the small galley kitchen filling her wineglass, Tori's milk glass, and Paris's bowl.

"And by someone else, do you mean Police Chief Dallas? Because you know as well as I do that he's going to go with what's easy. He always does. And the fact that Charlotte drew a veritable treasure map right to Parker's body makes her the easy suspect."

"Maybe, in this particular case, the easy suspect is the *right* one." Leona carried a serving tray into the living room and set it on the coffee table between the lounge chair and the sofa. "Look what Mamma brought you, precious . . ." Reaching onto the tray, Leona removed a pink-and-white ceramic plate with three thinly sliced carrots in the middle and placed it on the sofa, her collagen-plumped lips stretching into a smile at the rapid and appreciative response from Paris.

"I wish it was, I really do. Because then I wouldn't look like this," Tori pointed out before accepting the plate of cookies from Leona and placing them on her lap. "But I look like this because my gut has been telling me the easy suspect is the wrong suspect. And now, after talking to Frieda at the center today, I'm more convinced than ever that Charlotte didn't act alone when she killed her husband."

Leona lifted her wine goblet from the tray and returned to her lounge chair. "As you know, I found it rather perplexing myself, how a woman of Charlotte's age could not only dig a hole but deposit a grown man's body inside . . ."

"See? That's how it starts for me. I have a thought like that and then it leads to another one—like if she didn't dig the hole, then who did?" Tori wrapped her hands around her milk glass and stared inside, the image of Frieda's tearstained face tickling her subconscious. "And if someone helped her, why were they involved? Were they merely helping Charlotte or was Charlotte helping them?"

Leona looked at Tori over the rim of her glasses. "Why would Charlotte help someone kill the love of her life?"

"To which I counter with, why would *Charlotte* kill the love of her life?" When Leona's gaze drifted back to her wineglass, Tori raised her milk glass in response. "Now you see why I look like this."

"So tell me what you learned today," Leona prompted before taking a long sip from her glass. "Tell me what moved you from speculating to being sure?"

"Not a *what*, Leona . . . a *who*. A who who just happens to be Charlotte Devereaux's nurse—Frieda Taylor."

Slowly, she took Leona through the discussion she'd had with Frieda at the center, including the woman's absolute certainty that Charlotte had been trying to tell her something. "And I'll admit, I found the first part of what Charlotte had said peculiar all on its own, but when she added that last sentence, the one about having been wrong, it sent a chill down my spine."

Leona lowered her glass to her lap. "Say them again, dear?"

"Which part? The first part? Or the second?"

"Both . . . together."

Tori leaned her head against the back of the couch and repeated the words exactly as Frieda had shared them. " 'I couldn't tell. I couldn't stand to lose them both. But I was wrong.'"

A blanket of silence descended across them as each considered the words Charlotte Devereaux had been desperate to share, only to have them written off as the ramblings of a mind ravaged by illness. After a while, Leona spoke, her voice, her demeanor, commanding attention.

"And this picture she was determined to give her son was the one that led us to Parker's grave, yes?"

Tori nodded.

"Well, it seems to me that the first part of what she was trying to get across was her way of justifying the fact that she'd kept Parker's death a secret for so long," Leona mused. "At least that's the only thing that seems to make sense."

Tori took a sip of her milk then poured the rest into Paris's bowl. "And the second part?"

"I don't know. Both could refer to people or, perhaps, things. Or a combination of the two, I imagine."

When Paris had had her fill, she hopped to the edge of the couch and waited for an assist down to the ground. Several hops later and she was across the room and safely in Leona's arms. "You're really good with her, Leona."

"She's the child I never had," Leona replied. "And I'd do anything to keep her safe."

Tori nestled into the corner of the couch and watched in quiet awe as Leona kissed and cuddled the garden-variety bunny. There was no doubt about it—the mother-child bond, whether biological or not, was truly something to behold.

And one day, when the time was right, Tori would get

to experience that bond for herself. Like Leona was experiencing it now.

"I know it's different in some ways, but I feel the same about Milo. There's nothing I wouldn't do for him."

Leona looked up from a sleeping Paris and nodded. "From what I've heard, that feeling will only grow stronger once he's your husband."

"My husband," she whispered in echo. "I love the sound of that, Leona."

"I know you do, dear. And if all goes well, you'll still be saying that fifty years from now rather than sitting in a chair drawing a map to where you buried his body."

Chapter 22

Tori hadn't realized just how worried she'd been about her comment to Ethan Devereaux until after she'd hung up with the president of the library board and felt her body slack in relief. Whatever Charlotte's younger son may or may not be plotting in retaliation for being told off, he hadn't exercised it yet.

"Victoria?"

Lifting her head off the desk, she acknowledged her temporary assistant with the closest thing to a smile she could muster. "Yes, Dixie . . . what can I do for you?"

"Did everything go okay with Winston just now?"

Tori gestured toward the empty chair across from her desk, only to have the offer turned down flat. "I can't, I've got to keep an eye on the floor. But I'm worried about you. Did it go okay?"

It never ceased to amaze her how much things could

change over a period of time—even things that had seemed chiseled in stone for all eternity. Like Dixie's feelings toward Tori.

Two years earlier, when she'd accepted the job of head librarian, Tori had unknowingly placed herself on Dixie Dunn's personal Most Hated list. It didn't matter that the woman had been forced into retirement by the library board. It didn't matter that someone was going to be brought in to fill her shoes whether it was Tori or not. In Dixie's eyes, Tori had stolen her job.

Yet somehow, someway, the two of them had not only gotten past their rocky start but managed to develop an actual friendship based on mutual respect and admiration.

"Everything was fine with Winston. It was just a routine check-in call, and nothing was said about Ethan Devereaux at all."

Dixie's shoulders dipped in relief. "Phew. I think that's a very good sign. Ethan is all about the immediate, never showing interest in anything for longer than a day or so. If he hasn't said anything yet, I doubt he will."

"I hope you're right," Tori mused before burying her head in her hands. "Ohhh, Dixie, I was so sure he was calling to give me my walking papers."

Dixie sliced her hand through the air, releasing the hint of a snort as she did. "While I'm not one to put too much stock in the current board, I do have to give them credit for knowing a good thing when they find it. And they found you."

Tori dropped her hands to the desk and mouthed her gratitude for Dixie's support around the growing lump in her throat.

"You're welcome, Victoria. I'm just glad it worked

out." Dixie leaned the top half of her body out into the hall and turned her head toward the main room for a quick sound check. "I better get back out there. But first, I wanted to tell you you've got a visitor out at the information desk."

Closing her eyes against the image of the walk she'd hoped to take, Tori took a deep breath and made a mental count to ten. "Who is it?"

"Jerry Lee Sweeney. With the box of look-and-find books he's donating to our Cookies and Books with Mrs. Claus. Would you like me to just accept them or do you want to come up and get them yourself?"

Tori pushed back her chair to stand and then stopped, the opportunity the man's presence provided hitting her squarely between the eyes. "Actually, could you just send him back?"

"Of course." And with that, Dixie Dunn was gone, the quiet pitter-patter of her shoes soon replaced by a heavier, more authoritative step that slowed as it reached Tori's office.

Rising to her feet, Tori came around her desk and extended her hand to the same tall man with the same salt-and-pepper hair she'd seen twenty-four hours earlier, only this time, he was carrying a box teeming with small puzzle books ideal for stuffing into the circle's stockings.

"Jerry Lee, what a nice surprise. Though if I'd thought about it, I could have gotten these from you yesterday and saved you the trip today."

At her nod, he set the box on top of her desk. "I was out here anyway for the regular job."

The regular job . . .

She waved to the same chair she'd offered to Dixie and

was glad to see him accept. If he sat, he'd stay for a little while. And if he stayed for a little while, she could ask questions.

Rounding her desk once again, Tori took her seat and quickly hatched a conversation that would open the doors she needed to open. "Ever since I saw the Devereaux Center for the first time the day after Thanksgiving, I haven't been able to get it out of my mind. I mean, you really have something special there."

A genuine smile lifted his mouth upward, only to fade from his face as quickly as it had appeared. "Yes, we do. And that is what's making this waiting game so hard for everyone involved."

She rested her elbows on the arms of her chair and tented her fingers beneath her chin. "I met him the other day."

Jerry Lee furrowed his brow. "Him?"

Swallowing, she took a gamble and hoped it would pay off. "I believe you referred to him as The Prince."

"Ahhh . . ."

"He's a rather . . . *difficult* person," she said as diplomatically as possible.

"The Prince was, is, and will always be a spoiled brat who took advantage of the gift he had in his parents and never, ever appreciated any of it." Jerry Lee stood, walked to the plate glass window behind Tori's desk, and stared out toward the Green. "Ethan was the golden son, the one with the looks, the brains, and the impeccable grooming. In contrast, Brian was the special needs son, the one who inspired pitying looks and understanding pats on the shoulder and couldn't possibly amount to anything more than a sweet cross to bear."

Tori heard the gasp as it escaped her lips but not before she had a chance to squelch it completely. "Frieda told me that Charlotte adored Brian!"

Jerry Lee rested his forehead against the glass. "Because she did. But even Charlotte saw Brian as some sort of delicate flower that needed to be shielded from life when, in actuality, he could do anything as long as he had the proper guidance. Still can."

"Like what?" she asked.

"Anything and everything. Heck, I truly believe he would have done a fine job running Parker's company if Parker had changed his will the way he'd intended."

She dropped her hands back to the armrests and gripped them tightly. "What did you just say?"

Jerry Lee parted company with the window and turned to face Tori, his eyes hooded. "I said, I truly believe Brian would have done a fine job running Parker's company if Parker had changed his will the way he'd intended."

She worked to make sense of what she was hearing, her thoughts spinning off in a million different directions.

"Parker Devereaux was going to leave his company to Brian?"

"He'd finally come to realize that Ethan was worthless. That he would run the company into the ground if he was at the helm."

"But Brian is mentally challenged," she protested.

Jerry Lee's face hardened at her words. "Brian may have challenges, but with careful guidance and ongoing encouragement, he can do just about anything. And I have absolutely no doubt he would have done Parker and his life's work proud if given half a chance. Hell, we already were these past five years."

Piece by piece, a picture began to form in Tori's thoughts that looked very different from the one everyone else in Sweet Briar seemed all too willing to accept. But in order for it to be right, Jerry Lee, in turn, had to be right.

"Are you certain Parker was going to change his will, leaving control of his company to Brian?"

Jerry Lee wandered back around the desk and stood behind his chair. "Parker Devereaux was not only my boss but he was also my best friend. He made his company the success it was and is because of his larger-than-life personality. People were drawn to him because of that. But the behind-the-scenes stuff? That was my department. And it gelled the way it did because we trusted each other, talking through things on a daily basis." He raked a hand through his hair and exhaled deeply before continuing. "Parker struggled with my recommendation to cut Ethan out of the company should anything happen to him, but as time went on and he saw more and more examples of Ethan's worthlessness, he began to see the light. It was tough on him, no doubt, but he'd gotten where he was by being smart. Ethan was no longer a smart choice—if he ever was at all."

Wow. It was all right there. And it made perfect sense.

Charlotte Devereaux may not have been strong enough to dig that hole on the grounds of the library five years ago. But Ethan surely was.

Charlotte Devereaux may not have been strong enough to get Parker's body into that hole by herself. But once again, Ethan was.

And now, thanks to Jerry Lee, Ethan also had motive.

"You realize you need to tell Chief Dallas all of this, don't you?" she said.

Jerry Lee held up his hands, palms out, and waved them back and forth. "Oh, no. I can't prove anything I'm saying. And without that, we've got a map . . . drawn by Charlotte. I start pointing fingers at Ethan for something that can't be proven, and Brian and I will both be out of work. With my age and his challenges, we'll both be hard pressed to find a job of any kind in this climate."

She felt the man's frustration, recognized the anguish in his eyes, and knew there was only one option.

"Well then, maybe someone else should do the pointing," she said even as her mind was jumping ahead to the remaining holes that still needed to be closed.

Tipping his head in her direction, Jerry Lee made his way over to the door, stopping when he reached the hallway. "Maybe someone should . . ."

Chapter 23

Tori pushed her way through the door and onto the back stoop, the unseasonably warm evening temperatures instantly making her rethink her initial decision to drive to Debbie's Bakery. Granted, winter in South Carolina was nothing like winter in Chicago, but still . . . mid-seventies were mid-seventies.

Stepping to the right as she reached the parking lot, Tori headed in the opposite direction of her car, her feet every bit as capable of making the four-block jaunt as her compact. Besides, a little fresh air was good. Especially in light of everything she'd learned.

Ethan Devereaux had murdered his father. Of that, Tori was certain.

It was the missing link that made everything else fit together. Now all she needed was the surefire proof.

She glanced at her watch as she walked, her scheduled meeting time with Frieda still twenty minutes away. But that was okay. It would give her time to spit-shine her proposed plan before launching it on the unsuspecting nurse.

From the moment Jerry Lee had left her office, she'd considered all angles, even the possibility that he'd gotten it all wrong. And then she'd remembered Charlotte's words—the words she'd uttered to Frieda again and again during her descent.

I couldn't tell. I couldn't stand to lose them both. But I was wrong.

Suddenly, a dying woman's desperate confession made all the sense in the world. Yes, Charlotte Devereaux had loved her husband. But she'd also loved her son. And when she realized what her son had done, she'd been faced with an unthinkable decision—turn in her son and lose him along with her husband forever, or stay quiet and help him cover his tracks.

It was a decision the woman had stood by for five years, a decision she'd apparently come to regret as the end of her life drew near.

Tori slowed her pace as she neared Turner's Gifts 'N More, a familiar face pressed against the shop window pulling her out of her thoughts and propelling her into the here and now. "Kyle?"

Kyle Jordan pivoted his head just enough to allow a glimpse of her face before focusing on the holiday gift display cleverly arranged for optimal impact. "Hi, Miss Sinclair."

"Hi, yourself." She allowed herself a moment to study the little boy, his wide eyes and freckled cheeks reflecting back at her from a decorative mirror that served as part of the display. "So what's in there that's got you so mesmerized?"

"That," he said, pointing his finger against the glass.

She moved in behind him for a closer look, confident she'd see a model airplane or a race car or some other toy that appealed to a boy of Kyle Jordan's age. Yet try as she might, she couldn't find a single item that warranted the look of utter wonder on the third grader's face.

"Tell me," she finally prodded. "Tell me what you see."

"That!"

She stepped in closer, her gaze following the path made by his finger and coming to rest on a crystal snowflake that glistened in the last of the sun's rays. "The snowflake?"

Kyle nodded hard.

"You like snowflakes?"

The pause that followed lasted so long she thought he hadn't heard the question. But just as she opened her mouth to repeat it, a second nod was followed by an answer so quiet she had to strain to hear it. "My mom and dad collected snowflakes together. They said it reminded them that everyone is different . . . and everyone is special."

Tori allowed her focus to return to the crystal decoration, the beauty of the snowflake and the earnestness in the young boy's voice bringing an unexpected mist to her eyes. "That's a lovely thought, Kyle."

"Every year they found a new one to add to their collection. Some were for hanging on the Christmas tree, some sat in little holder things on the shelf in my mom's special cabinet, and some . . . like that one . . . hung from strings my dad attached to the ceiling. But that one is the most sparkly I've ever seen."

"It *is* very sparkly." She looked from Kyle to the snow-flake and back again, the delight in the child's eyes every bit as mesmerizing as the object that had claimed his attention with an iron fist.

"Do you think I have enough money to buy it?" he finally asked, fully turning from the window for the first time since her arrival.

"I don't know. How much do you have?"

Kyle reached into the front and back pockets of his jeans and pulled out two crinkled dollar bills and a hand-ful of loose change. After a quick count, he looked up at Tori. "Two dollars and forty-three cents."

She didn't need to see the price tag to know his stash fell much too short. "Kyle, I don't think that's going to be enough."

"But I know my dad would love it."

She looked back at the snowflake once again, an idea hatching in her mind in record time. "I could help you with the rest if you wanted."

Kyle's body nearly rose up off the sidewalk, only to come crashing back down again. "I can't do that," he mumbled sadly. "Then it wouldn't really be from me."

"It would be if the money was yours," she pointed.

"But it's not . . . it's yours."

Bending at the waist, Tori got down to Kyle's eye level. "When people do a job for someone else, they get paid for their work, right?"

"Yes."

"Well, I was wanting to talk to you about a job anyway. Something really special that only you can do."

A flash of excitement lit the young boy's eyes. "A job? Really?"

"You see, we're getting ready to have Mrs. Claus at the library so she can read some special books with the children from Sweet Briar and we need to make sure the children's room looks extra special for her visit." She took a deep breath and plowed on, hoping against hope her suggestion would put a smile on his much-too-sad face. "Which is where you come in, Kyle."

"You want me to make some paper chains? Because I'm not the best cutter in the world. My strips get all cockeyed."

She nibbled back the urge to laugh for fear he'd think she was making fun. "Chains would be great, but I was thinking more along the lines of helping Ms. Davis and me decorate a Christmas tree with some of the ornaments from the town tree that weren't used this year."

Kyle's mouth dropped open. "You mean my mom's ornaments?"

"Yup."

"B-But won't Maime get mad?" he whispered, wide-eyed.

"Of course not. How could that make her mad?"

"Because my mom picked them out."

"Well, that's a silly reason. Besides, I'll just tell your dad I need your help with a project at the library." Tori straightened and hoisted her purse back onto her shoulder. "We don't really have to mention the ornaments at all, if you don't want to."

Lunging forward, Kyle wrapped his arms around Tori's middle and squeezed. "When? When do I get to help?"

Blinking back the tears that pricked the corners of her eyes, she willed her voice to remain as steady as possible.

After all, the last thing Kyle Jordan needed was a sniffling librarian on his hands. "Soon, Kyle. Very, very soon."

Slowly, he loosened his grip around her middle until they were standing separately once again. He pointed at the window. "What happens if someone buys it before I decorate the tree?"

"Well, to make sure that doesn't happen, what do you think of buying it now?"

"Now?" Kyle echoed.

"Uh-huh."

"But I haven't decorated yet," he reasoned.

"True. But you're going to, right?"

He gave an emphatic nod.

"You promise, right?"

Again, he nodded.

"Then I don't mind paying you in advance." Holding her hand outward, she waited for Kyle to grab it, the answering warmth of his soft skin bringing her close to tears yet again. "C'mon. Let's go inside and you can buy your dad that snowflake."

By the time Tori got to Debbie's, Frieda was waiting at a high-top table close to the front window, the nurse's rail-thin shoulders hunched over a barely touched piece of chocolate cake.

"Frieda, hi! I'm so sorry I'm late. I ran into a little boy I know who . . ." Her words petered out as Frieda pushed her plate across the table and released a tired sigh.

"It's all right, Miss Sinclair. I knew you'd come. I just hadn't counted on seeing *him* while I waited."

Tori slid onto the high-back chair across from the woman and set her purse on the empty chair between them. "Him? Who's him?"

"Ethan."

Swiveling her body to the right, Tori glanced around the bakery, noting the faces of each and every person either standing in line at the counter or seated at one of the other high-top tables.

"Don't bother looking. He left in a huff about ten minutes ago." Frieda pulled her plate closer to her spot at the table, only to push it away just as fast. "I guess he was as disgusted at seeing me as I was at seeing him."

Tori watched as Frieda picked up her to-go cup with trembling hands and took a long slow pull of whatever the steaming hot liquid was inside. "Why doesn't Ethan like you? You cared for his mother until the day she died."

She supposed she should feel a twinge of guilt over posing a question that was essentially rhetorical, since she knew the answer, but still, the reason Ethan gave might not necessarily match Frieda's take on the situation.

Setting her cup down, Frieda slumped in her chair and sighed. "Not terribly long after Mr. Devereaux disappeared, or at least everyone thought he'd disappeared, Mizz Charlotte was told by her doctor that she was developing Alzheimer's. Knowing what she was up against, she decided to hire a full-time nurse who would look after her. After interviewing a few different candidates, she asked Jerry Lee if she could steal me away from the center. At first he was hesitant, as we'd just gotten the health room open and he liked have a registered nurse volunteering, but when I assured him I'd stay on as a volunteer set of eyes over any other volunteers he might bring in in that capacity, he was okay with it. He understood that I needed a paying job and he gave me his blessing."

Tori's eyes drifted off Frieda's face long enough to take stock of the chocolate cake and the fact that half remained. She licked her lips.

"So I started working with Mizz Charlotte and everything was fine. She was a real treasure. Brian, too. But Ethan, he expected everything for nothing. He'd make a mess, he'd look to his mother to clean it up. He wanted something, he expected his mother to hand him the money to buy it. The one thing she wouldn't do for him, though, was hand over the reins of the company. She said she couldn't, that it was Parker's to hand over."

All thoughts of chocolate cake disappeared as Frieda's words sank in, their meaning assimilating its way through her lips. "Maybe that was her way of striking back at what Ethan had done. Because without a death, the company ran as if he was still alive."

Frieda's head tilted a hairbreadth to the right. "Why would Mizz Devereaux have to strike back at Ethan?"

"For killing her husband."

Chapter 24

"I suppose I shouldn't feel right about letting myself into Mizz Charlotte's house without permission, but the way I see it, she was trying to tell me what happened with Parker for weeks and I owe it to her to see it through to the end, don't I?"

Without waiting for Tori's answer, Frieda inserted her key into the side door and pushed, the smell of closed-up house assailing them where they stood. "See? I told you, Miss Sinclair, Ethan does nothing. He doesn't cook for himself, he doesn't clean up after himself, and he most certainly wouldn't open a window with his own two hands. In fact, if it weren't for the fact that he yearned for the day his mother didn't control his money, I'd point to all of this as a reason why Ethan couldn't possibly have killed his dad. He was too lazy."

She followed Frieda into the butler's pantry and set her purse on the counter. "So how did you finagle it so we could be here when he wasn't?"

Frieda moved through the house flipping on light switches and shaking her head at the disarray they found in each room. "It was easy. He takes boxing lessons every Thursday evening from six to eight. So as long as we're in and out by seven thirty, he won't have any idea we were here."

"And the people who help with Brian?"

"Ethan has cut their hours down to nothing," Frieda explained, "which is why Brian is spending the evening at the Devereaux Center with Jerry Lee."

Halfway down a back hallway, Tori nearly ran into Frieda when the woman came to an abrupt stop outside the large paneled room with the all-too-familiar fireplace adorned with framed photographs atop its wide mantel. It made perfect sense that every brick, every picture, every knickknack was there just as Charlotte had drawn nearly every day for the last two weeks of her life, but still, it was unsettling.

Tori stepped around the nurse and into the room that had once been Parker Devereaux's study before becoming an almost prison for his wife. Slowly, she made her way toward the upholstered recliner situated just left of center on a small hooked rug roughly eight feet from the fireplace.

"I—I don't want to be in here anymore," Frieda said, her voice breaking. "When I think of all those times she tried to tell me about Parker . . . and how I hushed her words away as if they were nothing more than jibber jabber . . . I hurt all over."

She braced her hand on the back of Charlotte's chair and glanced over her shoulder at the woman still frozen in the doorway. "It wasn't your fault, Frieda. You didn't know."

"I failed her, Mizz Sinclair. She trusted me with something she'd kept secret for five years and I failed her."

"It's not too late to hear her words, Frieda. That's why she drew them in the notebook you gave her. She's still talking to you through them."

Rounding the back side of the chair to the front, Tori backed her leg up against the edge of the chair and lowered herself onto it, the sketches she'd seen in Charlotte's book springing to life right before her eyes for the second time since the woman's death. "Wow. Even having sat here before, it's still shocking . . . like I'm sitting smack dab in the middle of her drawings."

Step by step, Frieda made her way into the room, stopping to the side of Tori's chair. "Mizz Charlotte noticed everything. Every crack, every spill, every fleck of dust that didn't belong, and I knew that. Yet I failed to recognize that when it mattered most."

Tori rested her head against the seat back and imagined the dozen or more pictures Charlotte had drawn looking at that same mantel, day after day, including the rolled-up sketch Frieda had placed on the end of it in the event Ethan came to visit his mother.

"So she showed you the picture of the library grounds with the patch of earth marked by an X of sticks, right?" Then without waiting for confirmation, Tori continued, the events of Charlotte's last few weeks on earth playing out her mouth. "She hands it to you and you don't understand the picture. So she says her son's name again and again until you promise to give it to him . . ."

Frieda wandered over to the fireplace, the sound of her

soft-soled shoes muted by the hooked rug. "I knew it was
a building, of course. Even figured it was one here in town
based on the way she enjoyed sketching her way through
Sweet Briar, but I didn't know which one and I didn't
think it was any more significant than"—Frieda gestured
her hand toward the half-dozen frames lined up across
the mantel—"the rest of these."

Anxious to steer Charlotte's confidante toward action
and away from further self-recrimination, Tori prodded
on. "Okay and then what?"

"Then I put it right here." Frieda pointed to the fateful
spot at the end of the mantel. "After I set it down, Mizz
Charlotte repeated Ethan's name one more time, to which
I promised—one more time—that I would make sure he
got it the next time he came in to see her. Only he never
came in after that."

She looked at the spot Frieda indicated and imagined
the paper just as it had appeared in the sketches—each
daily drawing a testament to Ethan's lack of concern for his
mother's declining health. It was sad, really. Pathetic, even.

"So where is it now?" she finally asked as the image in
her head skipped ahead to Charlotte's last drawing, the
one that had sent Margaret Louise, Leona, and Tori out
into the middle of the night with shovels.

"Where is what?" Frieda slid her hand down to the end
of the mantel and then tucked it into the pocket of her thin
cotton smock.

"The picture."

Frieda turned to look at Tori. "You saw it, remember?
It's how you knew to dig up that spot at the library in the
first place."

"No. Not the one showing Ethan's picture after it had

fallen down onto the hearth. The other one. You know, the actual picture she wanted you to give Ethan."

Frieda drew back, her eyebrows dipping downward. "The picture for Ethan? Why . . . I don't know." Spinning on the balls of her feet, Frieda backed away from the fireplace to afford a clearer view of the empty hearth. "I didn't notice it being gone until a day or so after Mizz Charlotte's passing, but I didn't give it much thought."

Pushing off the chair, Tori joined Frieda in front of the fireplace. "Did you see it later that day? Maybe put it back on the mantel?"

Confusion cast a shadow across the woman's dark features. "She drew the picture in the evening, I think. And then, the next day, when I would have noticed that the picture had fallen, I was mourning Mizz Charlotte's passing, making phone calls, and trying to come up with the best way for Mr. Sweeney to break the news to Brian." Frieda's face crumpled at the memory, prompting Tori to drape an arm around the woman's slight form. "I guess, in all the chaos, someone just picked it up and tossed it out, not realizing what it was."

"No worries. We know what the picture was thanks to Charlotte's last drawing and that's all that matters." She heard a clock chime in the distance and knew their window was closing. It was time to stop woolgathering and get to the reason for their mission. "Frieda, is there anywhere you can think of that Charlotte might have kept personal papers?"

"In a drawer in her room." Frieda disengaged herself from Tori's arm and strode across the room toward the hallway. "If there's a legal document to be found, it'll be there. C'mon, I'll show you."

They made their way through the rest of the lower level to a grand staircase and a closed doorway just beyond. "That used to be Ethan's room. But about six weeks before Mizz Charlotte passed, she had a fall on the stairs on the way up to her room. She was okay, thank heavens, but it underscored the need to keep her downstairs, where the chance for future falls could be minimized. When I first suggested it, Ethan refused. But when I pointed out he could have his mother's suite instead, he stopped protesting. Though getting him to remove all of his stuff was an ongoing battle."

With a quiet hand, Frieda opened the door and stepped inside, her shoulders slumping fast. "I still can't believe she passed when she did, though having her go in her sleep was better than the alternative."

Under any other circumstance, Tori would have let Frieda talk, knowing the woman's grief was still so raw. But she couldn't. Not now and not there anyway. Ethan was due back in less than forty minutes and they still had so much to do. "Where are her papers? We need to hurry."

"I think most of them are in her nightstand drawer, which she kept under lock and key."

"You have the key?" she asked quickly.

Frieda smiled. "I don't have the key but I know where she kept it."

Lifting a compact from the nightstand beside Charlotte's bed, Frieda flipped open the compartment usually reserved for a flat brush and retrieved a key instead. "We're looking for anything that would indicate Parker's intention to turn control of the company over to Brian in the event of his death, yes?"

"Yes," Tori confirmed.

"Well, I'll check the drawer and you can check her secret box."

"Her secret box?"

Frieda braced herself against the edge of the bed with one hand and slowly lowered herself onto her knees. Once there, she lowered her body still farther to peer under the bed and retrieve a lavender shoebox-sized box. "She showed me what was inside once—mostly pictures and notes from her courtship with Parker along with a few of Brian's little surprises. But"—Frieda rose to her feet once again—"who knows? Maybe you'll find something useful."

Tori settled on the bed beside the box and lifted the lid, Frieda's words settling in her thoughts. "Brian's little surprises? What does that mean?"

Frieda's laugh echoed softly against the walls of Charlotte's room. "Brian liked to bring his mom presents. Things he found around the house mostly. Like a cat bringing its owner a mouse. He'd bring her my glasses, one of his live-in aid's socks, even Ethan's journal from time to time. Most of the time, she tracked down the owner fairly quickly. But sometimes, when it was something like a dropped flower petal or a misshapen piece of candy, she'd put it into her box simply because it made her smile."

Sure enough, the box contained an assortment of odds and ends as well as a stack of letters tied together with a simple red bow. "Those were Mr. Devereaux's love letters to Mizz Charlotte when they were courting," Frieda said before opening the nightstand drawer and removing a hefty file of personal papers. "Mizz Charlotte often said that Mr. Devereaux was a saint for marrying her, but that by doing so, she knew he truly loved her."

Tori reached into the box, pulled out the bow-tied stack of letters, and ran the fingers of her free hand across the top, the slightly yellowed envelopes a testament not only to their age but to the history they held inside their flaps. "Do you really believe she loved him?"

Frieda dropped the document she was skimming onto the bed. "Without a doubt. Which is why, if she knew about his death as we knew she did, there must have been a very good reason she kept quiet."

"Like protecting her son?" Tori quipped before looking down into the box once again. "Oh, wait—there's another letter. Or maybe just a piece of paper . . ."

Sure enough, near the bottom of the box was a folded piece of thick linen paper that had been ripped from a notebook of some sort.

Frieda leaned in for a closer look. "I don't think she ever showed me that one before."

Lifting the paper from the depths of the box, Tori slowly unfolded it to find small masculine writing void of any punctuation beyond the bare minimum.

Dear ~~Journal~~ Dad,

I'm not sure if I should call you Dad any longer or if I should just call you Parker because the man I knew never would have hurt Mom the way that you did. I told Mom it didn't matter, that we didn't need you but that was a lie. Mom needed you and now I need you. Mom is dying. I don't know how long she has because I don't ask. But I know it will happen whether I ask or don't. I don't know how to care for Brian, you always made it look easy. And I don't

*know how to run a company. I know you were tired
of cleaning up after me all the time and I know you
don't want to do it again, but if I mess this up, Brian
will be hurt and then everything you promised for
him will be a lie.*

Please come home. I need you.

Ethan

She finished reading, only to start from the top once
again. Line by line, she read the words of a man who truly
didn't seem to know his dad was dead. And if he didn't
know, then everything she'd been so sure of in regards to
Parker's death was wrong.

Dead wrong.

Chapter 25

Tori could feel the weight of Margaret Louise's eyes as she moved around the children's room making sure each and every box was properly labeled and ready for a quick turnaround once Mrs. Claus had returned to the North Pole. It was a painstaking process but one that had been necessary in order to get the board's support to transform the popular destination into a temporary winter wonderland.

And even with some of the boxes still awaiting Milo's strong arms, the backdrop was taking shape nicely.

"I can't believe you reupholstered a chair just for Mrs. Claus." Tori stopped beside the room's storytelling focal point and traced her finger across the whimsical fabric of candy canes and cookie jars. "How long did it take you to do this? It's perfect."

Margaret Louise came out from behind the snack table

she'd just erected and waved aside Tori's praise. "It wasn't nothin'. The chair was just sittin' in my family room gatherin' dust, and I decided to give it a second life."

"But to go out and find fabric this perfect for an event that's going to last less than two hours?" Tori let the question hover in the air, knowing the reason for the extra special touch was standing less than two feet away. With eyes that were finally sparkling the way they were meant to sparkle.

"I love Christmas, Victoria. I love the warmth, I love the kindness, I love the homey feel that comes with this time of year. And if I can't help spread that 'round Sweet Briar in the way I have before, I'm goin' to seize the chance you're givin' me with this."

"And seize you have," she said, spreading her arms wide and slowly turning in a small circle. "The children are going to love this place."

"Well now, that's a relief." Margaret Louise returned to the slew of shopping bags she'd set beside the snack table and began to unearth everything from a Christmas tablecloth to paper plates and napkins adorned with Santa's jolly face.

"What's a relief?"

Margaret Louise reached into the second bag and pulled out a roll of fake snow and a jar of sparkly Christmas tree glitter. "That hint of a smile you had just now while you were turnin' 'round and 'round. It's been missin' the past few hours."

Tori knew it was no use. Try as she might, the visit to the Devereauxes' home the night before still weighed heavily on her mind. But did she really want to bring it into a room they were working so hard to holiday-ify?

No, she didn't.

Not yet anyway.

She needed the magic Margaret Louise was creating just as much as anyone at that moment.

"Victoria?" Dixie poked her head into the children's room then stepped to the side to allow Kyle Jordan entrance. "Your helper is here . . ."

"Hey there, Kyle! Boy, are we ever glad to see you." Tori crossed the room to welcome the little boy with a warm hand on his shoulder. "So? What do you think? Do you think it's a room that will please Mrs. Claus?"

Slowly, Kyle pulled his gaze upward until it was fixed on Mrs. Claus's reading chair and the bare artificial tree positioned to its side. "Is that where I get to put my mom's ornaments?" he whispered in a voice far more burdened than fit an eight-year-old.

"It sure is." She met Margaret Louise's raised eyebrow with one of her own yet continued on as if nothing was amiss. "In fact, Ms. Davis, here, secured all those wonderful ornaments from the basement of the Town Hall just this morning and she has them waiting for you now, don't you, Ms. Davis?"

Margaret Louise leaned to her left, lifting a long rectangular storage bin into the air for Kyle to see. "Your mom was the best ornament picker this side of the Mississippi."

Kyle blinked once, twice. "Y-You knew my mom?"

Margaret Louise carried the bin over to the tree and set it down on the ground for easier reaching. "You bet I knew your mom. Why, when you sprouted enough to go off to kindergarten, your mamma joined my Christmas Decoratin' Committee. Before I met her, I didn't know anyone loved Christmas as much as I did, but she sure proved me wrong. That's when I started callin' her Holiday Sue."

"Sue was her middle name." Kyle's eyes widened in earnest as he appeared to hang on Margaret Louise's every word.

"So the nickname fit, didn't it?" Bending down to the child's eye level, Margaret Louise took hold of his hands, rubbing their topsides with her thumbs. "I can't imagine a more perfect choice than you, Kyle, to hang all those purty ornaments your mom picked out. I reckon she'd be tickled pink to know you inherited her holiday spirit."

Tori leaned against the wall, looking from Kyle to the tree and back again. "We weren't sure whether you like white lights or colored lights, so we got some of both."

Kyle slipped his hands from Margaret Louise's grasp, his mouth gaping open as he did. "You mean, *I* get to pick?"

"That's right. And you also get to choose whether we use garland or tinsel."

"Wow! Thanks!" Kyle wiggled out of his lightweight jacket and practically ran to the box of decorations, completely oblivious to the relief that passed between the adults in the room. Whatever hurt the little boy had been harboring when he walked into the room was long forgotten as he rolled up his sleeves and set about the task of decorating the tree that would soon welcome Mrs. Claus to the Sweet Briar Public Library.

Ten minutes later, the first decision under his belt, Kyle wound his way around the lower half of the tree, leaving colored lights everywhere he went. Next, came the very tough garland-tinsel debate, with the notion of tossing tinsel at the tree winning out in the end.

"It's looking good, Kyle," Tori called from the top rung of the ladder she'd dragged into the room for the purpose of affixing some decorations to the ceiling.

"Just you wait and see, Miss Sinclair, it's gonna look even better when my mom's ornaments are on it." Flashing a thumbs-up at his own tinsel-tossing ability, Kyle returned to the bin and retrieved the first of several dozen tissue-wrapped mounds from inside. With careful, almost reverent fingers, he peeled back the paper to reveal the first of many ornaments that would inspire the kinds of oohs and ahhs that made Tori wish, for just a moment, that she, too, were a child once again.

When the tree was all but done, save for the star at the top, Kyle finally looked around the room, his big brown eyes a testament to the success of their collective efforts. "Wow. Mrs. Claus is gonna *love* this place."

Margaret Louise's hearty laugh filled the room, soliciting one from Tori in the process. "You bet she is."

Kyle snapped the lid of the bin into place and wandered over to Tori's ladder. "Whatcha gonna hang from all those strings, Miss Sinclair?"

She winked down at him. "Snowflakes."

When he didn't respond beyond a gaped mouth, she tried again. "They're not as pretty as the one you got your dad for Christmas, but they didn't come out too bad if I must say so . . ."

The words trailed from her lips as the boy's shoulders lurched forward and began to shake with the force of his sobs.

"Kyle . . . Kyle . . . what's wrong?" She climbed down the ladder and pulled the child into her arms, his tears quickly soaking a hole through the middle of her royal blue blouse. When he didn't answer, she simply held him close, quietly hushing his tears and wishing Margaret Louise would hurry and get back from the latest trip out to her car.

When the tears subsided enough to make speech even semipossible, she tried again. "I can't help you if you don't tell me what's wrong. And I'm pretty good at fixing problems. Just ask Ms. Davis when she gets back . . ."

"You can't fix this," he hiccuped. "Nobody can."

She rocked back on her heels and studied him closely. "Try me."

"M-Maime b-broke m-my d-dad's or-ornament."

"Did she drop the box?" Tori reached out and pushed a scrap of hair from his eye, only to have it fall back in place with the emphatic shake of his head.

"She *threw* the box!"

Certain the boy had misunderstood, she tried again. "Sometimes, when something falls, it can look like it was thrown but—"

"I asked her for some wrapping paper and tape. So I could wrap my dad's present. When she gave it to me, she asked what I needed it for." Kyle stopped, took a deep breath, and plowed on. "I showed her the sparkly snow-flake and told her it was for my dad—for his and Mom's collection."

Uh-oh . . .

"When I said that, she got all mad and said I couldn't give it to him. When I said I was gonna anyway, she took it out of my hands and threw it against the wall." Kyle's shoulders began to shake once again as the tears reappeared on his cheeks. "I told her she was mean and she said I—I sh-should get used to it."

It took every ounce of restraint Tori possessed not to start yelling, to rail against the mean-spirited woman who'd set her sights and her evildoing on an innocent child whose biggest offense was cherishing memories of his parents together. She took gulps of air. She nibbled her lower lip. She clenched and unclenched her fists. But in the end, she gave Kyle what he needed most—a smile and a promise that he'd get to give his father a snowflake for Christmas one way or another.

Tori had just hung up the phone when it rang again, Leona's vow to put The Grinch in her place still fresh in her ears.

"Good afternoon. This is the Sweet Briar Public Library, how may I help you?" She heard the slight shake to her voice, knew her anger was still close to the surface, but hoped and prayed whatever remnants remained from the latest Maime Wellington story would go undetected over the phone.

"Mizz Sinclair?"

Her head snapped up at the familiar voice. "Frieda? Is that you?"

"Yes, Mizz Sinclair. It's me."

Tori inhaled deeply, allowing the movement of air through her lungs to relax her as much as possible. "Did you see him today?"

"Brian was at the center just a little while ago and we struck up a conversation. I asked him about some of the presents he liked to bring Mizz Charlotte. He talked about his beloved storybook and the candy he used to bring to her in her chair.

"And then he said it. He said he brought her Ethan's journal. He took it from Ethan's room when he was looking for a hat to go with the costume he was wearing for the center's Halloween party that day."

Closing her eyes, Tori asked the question that needed to be asked. "When was the Halloween party?"

"October eighteenth."

Nearly five weeks before Charlotte's death . . .

"It fits, Mizz Sinclair. It fits with the time Mizz Charlotte added that line about being wrong."

"It fits . . ." she repeated in a whisper. "Damn."

Chapter 26

One by one Tori counted her way through the stockings piled on her dining room table in anticipation of the sewing circle's first-ever stuffathon the next evening. When she reached one hundred, she allowed herself a moment to breathe before moving on to the candy canes and miniature look-and-find books mounded together on the opposite side of the table.

It was official. An event that had been born on a whim in an attempt to cheer a dear friend had taken on a life of its own, proving to be therapeutic for virtually all it touched behind the scenes. Including her if she let it.

But ever since she'd locked up the library and headed home, no amount of forced thinking could keep her mind off Frieda's call or the fact that she was right back to square one where Parker Devereaux's murder was concerned.

Sure, there was a part of her that considered giving up.

After all, the person everyone assumed was responsible was already dead. But no matter how hard she tried to bow to that notion, she knew in her gut it was wrong.

It simply *had* to be.

Besides, Charlotte's own words and the drawing she'd been adamant Ethan see meant *something*. The key was figuring out what that something was before she fell over from sleep deprivation.

All the clues Tori had been so certain pointed to Ethan didn't. Not the pictures, not his father's mounting disappointment, not Charlotte's oft-repeated plea, and not Brian's storybook.

Brian's storybook.

She stopped midway through her candy cane count and opted instead to pour herself a mug of hot chocolate. With any luck, the steaming liquid, coupled with a moment to put up her feet and close her eyes, would do her body and her mind good.

But even as she made her way into the kitchen and over to the stove, she found her thoughts revisiting the story she'd read to Molly Sue at the last sewing circle meeting. Page by page the toddler had hung on Tori's every word, her wide blue eyes soaking up every detail of every picture. Something about the story of a messy kid who finally gets it right, yet is still seen as messy because of his past ways, struck a chord with both Brian Devereaux and Melissa Davis's youngest.

A modern telling of a Little Boy Who Cried Wolf.

Tori moved between the sink and the stove as she filled the kettle and turned its burner on high. She'd been so sure that Charlotte had folded one of her pictures and shoved it inside Brian's storybook for a reason. Yet now that Ethan's hand in Parker's death seemed virtually unlikely, that reason no longer held weight.

Besides, the boy in the book hadn't really made the mess. *And neither had Ethan . . .*

Tori grabbed hold of the counter's edge as her legs began to sway. Maybe Charlotte *had* put the picture in the book for a reason. Maybe Charlotte, too, had thought Ethan was behind her husband's murder and had only recently come to realize that she'd been wrong all along . . .

I couldn't tell. I couldn't stand to lose them both. But I was wrong.

Suddenly Charlotte's words and her drawings made all the sense in the world. For five long years, the elderly woman had lived with the fear that her son had killed her husband. As a result, she'd had to mourn the passing of her true love in silence for fear that speaking of it would rob her of her son, too.

No wonder Charlotte had tried so hard to share her mistake with Frieda. No wonder she'd been so desperate for Ethan to see the picture—so he'd know his father was dead. To know such things, yet be powerless to make others understand, had to have been maddening for a woman essentially trapped inside her own mind.

It was a heart-wrenching scenario, one that threatened to pull Tori into the doldrums if she thought about it for too long. Instead, she lifted the steaming kettle from the stove and poured its contents into a waiting mug and the mix of chocolate powder that would soon be her evening's treat. As she stirred, she allowed her mind to travel back through the day, skipping through the bad parts and zeroing in on the good. But even as she recalled the fun of decorating and the sweetness of Kyle's smile while he strung the lights and tossed the tinsel, her thoughts kept returning to Charlotte and Ethan, again and again, like a tongue unable to leave the lone wiggly tooth alone.

Yet as she poked at it for the umpteenth time since Frieda's call, an undeniable reality began to take shape.

If Charlotte knew where the body was buried, and the likelihood she'd done it without any help was slim to none, then how could she have thought Ethan was involved? Wouldn't she have known?

Hooking her leg underneath her body, Tori sat down on the couch and blew at the steam that rose from her mug. Had Charlotte buried her husband all by herself? And if she did, was it because she came across his body somewhere and assumed Ethan had killed him? Or was someone else involved? Someone who helped dispose of the body after the fact?

But who would do that? Who would help someone bury a body?

A trusted friend or loved one . . .

"Frieda," she whispered.

Frieda adored Charlotte Devereaux and had said many times that she'd have done anything for the woman. Whether that anything extended to helping dispose of a body, though, was anyone's guess.

Tori sat in the car, staring up at the Devereaux home, debating the merits of knocking against the pull of heading back home.

If she knocked, she'd have to come face-to-face with a

man she'd called a jerk not too long ago. And having done so, she stood a good chance of being dressed down or, even better, picked up on trespassing charges.

If she went home, she might be able to put on her comfiest pajamas and climb into bed, but even if she did, she'd spend the whole night contemplating what she might have learned had she only stayed and knocked.

Squaring her shoulders, she turned off the ignition and stepped from the car, the glow of light from the second floor confirming that at least one, if not both, of Charlotte's sons was in residence. Would either one of them answer her knock, or would one of Brian's aids shoo her from the property?

"There's only one way to find out," she mumbled as she climbed the now-familiar porch steps and bypassed the notion of knocking in favor of a doorbell capable of waking the dead three counties over.

This time, her ring was answered by a man she'd never met yet knew immediately upon first sight. "Hewwo . . . I'm Bwian, who are you?"

She stepped forward and extended her hand in the direction of Charlotte's older son, who shook it warmly. "My name is Tori. Tori Sinclair. I'm a friend of your mother's—"

"Who's at the door, Brian?" Ethan barked from somewhere just out of Tori's field of vision.

The short, brown-haired man turned toward the voice, shifting from foot to foot as he did. "It's Towi. Towi Sincwair."

"Oh . . . is it now?" Footsteps sounded from around the corner, bringing Brian's brother into view. "Have you returned to insult me further?"

Brian's face crumbled in the hallway light. "Towi is nice, Ethan. You should be nice to her."

"Brian's right. I really *am* nice. Or at least, I try to be."

"You should be nice to her," Brian repeated before covering his mouth for a not-so-whispered whisper. "Plus she's a giwl. A weal, live giwl."

Tori couldn't help it—she laughed, the man's endearingly sweet honesty magically dissipating the tension she'd felt in every nook and cranny of her body until just that moment.

"We should invite her in," Brian said. Then at the unexpected nod from Ethan, he did just that. "Come in, Towi."

Pushing aside her bent toward shyness, Tori stepped into the wide foyer that ran the length of the Devereaux home. "I'm sorry to bother you this late in the evening but—"

Brian peeked around her shoulder for a better view of the mahogany grandfather clock at the end of the hall. "Uh-oh. I need to go to bed." And then, without so much as another word, the mentally challenged man disappeared up the staircase at the end of the hall.

"Great. My brother invites you in and then I get stuck having to deal with you." Ethan rolled his eyes skyward then brought them back down to stare at Tori in exasperation. "Doesn't that just figure."

She rushed to make amends, even though a part of her cringed at the prospect. "Believe it or not, we're on the same side. And because of that, I'm sorry I was a little . . . harsh the other day."

Ethan folded his arms across his chest. "We're on the same side?" At her nod, he smirked. "And what side might that be, Miss Sinclair?"

"The side of the truth."

He dropped his hands, only to link them across his chest once again. "The side of the truth? What the hell is that supposed to mean?"

She considered asking him if they could move into the living room or the dining room or anywhere with a pair of chairs, but let it slide. Ethan Devereaux wasn't about entertaining. Instead, she leaned her shoulder against the wall and got to the point of her visit. "Your mother was trying desperately to tell you something about your father's death. She tried to tell Frieda at first, but then, when given a notebook and a pencil, she tried to tell you."

"Yeah, nothing like telling me the truth five years after the fact." The bitterness in Ethan's voice was overshadowed by a very real, very raw twinge of pain.

For a moment, she considered telling him why his mother hadn't informed him of Parker's death but opted to hold back on that truth until they had more answers. Telling a man that his mother suspected him of murdering his father wasn't exactly conducive to ongoing conversation.

Instead, she jumped in headfirst. "What can you tell me about Frieda Taylor?" she asked.

He shrugged. "You mean other than what I already told you about her being a hypocrite?"

Tori bit back the urge to defend the woman who'd cared for this man's mother when he himself was too busy even to walk in the room and say hello. But she knew that if she did, she'd lose all hope of chasing down yet another possible scenario in Parker's death.

"How was she a hypocrite?"

"Was and is," Ethan corrected with a vehemence that surprised her. "Frieda Taylor liked to talk the talk about community service and doing your part as a human being. She'd preach it to a doorpost if she had a chance. Even went after me a time or two saying I should give of my time to those less fortunate."

"Ooo-kay . . ."

His emerald green eyes flashed with irritation at the sarcasm in her voice. "She talked a good game, yet did the complete opposite in her own life. Which—the last time I checked—is the definition of a hypocrite."

Tori felt the checked anger bubbling up in her chest and willed herself to remain calm. Flying off the handle would get her nothing except a strong-armed assist out the front door. Instead, she questioned the validity of his information. "I'm not sure how you can say she doesn't walk the walk when she was volunteering at the Devereaux Center for months before she came here, to care for your mom."

"Volunteering?" he hissed.

"Just like she is again now while she tries to find a new job."

His hands moved to his hips as he squared his jaw. "I don't know what it says in your book, Miss Sinclair, but in *my* book, volunteers don't get paid. They"—he raised his fingers into the air to simulate quote marks—"give of their time freely and without compensation."

"Frieda doesn't get paid," Tori protested. "She—"

"The hell she doesn't! She's gotten paid to work at the center since day one and she gets paid damn well."

"But—"

"In fact, she got paid as a consultant at the center even while she was working here, for my mom, double-dipping her way through money that was supposed to be *mine*."

"And Brian's?"

"That's debatable," he spat through teeth clenched so tight she was afraid they'd break. "But Frieda's being a hypocrite. There's nothing the slightest bit debatable about that."

Tori worked to keep up with everything he was saying, the words coming out of his mouth not jibing with what she knew. Or rather, assumed.

"And sadly, in addition to Frieda and a handful of others over the past four years or so, now there's another one."

Somehow she'd lost him between the jealousy and the anger. "There's another what?"

"Another person slowly draining my father's company dry via a center that was supposed to be staffed with volunteers. And this latest one? She's some local award-winning cook who's been brought on staff to teach Brian-alikes how to bake cookies."

Chapter 27

They were all there, stationed around her dining room table waiting for instructions, the nonstop chatter barely registering in Tori's conscious mind as anything more than background noise for the thumping in her ears. All day long, she'd batted around Ethan's words yet never got beyond where she was at that moment.

But living in a constant state of confusion didn't do anyone any good. Not her. Not Ethan. Not Brian.

Something was wrong. Charlotte had tried desperately to set the record straight where her husband was concerned, but had died before she could be heard. And while that notion was at once both frustrating and heartbreaking, it was also incredibly motivating. Especially for someone like Tori, who hated to have a story without an ending.

"So are you going to tell us what you want us to do, or

are we supposed to sit here and guess?" Rose griped from her spot between Beatrice and Debbie.

"Rose!" Melissa shifted in her seat to accommodate a stomach Margaret Louise claimed was growing faster than it had with any of the thirty-something's previous seven pregnancies. "If any of us ran around the way Victoria does on a daily basis, we'd be scatterbrained, too."

Scatterbrained . . .

Melissa's description snapped Tori back to the present in time to look at each and every face assembled around her—waiting.

Beatrice, although young, was on the go nearly all the time in her role as nanny for the Johnson family. When Luke, her charge, was home, Beatrice was by his side, taking him to parks, hosting play dates, and supervising his homework. When Luke was in school, she was either volunteering in his class or cooking and preparing the house for his return.

Rose was on the other end of the age spectrum, filling her retirement days with doctor visits, gardening, bunko, and sewing.

Debbie was, for lack of a better description, a happy-go-lucky hardworking blur. If she wasn't at home caring for her school-aged children, Susanna and Jackson, or hanging with her author husband, Colby Calhoun, Debbie was trying out recipes or organizing the financial books associated with her wildly popular bakery.

Across from Debbie was Dixie, another busier-than-ever-now-that-I'm-retired member of the Sweet Briar Ladies Society Sewing Circle. In fact, since Nina's maternity leave, Dixie put in nearly as many hours at the library as Tori did.

Georgina, the town's mayor, was on call virtually twenty-four/seven, the invention of cell phones making it impossible for her to ever truly take off her official hat.

Leona, although the epitome of a pampered pooch, managed to keep herself on a tight schedule, too, between pop-ins at her antique shop on the square, weekly manicure appointments, a busy dating calendar, and her devotion to one very lucky little bunny.

Melissa was, no doubt, harboring a second pair of arms somewhere because the effortlessness with which she mothered seven children actually made it look easy when everyone in the room knew it wasn't.

And finally, there was Margaret Louise—a woman who could put the screws to one battery-plugging bunny known for having nonstop energy. She kept up on her seven grandchildren without the assistance of a calendar or an electronic planner, providing a third pair of arms when Melissa's first and second pair couldn't be in more than two places at one time. When all was quiet on the grandchild front, Margaret Louise was cooking her way through the cookbook she hoped to submit for possible publication by summer, lending a hand wherever she was needed—around town or with friends; visiting with her mother, Annabelle; and now, most recently, volunteering at the Devereaux Center for the Mentally Challenged in Tom's Creek.

Volunteering . . .

Shaking her head against the too-easy path back into her jumbled thoughts, Tori met Melissa's eye and allowed the laugh that followed to relax the knot of tension in her shoulders if only for a little while.

"You're saying *I'm* busy during the day? Isn't that like the pot calling the kettle black?"

Melissa ran the palm of her hand against her stomach and exhaled slowly, deeply. "We all might be busy, but you—"

Tori held up her palms in opposition. "Oh, no. Don't even go there."

"It's true. Victoria is just scatterbrained because she spent entirely too many years breathing in all that Chicago air before finally finding her way here to civilization that's wrapped in a southern hug," Leona mused before looking down at the floor for a quick check of Paris's whereabouts.

Tori considered arguing the scatterbrained tag but let it go. After all, her sewing circle sisters had been sitting or standing around her dining room table for close to thirty minutes and she hadn't registered a single solitary snippet of gossip in that time.

"So? What are we supposed to be doing?" Rose repeated.

"Well, we need to stuff the stockings we made so Mrs. Claus can hand them out to all the little girls and boys on Saturday morning." Dixie stood in front of her chair and swept her hand toward the cartons of candy canes, stacks of look-and-find books, mounds of cookies wrapped with plastic and tied off with red and green ribbons, and piles of pencils with Santa Claus erasers. "Margaret Louise, the cookies look wonderful. And Debbie, the pencils are a nice touch."

Margaret Louise beamed. "Mrs. Claus wants all of the kids to have another one of her special cookies before they go to bed that night. So they can remember her."

"I don't think they'll forget, Mee-Maw." Melissa reached out and gave her mother-in-law's hand a gentle squeeze, the love and admiration she had for the woman obvious to everyone in the room. "How could they? Mrs. Claus is the best."

"So what's *our* jobs?" Rose tapped at the face of her watch. "Some of us are old and need to get our sleep before the bladder alarm goes off at the crack of dawn."

She stifled the urge to laugh and instead forced herself to get on with the task at hand, moving in beside Dixie. "We need someone on stocking detail to make sure everything looks good and there aren't any missed stitches that were overlooked."

Dixie grabbed hold of her chair and moved it to the head of the table beside the pile of stockings. "I'll take that job."

"Thanks, Dixie, that's a huge help." Her gaze drifted to the box of look-and-find books. "Who would like to be in charge of making sure a book finds its way into every stocking?"

Margaret Louise raised her hand then positioned herself beside the box, ready to start stuffing at the proverbial crack of the gun.

"And the candy canes?"

Rose reached across the table and pulled the cartons of red-and-white-striped candy in her direction. "I've got those."

"And I'll do the pencils and erasers," Debbie volunteered while Beatrice claimed the homemade cookies.

"What about me? What can I help with?" Georgina spread her hands wide and glanced up at Tori. "Do we have some sort of note to put inside from Mrs. Claus? I could put that inside if we do."

"Notes," Margaret Louise remembered with the snap

of her fingers. "I must be losin' my mind. Melissa, did you see notes in the car just now?"

Melissa shook her head and offered an apologetic shrug.

"Well, don't you worry none 'cause if they're not, I can head home lickety-split and be back before anyone even misses me." Pushing back her chair, Margaret Louise gestured toward the look-and-find books. "Georgina, how 'bout you sit in for me here and I'll be back in two shakes of a lamb's tail."

Tori followed Margaret Louise out the front door and onto the porch, grateful for the opportunity the woman's forgetfulness had presented. All day long she'd replayed Ethan's words again and again, his adamant claim that Margaret Louise was being compensated for time spent at the Devereaux Center simply not adding up.

"I can find my way to my car by myself, Victoria. You don't need to worry none 'bout me." Margaret Louise lifted her hand and jangled her key ring in the air. "My car's right there."

Tori pulled a deep breath of air into her lungs and took an extra moment to let it back out. "I wanted to ask you something."

"I know."

She drew back. "You do?"

"Land sakes, Victoria. I didn't fall off my Daddy's turnip truck day before last. Why, I've known you long enough now to know when you've got a problem."

Slowly Tori nodded, unsure of how, exactly, to proceed.

"Most problems ain't no bigger than the little end of nothin' whittled down to a fine point."

"Do you get paid to work with the folks at the Devereaux

Center?" She hadn't meant to be so blunt, but it was time for answers.

Margaret Louise's eyes widened at the question. "Well, don't that knock your hat in the creek!"

"It's probably none of my business but—"

"Can you lick that calf again, Victoria?"

She felt her mouth gape open as her mind raced for a translation it could not find. "Lick a calf?"

Leona's sister swiped her hand through the air in frustration. "What did you just ask me, Victoria?"

Suddenly, Tori wished she'd stayed inside. If she had, she'd be preoccupied with the makeshift assembly line rather than standing there, on her front porch, insulting one of her very dearest friends. "You know what? Let's pretend I didn't ask that. It was out of line."

"That makes as much sense as tryin' to sling a hammock 'tween two cornstalks, Victoria. You asked it once, so just ask it again."

Margaret Louise was right. If Tori asked the question once, she could ask it again. "Okay . . . Do you get paid to work with the folks at the Devereaux Center?"

"Don't know how gettin' paid would be volunteerin', but since you felt the need to ask, I'll just say it out so there's no misunderstandin'. No. I don't get paid."

"Are you sure?" she whispered.

"I don't chew my tobacco twice, Victoria."

"And Frieda?"

Margaret Louise's eyes narrowed. "What 'bout Frieda?"

"Does *she* get paid to be at the center?"

"You can keep puttin' your boots in the oven, but that ain't gonna make 'em biscuits. Volunteerin' is volunteerin' and I reckon you know that. Ain't no pay for volunteerin' 'cept maybe smiles and thank-yous."

It was a question Tori shouldn't have had to ask. Especially of someone like Margaret Louise, who was one of the least selfish people she had ever met. She rushed to explain, hoping her words would smooth any ruffled feathers. "I don't know why, but Ethan Devereaux is convinced that you and Frieda—as well as others—are paid employees of the center. He said he's seen the invoices with his own two eyes."

"Then someone's tongue is waggin' at both ends."

Chapter 28

Somehow, one hundred Christmas stockings were stuffed and packed away in Tori's car, ready for distribution that weekend by none other than Mrs. Claus herself.

Somehow, eight friends had celebrated that feat with dessert, gossip, and only a handful of odd looks cast in Tori's direction.

And somehow, despite the dozens of forehead-slapping southern expressions Margaret Louise had thrown out while being interrogated on Tori's front porch, one had actually stuck, making her rethink everything she knew about the players in Parker and Charlotte Devereaux's life.

For nearly five years, Charlotte had believed Ethan was responsible for her husband's death. Charlotte had been so convinced, in fact, that she'd kept quiet in an effort to protect her younger son from prosecution and a life sentence behind bars.

But Charlotte had been wrong about Ethan just as Tori and Jerry Lee had been.

"You figure it out yet?"

Tori dropped her foot onto the wooden-planked porch and thwarted the gentle sway of the swing. "Margaret Louise? You came back?"

"I did. Got Leona and Paris settled at their place, and Melissa inside with Jake and the youngins, and all I could think 'bout was you frettin' over hurtin' my feelings."

Scooting to the side, Tori patted the open spot to her left. "I'm sorry, Margaret Louise, I really am. I didn't mean to insult you with that question but I was confused. I thought maybe *I'd* misunderstood about the work you and Frieda were doing at the center."

"No siree, you didn't misunderstand nothin'." Margaret Louise backed into the swing and came down with a thud next to Tori. "Oomph! Well, don't I reckon I'm a bit heavier than this contraption's used to."

Tori nodded but her mind was already on to something else, something Margaret Louise had said not more than an hour or so earlier. "What did you mean with that saying about somebody's tongue wagging?"

The swing creaked beneath their combined weight, making Margaret Louise grab on to the side arm with a steel grip. "What? I didn't say nothin' 'bout a—wait. You mean the part 'bout someone's tongue waggin' at both ends? That one?"

"That's it." Tori braced the toes of her sneakers against the porch and brought the swing to a slower, more even pace, the decrease in speed and subsequent creaks bringing color back to her friend's right hand. "But what does it mean?"

"It means someone's lyin'."

"Lying?" she echoed.

"You said Ethan saw these invoices with his own two eyes, right?"

"And so did I," she finally admitted. "When I questioned whether he was sure you and Frieda were being paid for your services, he took me to his computer and showed me the expenditures for his dad's company from just this past month alone. You're on there and so is Frieda."

"We don't belong on there," Margaret Louise protested. "'Cause if someone's gettin' a paycheck for my volunteerin', it sure ain't me."

Tori laughed at the thought. "Can you imagine sitting back, collecting an erroneous paycheck for months on . . ." Her words trailed from her mouth as a sickening thought took root, pushing all else from her head. "Wait! That's it!"

Margaret Louise stopped the swing completely and began to struggle her way out of it amid an array of grunts and groans. "What's it, Victoria? You lost me."

"Jerry Lee's been essentially running the center since it opened six years ago. He furnishes the rooms, gets all the equipment, hires the volunteers, and oversees the general day-to-day of the outreach program. He even said Parker was so busy traveling that operating the center was pretty much left to him."

"If he's doctorin' the books, he's takin' one heckuva chance, don't you think?"

"If Parker were alive, sure. But he's not."

Margaret Louise crossed Tori's front porch and landed in a single, stationary wicker chair. "But Jerry Lee didn't know Parker was dead, right?"

"*Someone* knew," she pointed out, her voice suddenly breathless. "*Someone* had to have helped Charlotte dig that grave. Why couldn't it have been Jerry Lee?"

"Because Charlotte herself thought it was Ethan?"

Damn.

She'd forgotten that part.

"Back to square one . . . again," she mumbled.

"Maybe. Maybe not. Maybe someone *convinced* her Ethan did it."

Tori considered Margaret Louise's statement from a variety of different angles, with one making her sit up tall. "Jerry Lee had pretty much convinced *me* he'd done it."

"Charlotte may have coddled Prince Ethan for far too long—lookin' the other way every time he did somethin' stupid and rushin' to clean up his mess so he could go on pretendin' he did nothin' wrong. But she wasn't blind. She knew Ethan was—"

Tori leapt up, the force of her jump smacking the edge of the swing into the backs of her thighs before she could clear its path. "Say that again! Please!"

"Which part? The part 'bout Charlotte not bein' blind or—"

"Before that!" she yelled. "About the mess . . ."

Margaret Louise hesitated as her eyes rolled up in recollection. "You mean 'bout her always rushin' to clean up his mess so he could go on pretendin' he did nothin' wrong?"

"That's it! That's why Charlotte thought Ethan had killed his father. Because Jerry Lee had convinced her it was true! And with Ethan's track record, she had every reason to believe it was so. Especially if the relationship between father and son was at a breaking point when all of this happened, as both Jerry Lee *and* Ethan have implied!"

"So you think Jerry Lee led Charlotte to believe Ethan had killed Parker?"

She nodded even before the question had truly sunk in. It all fit. Even the story Charlotte had told everyone to explain her husband's sudden disappearance. Parker leaving wouldn't set his will in motion. Only death would.

To that end, Jerry Lee had put himself in the role of cherished friend by helping Charlotte dispose of the body, and by looking after her special needs son while she quietly mourned the loss of her husband and tried to sweep her younger son's betrayal under the proverbial carpet in an attempt to keep at least part of her family intact.

Ethan's journal entry to his father, though, had changed everything. Suddenly, the story Charlotte had believed for so long was wrong. Her son hadn't killed her beloved husband . . .

"But someone did," she whispered into the night before grabbing hold of the porch railing for support as reality sprang into focus once and for all. "She tried to tell Frieda she'd been wrong . . . but since Frieda didn't know Parker was dead, Charlotte's words made no sense!"

"Thank heavens for that sketch pad, huh? Or else Parker'd still be buried outside the library and no one would be the wiser."

Except one . . .

Despite having outlined her theory a half-dozen times at least, Tori held Police Chief Robert Dallas's gaze rock steady as she took her theory from the top one more time. When she was done, and his expression hadn't changed, she tried a different tactic.

"Look, all I'm asking is to see the picture my friends and I used to locate Parker Devereaux's body." When he didn't react, she leaned still closer to the man who'd made her life a living hell a time or two over the past two years. "You do still have it, don't you?"

"Of course we still have it, Miss Sinclair. It's evidence."

That's what I'm counting on . . .

Shaking the thought from her mind long enough to plead her case, she infused as much sweetness into her voice as humanly possible. "I don't even have to touch it. You can just set it right here on your desk and I can give it a simple once-over."

For a moment, Chief Dallas said nothing, the only audible indication he was even still in the room coming from the staccato tap-tap of his fingers atop his desk. When he finally did speak, however, his words nearly sent her into shock.

"Okay. You can look at it. But you keep your hands to your side, do you understand?"

Her emphatic nod and promise to behave were followed by a press of the chief's intercom and a request for the evidence officer to deliver Charlotte's sketch. Seconds turned to minutes as they waited, but finally, mercifully, the picture arrived and was placed in front of Tori.

Hunching herself over the picture so as to afford the best view, Tori studied the broad details—the fireplace, the framed photographs along the mantel, and even the broken clock. Everything was as she remembered it, both in the sketch and from the vantage point she'd experienced firsthand in Charlotte's chair.

Next, she studied the finer details—the tiny crack in the third row of bricks from the bottom, the picture Charlotte had drawn for Ethan lying faceup on the hearth where it had fallen, and the roughly twenty-five percent of a nearby end table that was showing. Reaching into her purse, Tori pulled out the leather-bound sketchbook that had belonged to Charlotte and flipped it open to one of the many sketches that was a near-perfect copy of the one on the chief's desk—save, of course, for the drawing within the drawing that was lying some three feet below the mantel in this particular rendering.

Like the sketches in the notebook, Charlotte's vantage point never changed from picture to picture, though occasionally, details did. Aware of the chief's eyes studying her, Tori pointed to some of the subtle changes from picture to picture. The water glass in one became a stethoscope in another. The lone bookmark in one became Brian's storybook in the next. Brian's storybook in that one became a full glass of wine, a clip-on pearl earring, and the binding of what appeared to be a high school yearbook from nearly fifty years earlier in the sketch she'd been banned from touching.

A glass of wine . . .

And a clip-on pearl earring . . .

"Oh my God." Tori steadied herself against the chief's desk as everything she'd figured out to that moment was suddenly blown to smithereens right before her very eyes.

Chapter 29

Tori let herself into the library through the back door, Charlotte's high school yearbook tucked under her arm and more than a few questions pecking at her brain. All night long, she'd found herself replaying snippets of conversations from the past few weeks that had seemed so innocent when first uttered, yet now, when seen in a different light, were anything but.

But as she'd learned many times in her quest to track down Parker Devereaux's killer thus far, the ground tended to shift beneath her feet when she least expected it, proving her wrong again and again.

It had been hard summoning her best poker face when she walked out of the chief's office with nary a word about her latest head-spinning suspicion. And it had been hard convincing Ethan she needed to see his mother's yearbook, only to send him back inside for the one that matched the earlier year noted in his mother's final sketch without giving him any reasons as to why.

By the same token, though, if her latest hunch proved true, she might be able to have her first full night's sleep since finding Parker's body.

"Dixie?" she called. "Are you here?"

The stocky woman she'd come to count on in more ways than one peeked her head down the hallway and waved. "I'm here, but I'm busy with those two boys from the high school who were interested in the Vietnam era."

She knew she should be happy for Dixie, happy for the smile the boys' continued interest instilled on her friend's face. But it was hard. *She* needed Dixie, needed her knowledge of a different time and place that couldn't be researched in a book.

Or could it?

Glancing down at the book tucked under her arm, she willed her voice to sound as natural as possible. "Okay. But will you come to my office when you're free, please? I have something I need to ask you."

At Dixie's nod, Tori flicked on the light in her office and carried Charlotte's eleventh-grade yearbook over to her desk and sank into her chair. A call to Frieda had confirmed what Charlotte's final sketch had revealed at the police station. Sadie Sweeney had stopped by for a visit that last night, her presence enabling Frieda to sign off for the night far earlier than normal. But even with that, Frieda had made sure, before leaving, that the women were all set for their long-overdue visit—Sadie with her wine and memories, and Charlotte with a fresh sketching pencil.

It was a visit that, under normal circumstances, wouldn't

have even raised Tori's eyebrows—as it apparently hadn't for Frieda, either. But considering the woman's marital relationship with Tori's chief suspect *and* the unsettling fact that Charlotte had died later that same night and, well, her eyebrows were raised. Big time.

Opening the book, Tori flipped straight to the junior class, slowly searching page after page for a Charlotte. Sure enough, roughly forty students in, she came to a slightly younger face than the one she'd seen in the wedding photo buried alongside the woman's husband.

The senior class followed, but Tori passed those pages by, skipping ahead to the open pages in the back designed specifically for signatures and notes from classmates. A note near the bottom of the second such page caught her eye, the masculine writing marred by a reddish-colored stain.

Intrigued, she held the book to her nose and inhaled, a faint, yet still present smell catching her by surprise.

"Wine?" she whispered.

Her gaze traveled back down to the stain and the writing still visible beneath its mark.

Charlotte,

Before I met you, I thought my path was clear and my destiny set. That may still be true, but now, rather than look ahead on that path, I will forever be glancing back over my shoulder . . . wondering and imagining what might have been if only I'd seen you first.

Stunned by your presence,
Jerry Lee

"Jerry Lee?" she read aloud with a voice that was as stunned as it was quiet. "Jerry Lee Sweeney?"

"And aside from an underclassman who caught his eye midway through their senior year and periodically throughout the next year or so, Jerry Lee was pretty smitten with Sadie."

Dixie's words from weeks earlier filtered through her thoughts as if the woman were in the room with her at that moment, single-handedly tying the seemingly odd strings in her hands into something resembling a bow.

Flipping backward, Tori stopped on the page devoted to members of the high school's senior class whose name began with the letter "s." And, sure enough, there was Parker Devereaux's best friend and longtime business partner, Jerry Lee Sweeney. The next page revealed a student listed as Sadie Underwood . . .

Sadie.

Suddenly, the bow that was taking shape in her head got a good, tight pull from yet another inscription—this one written by *Charlotte* inside a very different book.

My dearest Brian,

I love the you that you are—the you that you are because of a father's love.
Forever and Always.

Love,
Mommy

Charlotte hadn't written "your father's love." She'd written "a father's love" . . .

"Sorry about that, Victoria. But I just had the most fun with those two young men. Their paper is done, yet they came in to ask me more questions, if you can believe it. Said they wanted to know more about that time in our history."

"How did Charlotte and Parker meet?"

Dixie stopped midway across the office. "Charlotte and Parker? They met about the time Charlotte was graduating from high school. Apparently, Jerry Lee had a party and invited Parker—someone he'd been friends with throughout his childhood. Charlotte was there, too, and she said it was love at first sight. Must've been because they married less than three months later."

Tori forced herself to look up from the yearbook picture of Jerry Lee, as a question she hadn't even been aware she was contemplating found its way out from between her lips. "Parker Devereaux wasn't Brian's father, was he?"

Dixie stopped mid-step, her face draining of all color. "Why do you ask?"

"I just need to know."

For a moment, she thought Dixie was going to turn on her heel and head back into the library, Tori's question unanswered. But finally, the woman spoke, her voice hesitant. "No. He wasn't. But he knew Charlotte was pregnant when they married and he agreed to raise the child as his own, giving him his name on the birth certificate despite the obvious issues that presented themselves at Brian's birth."

"Who was the father?"

A second, longer pause was soon followed by an answer Tori didn't expect. "I don't know. Charlotte never said and I never asked. In fact, other than telling me that

Parker wasn't the father and that only she, Parker, and the biological father knew the truth, she never spoke of it again."

Mustering up every ounce of courage she could via a deep breath, Tori shared her suspicions aloud. "I think it was Jerry Lee Sweeney."

Dixie gasped. "Jerry Lee? No. Where on earth did you come up with that?"

She spun the yearbook around so Dixie could see, flipping ahead to Charlotte's junior class picture and then back to the senior class pages depicting Parker, Jerry Lee, and Sadie. "Didn't you say that Jerry Lee and Sadie were high school sweethearts? That aside from an underclassman who caught Jerry Lee's eye midway through his senior year, he was pretty smitten with Sadie?"

"I did. But from what I gather, he kept that girl's identity a secret from everyone, including Sadie. So I don't see how you can take a few pictures and make the leap you're making."

Without saying a word, she flipped to the back of Charlotte's book and the wine-stained inscription from Jerry Lee to Charlotte.

Wine-stained . . .

She matched Dixie's gasp as the items Charlotte had depicted in her last drawing flashed before her eyes.

The yearbook Dixie was reading now . . .

A lone pearl clip-on earring . . .

A full glass of wine . . .

"I had no idea—"

She waved off her friend's rant with one of her own. "Dixie! That's it! Sadie must have put two and two together that night while looking through Charlotte's yearbook.

She must have been so stunned she spilled her wine on the page. She did it! She killed Parker."

Dixie began shaking her head before Tori was even finished. "If she *just* found out Charlotte had been the underclassman her husband had been mooning after all those years ago, what reason would she have had to kill Parker five years ago? And why *Parker*? What did *he* do to Sadie?"

She felt the air whoosh from her lungs as she realized Dixie was right. Maybe Sadie being in Charlotte's house that last night was nothing more than a coincidence.

A wine-stained coincidence.

No. There had to be a connection. Somehow, someway.

"If Sadie killed anyone after reading what Jerry Lee wrote, my money would be on Charlotte."

Her head snapped up. "Charlotte?" But even as the question hovered in the air between them, she knew.

Charlotte hadn't died earlier than Frieda expected.

She'd been *murdered*.

By Sadie Sweeney.

The same Sadie Sweeney who touted herself and her life as picture-perfect.

It all fit. Perfectly.

The only question that still remained was whether Charlotte had been murdered in a fit of jealousy or as a way to keep her quiet.

"My bet's on jealousy," she whispered.

Tori made her final lap around the outside of the library before heading back toward the stone steps that called to her in much the same way a lighthouse called a ship home. She'd been walking for nearly an hour, her thoughts a jumbled mess despite the list of questions she'd jotted down in her notebook with Dixie's help.

Question by question, the answer had come up the same.

Jerry Lee.

Jerry Lee.

Jerry Lee.

Slowly, she climbed the stairs, the absence of cars in the lot and the lack of pedestrians going in and out of the front door letting her know she'd walked right through closing. When she reached the front door, she pulled, the give of the door quelling any fear Dixie might have locked her out in the woman's haste to get home.

"Dixie, I'm back," she called as she turned and locked the door in her wake. "I'm sorry I walked so long. I guess I just lost track of time."

She turned to find the library's main room empty and several stacks of books lined up around the information desk.

Hmmm. That's very un-Dixie-like . . .

After a quick peek down several aisles, Tori headed down the hallway toward her office, her thoughts jumping to the various motives she and Dixie had schemed where Jerry Lee was concerned.

He was angry at Parker for raising his son?

He was bilking thousands upon thousands of dollars from Parker's company?

They were possibilities, she supposed, but they didn't sit right. Not completely anyway. There was something missing; she was sure of it.

She rounded the corner into her office and froze.

There, standing behind Tori's desk with eyes open wide in terror, was Dixie . . . with Jerry Lee Sweeney's arm around her neck. Gasping, Tori spun around and ran into the hall, only to be stopped by Jerry Lee's halting words.

"You walk out of here to call the cops, Miss Sinclair, and I swear I'll snap her neck."

She looked from Jerry Lee's angry face to Dixie's terrified one, her gut telling her to get the man talking.

"Why did you k-kill them?" she stammered.

"*Them?* I didn't kill *them*."

"Sadie killed Charlotte, didn't she?" It was a risky question to ask, but it was all she could think of to buy herself time and a moment to think.

A flash of pain crossed Jerry Lee's face, only to disappear as quickly as it had come. "I suppose the notion of me fathering another woman's son—and a mentally challenged one at that—was more than she could take. It doesn't really mesh with her image."

Tori took a slight step to her right and then followed it up with a second and third, finally leaning her body against the doorjamb as her focus alternated between Jerry Lee, Dixie, and the cell phone she was all too aware of in the back pocket of her jeans.

Jutting her chin toward the yearbook on her desk, she hoped the momentary visual distraction would afford her the second or two necessary to slip her hand behind her back and pull out her phone. "I saw what you wrote to Charlotte when you were kids."

Bingo.

Jerry Lee looked down at the still-open yearbook, the now wine-stained inscription claiming his attention just long enough for her to do as she'd hoped. Flipping the phone open against her pant leg, she slid her fingers across the keypad until she reached the speed dial number assigned to Milo and then hoped and prayed he would be able to make out the confession she was determined to get, as well as their location.

"I know you were putting your volunteers on paper as paid employees at the center so you could pocket the money for yourself. But I also know you didn't start that until *after* Parker was dead. Was that the plan all along? Is that why you killed him and tried to pin it on Ethan? So you could set your plan in motion?"

Jerry Lee looked up from the yearbook with a snarl. "I trusted Parker to raise my son as his own while I held up my end of the bargain and never told a single solitary soul—including my wife—that I was Brian's biological father. I knew Charlotte loved Parker and that she'd always resent me if I kept her from him. So I signed over my parental rights prior to his birth with the understanding that he'd be given the same life and privilege as any future children they might go on to have. When Brian was born the way he was, I guess I gave up on some of that, thinking, like everyone else, that there wasn't much life to be had by someone like that.

"But after I came on board with the company and saw how diligent Brian was with every menial task he was given, I began to wonder if he could do more. Little by little, as the years went on, I started giving him more and more things to do around the office. Some of those things had him working with the computers and the programming, and he was able to do almost everything I put in front of him to do. He was a hard worker. A really hard worker. And day by day, I watched him plug away while

Parker's real son—Prince Ethan—proved himself a disgrace again and again. When I tried to make him see that Brian was the only choice to run the company should something happen to Parker, he almost changed his will. But in the end, he opted not to. And so I knew it was time to make him disappear. Permanently."

"Because if he disappeared, things would continue as they were—with you running Parker's company alongside Brian, right?" Oh, how she prayed Milo had answered, that he was listening, that he was calling for help.

"Smart girl."

"That's why I'm at the library," she said as clearly as she possibly could without raising too much suspicion. "So you killed Parker, convinced Charlotte that Ethan had done it, and then had her help you bury the body and craft the whole philandering story in order to keep Ethan out of jail and keep you running the company through Brian. Before long, the bilking of money from the center started . . ."

"That about sums it up. Sadie even helped me out by getting rid of that blasted picture Charlotte drew pointing to Parker's body like it was some sort of treasure chest. Though even I know she didn't dispose of it to help me. She was just cleaning up hoping not to leave a trail back to herself. Too bad she missed that damn sketch book. If she hadn't, Parker's will wouldn't be an issue and I'd still be running that company by way of my son."

"Your son or your puppet?"

A near silent click from the end of the hallway let her know her call had worked, yet she resisted the urge to sigh until after Dixie was safe.

"The writing was on the wall, huh?" she asked, her gaze locked on Dixie's.

"The writing's on the wall, all right." Chief Dallas rounded Tori's office door, his revolver pointing straight at Jerry Lee Sweeney. "Put your hands in the air . . . *now*!"

Chapter 30

If Tori could only point to one thing as proof that the first annual Cookies and Books with Mrs. Claus was a success, she'd have to say the smiles of the children as they'd sat in front of Santa's wife, eyes wide, listening to her tales of life in the North Pole with the jolliest of jolly men.

But she didn't have to point to just one, especially when there were dozens to choose from.

Not the least of which was the face-splitting smile worn by Mrs. Claus herself as she savored the utter worship of the children assembled around her, knowing they were hanging on every word she read and happily devouring every cookie she'd made.

"Every time I think we've outdone ourselves, we do it again," Dixie said, moving in beside Tori in the doorway of the almost-empty children's room. "And this on top of what happened yesterday."

She heard the slight hitch to her friend's voice and knew the horror of being held captive by a killer hadn't truly worked its way out of the woman's system quite yet. Turning to Dixie, she placed a gentle hand on her arm and gave a little squeeze. "What happened yesterday was this—you were brave and you were steady and you helped put a killer behind bars."

"*Killers,*" Dixie corrected.

Dixie was right.

Parker's confession and subsequent arrest had led, in a way, to Sadie's arrest, too. For suffocating Charlotte with a bed pillow.

Shaking her head against the thought that threatened to undermine all the good that had come from the library event, Tori focused instead on the few remaining stragglers still left in the room, including Melissa, Lulu, Sally, and Molly Sue.

Tori bent at the waist to address Margaret Louise's three youngest grandchildren. "Did you enjoy yourselves today, girls?"

Three heads nodded in unison.

"I just wish Mee-Maw had been here, too. She'd have loved Mrs. Claus."

Her eyes traveled upward to mingle momentarily with Melissa's. "Well, sometimes mee-maws have things to do, like moms and little girls."

"And my youngest has something she'd like to do, too, don't you, Molly Sue?" Melissa asked, reaching down to give Molly Sue a pat on her strawberry blonde head before pulling a book from her oversized mom purse.

Nodding, her eyes solemn, Molly Sue took the book from her mother's hand and held it out for Tori.

Confused, Tori looked from the book to the toddler and back. "Why are you giving this to me? It's yours, sweetie."

Lulu stepped forward, placing a reassuring arm around her little sister's back. "Mama says we're going to order another copy for Molly Sue so she can give this one back to the boy who owns it. So he can remember his own mama, isn't that right, Molly Sue?"

The little girl nodded again, her understanding of the whole situation more than a little tenuous. But she trusted her mother and her big sisters, so she did as they asked.

Swallowing against the sudden lump in her throat, Tori took the book, hugging Molly Sue in return. "When your copy comes in, sweetie, you bring it to me at the library and we'll read it together, okay?"

Molly Sue's mouth exploded in a smile just before she buried her face in her mother's leg.

"Thank you, Victoria." Melissa nudged her chin toward the little boy nervously watching them from the other side of the room. "I think someone is trying to catch your attention."

She followed the path made by Melissa's chin and smiled.

Kyle.

Turning, she readdressed Dixie, who was still standing in the doorway. "Dixie, it's time . . ."

Dixie nodded knowingly. "I'll alert Rose and Leona that Operation Destroy Grinch is under way."

Oh, how she hoped it worked.

For Kyle's benefit, and for his father's . . .

She strode across the room to the freckle-faced little boy who'd enjoyed the stories Mrs. Claus had shared as much as every other child in the room, the lighthearted holiday fun something he'd needed desperately. "Are you ready?"

Kyle beamed. "I'm ready." Then, waving to his dad, who was standing a few feet away with The Grinch, he called, "Dad? I have something for you."

A flicker of surprise lit Maime's mud brown eyes, only to recede into full-fledged irritation as Councilman Jordan left her side to join his son. "What is it, son?"

Reaching onto one of the only remaining shelves in the room, Kyle plucked a Christmas-wrapped box from the top and handed it to his dad. "I—I hope you like it. I bought this all by myself with money I earned decorating that tree"—he pointed at his masterpiece beside Mrs. Claus's now vacant chair—"with Mom's ornaments."

Maime gasped as she, too, turned to look at the tree.

"You did a great job, Kyle," Avery said. "Mom would be proud."

Kyle nodded, hopping from foot to foot as he did. "Open it, Dad! Please, please open it."

With careful fingers, the councilman tore off the wrapping paper to reveal a plain white box, Kyle's exuberant anticipation claiming the attention of the volunteers who'd stayed behind to clean up the children's room. "Keep going, Dad. I just know you're gonna love it. You have to!"

Avery Jordan smiled down at his son then flipped open the top of the box to reveal the very same snowflake Maime had thrown at the wall less than a week earlier. "Oh, Kyle, it's—it's perfect," the councilman said in a voice choked with raw emotion. "Your mom would have loved this, too."

"His mom? His mom?" Maime yelled from her spot beside Avery's elbow. "His mom is *dead*. She's gone. *I'm* here now. And I told you that when you were trying to wrap the first one, didn't I, you little brat!"

Avery's eyes widened. "The *first* one?"

Kyle nodded, his shoulders slumping at the memory. "She threw it against the wall and broke it."

"You broke my son's gift to me?" Avery asked in a voice that was suddenly wooden.

Before she could speak, Kyle looked up, pointing to Tori as he did. "Miss Sinclair's friends—Ms. Winters and Ms. Elkin—took me to the store so I could buy a new one."

Maime turned on Tori. "Who the hell do you think you are? You had no right to stick your nose where it didn't belong. This is *my* life—my life with Avery."

Holding the ornament box to his chest with one hand, Avery pointed to the door with his other. "You have no life with me. *My son* is my life. You hurt him, you hurt me. And while I might be desperate enough to put up with you hurting me, I could never be desperate enough to put up with you hurting him. Now get out!" Then, turning to Kyle, he held out his hand for the boy to take. "As for you, let's go find the perfect place to hang my new snowflake."

When the pair was gone, Leona, who'd entered the room with Rose in time to watch the fireworks, wrapped her arm around her cohort and gave a gentle squeeze. "We sure showed The Grinch a thing or two, didn't we, you old goat?"

Sewing Pattern

Christmas Stocking Pattern

Want to make Christmas stockings the way Tori and the rest of the Sweet Briar Ladies Society Sewing Circle do in this book? Here's how . . .

🪡 Decide on the size stocking you'd like to make and cut the shape from fabric—remembering to cut both a front and a back.

🪡 Once you've cut, place both stockings together—with the right side of the fabric facing inward against each other—and sew around the edges, leaving the top of the stocking open.

- Turn the top edge of the stocking down (roughly ½ inch) and hem in place.

- Then, turn right side out and attach a ribbon loop for hanging if desired.

- Once the stocking is sewn, you can decorate it with ribbon, buttons, jingle bells, or whatever you decide.

- Fill with items designed to fit your size stocking.

To view a photograph of a completed Christmas stocking, click on the "projects" tab at the top of my website at www.elizabethlynncasey.com.

Holiday Gift Idea

Personal Organizer

Take a fabric place mat (line it if it's too floppy—damask/tapestry works best) and fold up the bottom third (this section will become your pockets when done).

Then, fold it lengthwise into thirds to make a folder. Velcro can be added at each end so your organizer can be closed.

Finally, stitch up some pockets that can be used to hold notepaper, stamps, pens, etc. Add a few of these items along with the organizer and you have a great gift!

To see a photograph of the completed project, visit www.elizabethlynncasey.com and click on the "projects" tab at the top.